REJECTED by her MATE

Other books by Jaelynn Woolf

Rejected by the Pack
Rejected by Her Mate

Co-written with R. A. Steffan:

Circle of Blood Book 1: Lover's Rebirth
Circle of Blood Book 2: Lover's Awakening
Circle of Blood Book 3: Lover's Sacrifice
Circle of Blood Book 4: Lover's Absolution
Circle of Blood Book 5: Lover's Atonement
Circle of Blood Book 6: Lover's Victory

The Last Vampire: Book One
The Last Vampire: Book Two
The Last Vampire: Book Three
The Last Vampire: Book Four
The Last Vampire: Book Five
The Last Vampire: Book Six

Rejected by her Mate

JAELYNN WOOLF

Rejected by Her Mate

ISBN: 978-1-955073-78-3 (paperback)

For information, contact the author at
http://www.otherlovepublishing.com/contact/

Cover by AddictiveCovers.com

First Edition: April 2024

AUTHOR'S NOTE

This book contains cursing, descriptions of violence (including bullying), and a couple of graphic sex scenes. It is intended for a mature audience.

TABLE OF CONTENTS

1

ONE

"ONCE UPON A TIME, an evil Faerie King seduced a mortal wolf-shifter and sired a half-breed child on her, not knowing that his illegitimate daughter would grow up to become one of the most powerful creatures in all the cosmos. When he found out, rather than tremble in fear at what he had wrought, he decided to use her as a weapon to gain control of Earth as well as the fae realm of Elfhame.

He sent his best general to capture his daughter and bring her to his palace. When that didn't work, he abducted her best friend instead, using the threat of the friend's public execution as blackmail.

Rather than submit, this powerful half-fae shifter discovered the truth about her heritage. She decided to take on the mad king in an effort to defeat him and rescue her best friend.

With the help of her fated mate and the mad king's noble general, the half-breed killed the evil king and formed an alliance with Elfhame's new queen, bringing peace to the realms and saving her friend from certain death."

It was a good story, one made even better by virtue of being true. It was also a tale I'd told many times. Ember Valentine was a hero who had saved two worlds from a madman's devastating war, with the help of her shifter mate, Cai Greystalker, and their fae co-mate, Tamlain. Happily, Queen Titania had proven herself a fair and capable ruler after the death of her much-reviled husband, King Oberon.

And then there was me.

I was the kidnapped friend.

I was the one that Oberon's pet witch—a vile woman who'd infiltrated Ember's life and gained her trust while spying on her for the king—had stolen away from Earth to use as *bait*. It had been the most horrific thing that ever happened to me. Beaten and chained; tortured because my pain would in turn torture Ember, my good friend. Then I'd been rescued, and it was as though everyone just sort of expected me to… *get over it*.

I shuddered, pressing my fingers into my temples.

Don't think about it, Darby. They're right. It's over. It's stupid to keep replaying it in your head like this.

It was bad enough that I had to revisit the bowels of Oberon's dungeon in my dreams without obsessing over things during my waking hours as well.

Besides, I had a job to do.

Despite my unease at being back on Elfhame, far from my pack's home on Earth, part of my new responsibilities included liaising with Queen Titania. The four of us—Ember, Cai, Tamlain, and I—had arranged for educational exchanges to be developed between our two worlds, with the queen's blessings. The idea had been to establish a sort of haven in our packlands for those who had no place else to go—whether fae, human, or shifter. We'd hoped it would eventually reduce the fear and stigma between our peoples.

I wouldn't lie. After all my years living as a low-status omega within the Greystalker pack, I had private doubts that human, shifter, and fae natures could ever truly overcome the friction between them—but I owed Ember my life, and it was a worthy goal. Trying to help bring her vision into reality was the least I could do.

Besides, it wasn't as though things hadn't improved within the packlands since Cai became our new alpha. They had. I just remembered all too well how much abuse had rained down on our heads under the rule of Cai's sire, when Ember and I had been pups.

Shifters could be cruel. Though maybe not as cruel as fae could be.

After stepping between the two realms through Tamlain's magic travel portal, I had to swallow the hot wave of panic that tried to overwhelm me. I squeezed my eyes shut, blocking out the vibrant colors and strange smells that assaulted me the moment the portal snapped shut behind me.

This was fine.

Being here was fine.

I could do this.

Elfhame had the power to drive humans and shifters mad. That insanity had overwhelmed me completely during my previous captivity, leaving me nearly catatonic by the time I'd been rescued. But Ember was a child of both worlds. Her mental touch was a balm that could pull others back from the madness. She'd showed me how to survive here in the fae realm. I latched on to the psychic memory of the peace she'd shared with me during that horrible time.

Opening my eyes slowly, I checked that my equilibrium had returned, and found I was back in control. In front of me lay a rustic cottage that I knew very well.

This little slice of Elfhame was safe, I reminded myself firmly. It always had been. Here, I would find Dianthe—one of the very few fae I called a friend. She was Tamlain's cousin, and she had risked her life along with the others to defeat Oberon and free me from captivity. Today, I had arranged to meet up with her for a few hours before attending my appointment with Queen Titania.

Despite my familiarity with this little house tucked away in the forest, I couldn't help but throw an uneasy look over my shoulder as I knocked on the door. On Elfhame, I always felt like unseen eyes were watching me from the shadows.

"Darby!" Dianthe's melodious voice greeted me as she pulled the door open. "It's good to see you, my friend."

The fae warrior looked the same as ever—tall and strong, her green eyes glowing with good humor and her strawberry blond hair done up in intricate braids. We embraced, her familiar sweet scent swirling around me. Grounding me.

"It's good to see you too," I told her. Pulling back, I gave her a teasing onceover. "Don't lie, though—you were five minutes away from ditching me and heading out for a solo hunt."

A mischievous grin spread across my friend's face. "Well, you are a *bit* late."

I pretended to scowl at her. "I am *not* late! Ember specifically had Tamlain open the portal for me early, because she knew you'd be itching to leave."

Dianthe's smile grew devious. "Then Tamlain should have known to open it ten minutes ago."

My fake scowl broke. We laughed and embraced again. Goddess, I'd missed her. Elfhame was far from being my favorite place, but Dianthe was one of my favorite people. Maybe I should invite her to come hunt with me on Earth more often. That way I could see her without having to fight the fae realm's influence during our visits.

She ushered me inside and wordlessly pointed to the back of the cottage, where a cozy bedroom was tucked away. I ducked inside and stripped quickly out of my clothes, tossing them into my backpack and placing the bag on a chair in the corner.

Shifting into my wolf form made everything somehow more bearable. I padded back to the front room and blinked up at Dianthe, licking my chops in anticipation. We went outside, and she closed the door behind her, waving her hand to activate the magical wards that would protect the premises in our absence.

With a mischievous light in her eyes, she winked at me and sprang away, sprinting silently into the depths of the trees. Grinning a wolfish grin, I tore after her.

As I ran, my breathing settled into a deep, steady rhythm. In many ways, my emotions were muted in my wolf form—the bad ones, especially. It was easier to deal with the traumatic memories and the magic of Elfhame as a wolf than as a human. Tracking Dianthe through the trees was simple. It didn't take long before my easy, loping strides caught up with her. I slowed, moving noiselessly to join her.

She was crouched behind a thick shrub, her attention focused on a deer that seemed to shimmer faintly in the dappled light as it picked its way daintily through the underbrush.

Without a word being necessary between us, I stalked around to the side on silent paws, eager to flank our prey. My mouth watered in anticipation of the kill, when suddenly the deer's head popped up in alarm.

I froze, afraid for a moment that I had somehow alerted the animal to our presence. But how? The wind was in my favor, and I hadn't made a sound.

Then all became clear. The deer wasn't looking at me. A low murmur of noise from somewhere behind the creature reached my perked ears. Then the deer sprang away, bounding out of sight into the dense forest. A moment later, Dianthe rose from her hiding place with a frustrated snarl, storming through the undergrowth towards the sound of the voices that had startled our breakfast.

With a huff, I trailed after her. Well before she came into view, I could hear Dianthe's irritated voice over the rustle of purple and gold leaves.

"—*completely* careless and out of bounds! You call yourselves hunters? I've seen *humans* with more stealth than you three cretins."

I stepped into the clearing where the rather one-sided confrontation was taking place. There, three males were facing off with Dianthe—or rather, *she* was facing off with *them*. Two of the males were fae, while the third was unmistakably a shifter. He turned at my approach, his expression wary, and my breath caught on a low, involuntary whine.

I knew this male. Or, more accurately, I'd seen him at Titania's Court and nearly stumbled over my own feet like an idiot… because how in the goddess' name was *anyone* that beautiful? Dark hair falling in messy waves over brilliant blue eyes. High cheekbones, sharp jaw, and the graceful body of a predator.

Goddess help me, I was *drooling*.

The shifter male and his mother were advisors to Titania, and supposedly they'd been tied up somehow with whatever disagreement had originally estranged Titania from her husband Oberon. That was the extent of my knowledge about him. Yet even when I was in wolf form, his perfect features made my heart thrum fast and hard in my chest. I rumbled a low growl of irritation, because this unexpected coincidence was an added distraction that I did *not* need today.

One of the fae males cocked an eyebrow at Dianthe in an appraising way, clearly taking note of her empty hands. He was pretty in the way that so many male fae were pretty, with sculpted features, a lithe body, and pale, platinum blond hair. His bearing practically reeked of high breeding.

"We aren't hunting," he said, "and therefore we had no need for stealth. We've already made our kill." This, apparently, was his justification for the way they'd been heedlessly crashing through the forest, scaring away the game. He gestured to his companion, a broader, rougher looking fae with red hair and a smattering of freckles dusting his nose and cheeks. The second fae had an animal slung over his shoulders—something resembling a small boar, but with vicious spiral tusks jutting from its lower jaw.

"How nice for you. *That* was our kill." Dianthe pointed emphatically after the departed deer. "And *we* only started hunting a few minutes ago."

I realized rather abruptly that the male shifter was hunting in human form rather than as a wolf, with a bow slung over his shoulder. His muscular arms hung loosely at his sides, his fingers resting on the hilt of a dagger sheathed at his hip in a studiously casual way.

Screwing up my courage in the face of way too much male prettiness on display at once, I crossed to Dianthe's side and gave her a meaningful look. She sighed and flicked her fingers in a complex magical sigil. I drew my human skin back around me, shifting form, and her magic settled around my body in the form of simple clothing as I rose to my feet.

The shifter male frowned at me. The moment his eyes met mine in human form, sudden pain flared hot and insistent in my chest. I swallowed a gasp, my hand rising instinctively to cover the burning place just above my heart.

Utter shock overwhelmed me. I didn't need to reach beneath Dianthe's ephemeral robes to recognize the burn of the unmatched fate-mark that had lain dormant on my skin for months. Dormant and totally dead… until this very moment.

TWO

NO, I THOUGHT, followed closely by, *seriously, no. I really don't need this right now. C'mon, fate — do me a solid, here. Don't be a total bitch like this, okay?*

It was all I could do not to trace the outline of my fate-mark with my fingertips, following its figure-eight shape like an infinity symbol. The terrible burning sensation abated almost as quickly as it had come, but the skin over my sternum still felt inflamed and itchy.

I was an outlier in our pack; very few people manifested a fate-mark after the coming-of-age ceremony we called the wolfbirth. After the mark had bloomed so unexpectedly upon my skin during the ceremony, Cai had used his influence as the pack alpha to help me make discrete inquiries within the Greystalker clan and all the surrounding packs. No one else had a matching fate-mark shaped like an infinity sign — the mark of my soulmate.

I had begun to think it was just part of my destiny as the most unlucky and ill-fated member of the pack. After being kidnapped and held as bait by the most insane ruler that Elfhame had ever known, *of course* I'd also end up with an unmatched fate-mark. In the brief, rather pathetic history of my life, this latest mild scandal had barely registered.

"Darby?" Dianthe's voice shook me from my bitter thoughts.

I looked up quickly and found that four sets of piercing eyes were pinned on me. I could tell by

Dianthe's tone that this wasn't the first time she'd called my name.

The shifter male's brilliant, summer-blue eyes were wide with… shock? Outrage? I wasn't sure. A queasy feeling began to roil in my stomach.

I cleared my throat, tearing my gaze away to meet Dianthe's. "Sorry, what?" I rasped.

"Are you well?" Dianthe searched my face with clear concern.

Steeling myself not to rub at the inflamed fate-mark, I drew in a shuddering breath. How could I possibly explain what just happened? What were the chances that my fate-mark would come alive at this exact moment… the same moment I met the eyes of another shifter? A shifter I'd been hopelessly attracted to on the one other occasion I'd seen him.

"Peachy," I croaked. "Seriously. Never better."

She would see right through me, of course, but I tried to communicate to her with a glare that she should let the matter drop, at least for now.

Dianthe, though, clearly had other plans.

Her eyes landed on the queen's shifter advisor, who was mindlessly rubbing at the same spot above his own heart. I knew it could only mean one thing—this mysterious male had the fate-mark that matched mine.

This was completely insane. In my distraction, my hand crept up to my chest again. I couldn't help it.

Dianthe's gaze flicked back and forth between the two of us, each trying to massage the pain from our stinging skin.

"There's some kind of weird shifter thing going on right now, isn't there," she said, not making it sound like a question.

"What are you prattling on about, woman?" The shifter snarled at her, his head snapping up with a look of pure defiance. "What business is it of yours?"

How was this possible? I blinked rapidly, still trying to wrap my mind around this stunning revelation. Almost despite myself, a fragile thread of hope and excitement crept through me.

I have a mate. A real mate. He's here! He's been here on Elfhame this whole time… and he's the most stunning creature I've ever seen in my entire life!

Could… could this mean that I wasn't some impossibly damaged shell of a she-wolf after all, doomed to misery and misfortune all my life? He looked so strong. Could he be an alpha? Was it possible I might finally escape the low omega status that had dogged me my entire life, once and for all? Good goddess, he was an advisor to a *queen* —

The wolf inside me grew restless, longing to get closer to our mate. Almost against my own will, I crept forward, my feet carrying me towards the male who would complete my soul with his.

What was it that Ember always told me? That she could feel the presence of both her mates on an almost spiritual level?

I wondered if it would be the same for me.

Never taking my eyes off the male who was now scowling at the forest floor as though it had personally offended him, I let my wolf's senses reach out towards him, feeling the air around him until I found the bright spot of our connection.

A low growl erupted in his chest and he jerked backwards, severing the delicate silken thread between us in one swift slice.

The sudden loss stopped me in my tracks, stealing the air out of my lungs. A whimper escaped my throat.

"Edric, Aiwin, we're leaving," he said, his tone biting. "I've no time for mutts and harpies."

The insult tore a gasp from my chest and sent blood rushing to my cheeks. The two fae—Aiwin and Edric, apparently—looked at each other in bewilderment.

"Oy, Vale! That's well out of order," said the redhead, glancing at me as though in secondhand embarrassment. "What's got into you?"

"*Mutts*?" Dianthe's tone was indignant with disbelief. "If this is how the queen's advisor behaves in public, then I daresay we've no time for you either!"

The shifter directed a glare at her. She didn't back down.

"Dianthe," I murmured, a horrible, sinking feeling making my chest feel like lead. "Leave it."

All my enthusiasm for our hunt had fled in the time it took my mate to insult me and look at me like I was dirt on his boot. Right now, the only thing I wanted was to return to the safety of the cottage. Shame welled up inside me as the beautiful shifter that fate had tied to my soul turned a cold shoulder to us. My cheeks burned hot, and I stood blinking back stinging tears.

"They can't even take down a deer," he muttered, herding his companions away from us. "We shouldn't linger. I'd hate for their incompetence to rub off on us somehow."

Dianthe took a hostile step forward, but I clutched her arm, desperate to escape the situation.

"Please," I whispered, barely loud enough for her to hear me.

Cocking her head at me, Dianthe glanced down at my trembling fingers on her arm, and then up at my pinched face. I was sure my cheeks had gone beet-red with humiliation.

"Fine. I'll let the disrespectful little whelp live," she assured me, though her voice sounded like gravel. *"For now."*

"This isn't like you, Vale," the blond fae said. His voice was barely audible as the trio walked away from us. "What aren't you telling us?"

The shifter who should be my mate didn't answer. Instead, he cast a final, narrow-eyed glance over his shoulder at me. *I don't want you,* his expression said. *I don't need you. Not for anything.*

THREE

Eleven months ago

*

"YOU'VE SUCCESSFULLY SHIFTED into your wolf form before. Is this correct, Darby Adalwolf?"

I stared hard at my feet, wishing I could escape from this embarrassing situation by disappearing straight into the ground. I could feel the gazes of the entire village on me, gathered here to bear witness to my induction into the pack as an adult member.

Without raising my eyes, I nodded in response to the alpha's question. Cai Greystalker already knew the answer. He was only asking for the form of the thing.

"Ember helped you bring your wolf to the fore?" he asked, his tone exceedingly gentle.

I took a deep breath and willed the tears from my eyes. Like *hell* I was going to get emotional in front of my new alpha during my own freaking wolfbirth ceremony. It was bad enough that my feelings frequently felt like they'd been hijacked by an absent ghost, without showing the whole world just how damaged and broken I had become after my ordeal with Oberon.

I knew that it was highly improper for a wolfshifter to transform for the first time prior to the ceremony that marked their coming-of-age within the pack. It simply *wasn't done*.

Most alphas would have seen it as usurping their power for someone else to assist with a new wolf's transformation before the official wolfbirth. Even though I knew it wasn't going to happen, the broken thing inside me whispered that it would be within Cai's rights to punish me severely. My irrational dread must have shown on my face, because Ember—who was present in her new capacity as the alpha's mate—wrapped a comforting arm around my shoulders.

"Easy," she whispered to me, "it's okay. Remember where you are. Cai isn't like his father, and this was an exceptional circumstance."

She meant to ease my worry, but instead the burgeoning seed of panic inside of me only grew larger. I didn't *want* any exceptional circumstances. I didn't *want* to have achieved my transformation early. I'd never wanted *any* of this.

"Exceptional circumstances, indeed," Cai said kindly, his alpha rumble soothing my inner wolf almost despite myself. "You are not at fault, and there will be no consequences to you or your family."

Chewing on my bottom lip, I nodded and tried to utter a thank you. Unfortunately, I couldn't seem to form words, only a graceless whimper.

Fresh concern filled Ember's face. "Darby?"

I tried to answer but found my throat was still constricted.

"You don't seem well," Cai said. "Given everything that's happened recently, no one will judge you if you prefer to forego the ceremony."

My eyes flew up, meeting his in defiance of protocol. No one would judge me? Was he *joking*? *Of course* people would judge me! They always had.

"No, I want to do it." The words tumbled out of my mouth before I had a chance to stop them. Heat rose in my face, and I returned my gaze to the ground again, shamefaced.

"We can still do it, obviously," Ember said, hurrying to fill the silence as the nearest onlookers began to murmur to each other. "Right, Cai?"

"Yes, if you wish," he replied, watching me closely. "But Darby, can you help me understand why you're so upset?"

"I just want a normal life," I managed, not meeting his gaze. "I didn't want any of this, and I just want to be treated like everyone else. Including a normal wolfbirth ceremony."

"I see." Cai sighed unhappily; the sound too low to carry to the watching crowd. "After everything you have done to help this pack, a normal wolfbirth is the very least I can offer you."

Ember had arranged this ceremony for me after we'd returned to Earth from the fae realm. At first, my family had been confused. We were low status. We had been for generations. They'd been relieved beyond measure to have me back safely, but they, like me, had expected punishment for my early transformation—or at the very least, ostracization. It had taken Cai and Ember meeting with my parents to assure them that I wasn't in trouble for transforming early.

"I had to help her shift into her wolf form to combat Elfhame's madness," Ember had explained to them.

Meanwhile, Cai had deferred to her, remaining in the background as she reassured my mother and father that my unusual circumstances didn't reflect badly on me. Even now, I couldn't help but marvel how such understated leadership seemed to come more naturally to Cai than it ever had to his sire.

"We understand," my father had replied, glancing nervously between Ember and the new pack leader. "And we appreciate it, Alpha. It's just highly unusual, is all."

Cai lifted one shoulder in a casual shrug. "Welcome to my world for the last few months."

Ember had snorted in amusement at that, bumping Cai's shoulder with hers in an affectionate gesture. "At least we haven't been bored."

Goddess. By that point, I would have *killed* for a few weeks of boredom.

"So, there will be a normal ceremony on her twenty-first birthday, and Darby will officially come of age?" my mother asked, ever the practical one.

"Yes," Cai said easily. "Just as she has requested."

My parents looked at me, as though surprised that I'd had the boldness to make a request of an alpha. I couldn't really blame them. I'd been a little bit surprised myself.

Ember looked back and forth between us. "So, it's all settled, then?"

Cai had nodded, his agreement as good as a decree.

Still, I couldn't help glancing at my parents for their opinion.

"It's whatever you need, my darling," my mother had insisted, wrapping a warm hand around my wrist. I stared at her callused fingers, willing my heart not to race into a panic in response to the unexpected physical contact.

"I just want things to go back to normal," I said again, willing it to be so.

———◆———

And that was how I found myself standing naked before Cai, Ember, and the entire damned village, waiting to transition into my wolf form. Although I had shifted before, I allowed Cai to lead me through the process, feeling his alpha power flowing around and through me.

It felt like a warm light inside me, pushing the panic away, and I bathed in that comforting glow of protection for the few moments of respite it offered me. As soon as I transformed back into my human form, I felt a sharp pain on my chest.

"Oh, goddess. What now?" I muttered, looking down to find the unfamiliar figure-eight shaped mark etched into my naked chest like a fresh burn.

My stomach plummeted, even as Ember drew in a sharp breath of surprise. It was a fate-mark. *I had a brand new, shiny fate-mark.* The irony was too much to bear, and I started to giggle. I bit on the inside of my cheek hard, trying in vain to hold in the hysteria that threatened to overwhelm me. Despite my best efforts, the giggles grew worse. Covering my mouth with my hand, I tried to stifle the ugly noises escaping my throat. The onlookers glanced between themselves, obviously concerned for my sanity.

"Darby. Breathe," Cai said, stepping forward and clasping my left shoulder, even as Ember clasped my right.

Flinching backwards from their touch, I whirled away and stumbled back a couple of steps.

I felt Ember at my side again a moment later, followed closely by my mother.

"You have a fate-mark," Ember said, wonder in her tone. "This is a good thing, Darby! There's no need to be upset."

My mother smoothed my dark chestnut hair away from my face. "Yes, my dearest. It's just a fate-mark. It's perfectly natural. It means you have a mate out there waiting for you."

It was only then that I realized tears were streaming down my face. I was giggling hysterically and crying at the same time. No wonder everyone was looking at me as if I'd lost my mind. Maybe I had.

I pushed them away from me and tried to regain control of myself.

"I know," I told them, my voice emerging choked and strange. "I'm okay."

No one looked convinced. I really couldn't blame them, but I needed to escape the situation so I could gather myself. I just needed to think.

Rubbing at the new scar I would carry for the rest of my life, I forced on a smile that felt entirely strained and fake.

"Really, I'm fine."

FOUR

The present day

*

MY FINGERS TRACED over the mark again as I pulled myself free of the bitter memories. After months of searching, I had finally found my mate… only to discover that he was apparently a complete asshole.

Why couldn't it have been someone sweet and amazing like Cai or Tamlain? Ember was so lucky.

Though, to be fair, it hadn't started out that way. If anything, Ember's own wolfbirth ceremony had been far more bizarre and humiliating than mine. When their matching fate-marks had been revealed, Cai was already under the magical influence of a fae agent called Pavia. She was Oberon's pet witch, and she'd been hiding in plain sight as a shifter using the alias, *Geneva Padfoot*. Though it hadn't technically been Cai's fault since he was under a fae spell, he'd rejected Ember publicly and demanded their fate-marks be burned out to sever the bond.

The burning of a fate-mark was sometimes seen as necessary in shifter society, but it was still the ultimate shame for the rejected party. Worse yet, it hadn't even worked—not completely.

I shuddered, unable to even imagine the pain that Ember had gone through on that first night, when Cai had slept with other females in an attempt to complete the severing.

Okay, so maybe Ember hadn't been lucky after all. At least, not at first. She did end up having the world's worst father in the form of the mad king Oberon, not to mention a fae-controlled mate who'd rejected her until he'd come to his senses and realized what a horrible mistake he'd made.

And all that was *before* you took into account the fate of two worlds balanced on her slender shoulders.

Remembering Ember's plight brought my own into better perspective. Feeling slightly steadier, I turned my attention back to the retreating group of hunters. And—joy of joys—the posh-looking fae had dragged my asshole of a would-be mate to a halt and was quietly berating him. Beside me, Dianthe watched with a jaundiced expression as the two fae physically hauled their companion around and dragged him back in our direction.

Despite my best efforts, my wolf perked up hopefully at my fated mate's approach. I tried to rein her in, confident that extending this confrontation would only bring more heartbreak and humiliation.

"Sorry, can we try this again?" the high-bred blond fae said, stepping forward to offer a slight bow. "My name is Edric, and these two are Aiwin and Vale. My friends, although at least one of them is in need of a refresher regarding basic manners."

Aiwin also stepped forward, bowing as much as he could with a dead boar draped across his broad shoulders. Meanwhile, my mate—*Vale*—stood back resolutely, his arms crossed. Dianthe, too, seemed to radiate hostility.

The red-haired fae, Aiwin, gave his companion a bemused look. Returning his attention to us, he stumbled through an awkward greeting. "Um, we're… honored to meet you. What brings you to the forest today?"

"I live here," Dianthe told him, her cold green eyes still fixed on Vale. It was clear that her disgust with his behavior was mounting, and it would likely reach a boiling point before long.

Honestly, I was a bit surprised she hadn't punched him in the face yet, based on her murderous expression. Dianthe had never been shy about expressing her opinions, being bold to the point of recklessness. After a moment, it occurred to me that as a direct advisor to Queen Titania, Vale must outrank Dianthe by quite a margin within the fae court.

The idea that she was constrained from putting the insolent ass in his place by the concerns of politics was… disquieting. I wasn't used to seeing Dianthe stifled.

"And you, my lady?" Aiwin asked politely, turning towards me.

Startled out of my thoughts, I took in his pleasant features and the smattering of freckles dusting his cheeks. He was the blond fae's opposite in almost every way, and yet they were both equally appealing.

"Oh," I stammered, "I, uh, I have a meeting with the queen, but I came early to visit Dianthe."

"The queen?" Aiwin echoed, sounding impressed. "Clearly, my ass-headed friend should think twice before hurling insults at random strangers."

"That he should," Edric muttered, shooting Vale a sidelong glance. "And might we know your name, my lady?"

"Um." I fought a blush, silently cursing myself. "It's Darby. Darby Adalwolf."

"Well, Lady Adalwolf, please accept our welcome to Elfhame," Edric said.

"Yes," Aiwin agreed. "We don't often have shifter visitors. In fact, I can't say I've ever met any shifters except for Vale and his mother, the Lady Zara."

"Uh, thanks," I said, fighting the urge to shuffle my feet. My gaze slid to Vale without conscious volition. What did you say to someone that you were supposed to spend the rest of your life with, while sharing an unbreakable spiritual and physical bond?

"Why do you hunt as a human?" I blurted. "Why not use your wolf form?"

Internally, I cringed. *Smooth, Darby. Real smooth.*

Hunting. Here I was meeting my soulmate for the first time, and the best conversational ice breaker I could come up with was a stupid question about his hunting style. This, after he'd already insulted me to my face and treated me like dirt.

Still—once a wolf shifter, always a wolf shifter. Hunting was an important part of our culture. Maybe Vale shared the same traits, despite being raised on Elfhame.

My would-be mate only sneered at me. "I don't share information about my wolf with the unworthy."

And… *okay, then*. I blanched, recoiling from the venom in his voice. A quick glance at Dianthe revealed that she seemed just as shocked as I felt. It was as though he'd slapped me across the face or doused me in icy water.

What had I done wrong? I thought in bewilderment, unable to stop my pained gasp or the hot tears threatening to spill over. I stepped back, hiding my emotional reaction behind Dianthe's shoulder. She bristled on my behalf.

Omega instinct had me hunching in on myself… trying to make my body appear small. Fruitlessly attempting to wrap a cocoon of protection around my injured wolf. I had always been one of the lowest ranking members of the pack, I knew how to be submissive, but that didn't stop the anger from boiling in my stomach at Vale's treatment of me.

The old submissive instincts were strong, but I had gained significant status under Cai and Ember's new regime. I had been elevated to an advisory position, and I was Queen Titania's liaison, for fuck's sake. My whole family had benefitted from the reflected glory of my new position.

But apparently, none of that mattered in the end. Whatever I'd accomplished, I would never be good enough for a mate-bond.

Fresh anger seared through me, but at least my eyes no longer leaked bitter tears.

"Ah, Vale, that's far too harsh, don't you think?" Aiwin said in an uneasy voice.

Edric looked positively scandalized. "*Harsh?* You're being a fucking arsehole, you mangy cur. What in sanity's name has got into you today?"

Out of the corner of my eye, I saw Dianthe open her mouth as though to voice her opinion on the matter. But before I could elbow her in the ribs to shut her up, a loud caw from the sky above us drew every eye in the clearing.

As we all looked up, a large, black raven flew through the open space. Everyone ducked, and I yelped as its claws scraped over my head, tangling in my hair.

With a strangled cry, I tried to beat the bird off, but it tightened its hold on my long locks. I struggled wildly against the flapping creature as the world around me grew unnaturally dark. Heavy black storm clouds rolled overhead, barely visible in the murk. It was as if night had fallen in the space of a handful of seconds.

"Dianthe!" I screamed, trying in vain to pry the talons from me… batting at the bird in desperation.

A blast of wind sent me to my knees, shaking the vicious bird loose. It tumbled away with another loud caw that seemed to reverberate off the trees in the shattering wind.

Dust and leaves swirled around me, cutting me off from the others. But almost as soon as the storm had begun, it was over. Everything began to settle, revealing the clearing—empty now, except for me and one other person.

Everyone had disappeared except for Vale.

We both whirled around, taking in the absence of our friends. Then our eyes met, each of us mirroring the horror of the other.

FIVE

I GASPED IN SHOCK. "What's *happening*?" I demanded. My adrenaline surged, even as my breathing grew ragged with fear. Vale made a snarling noise in response, pacing around the clearing and shooting wary looks at the sky, as though he expected more ravens to dive-bomb us.

My heart had leapt up into my throat at the first sign of danger, constricting my airways and making my head spin. Pressing my fingers to my temples, I tried to calm the tide of panic that was threatening to overwhelm me.

Broken images from the past flashed through my mind. The chaos of the palace square when I'd been dragged there for torture by Oberon. Hooded guards, too large and strong to fight, pressing in on me, hemming me in. Hard hands gripping my arms, holding me down as the metal shackles were put on. And then, the pain had come.

The hands restraining me began to shake, sharp nails digging into the skin.

But… no. That wasn't right.

I opened my eyes with a jolt, abruptly aware that the vice-like grip on my upper arms was only my own fingers. I had fallen to my knees and wrapped my arms around myself, trying to ward off the flashbacks that felt every bit as vivid as the real world around me. My fingernails dug into my biceps like claws.

I needed Dianthe here. She might know what had caused this magical shift in our surroundings.

Even if she didn't know the reason, she'd at least know what to do about it. And, more importantly, I wouldn't be alone.

But… I wasn't alone, was I? My *mate* was here with me. My mate, who wanted nothing to do with me.

Joy of fucking joys.

Vale didn't seem any happier about things than I was. He let out a cry of frustration and pulled an arrow from his quiver, fitting it neatly into his bow. Swinging around, his aim moved from the trees to the line of bushes all around us, looking for a target.

When he couldn't find one, a low growl rumbled in his throat. The bow and arrow dipped in defeat.

The raven took that moment to break from hiding. It took off from high in one of the trees above us, letting out a terrible shriek as it flapped toward us. To my shock, it dove at us again, beak opened wide.

This isn't how birds behave, I thought, more than a little hysterically. *They don't attack shifters! Not unless they're sick, or crazed, or—*

Vale released an arrow, which whistled through the air, straight and true. It passed beneath the raven's outstretched wing, close enough to ruffle its feathers. The large bird was knocked off course, fluttering wildly in response to the close call. Shrieking, it beat the air frantically for a second or two before it was able to right itself.

Through the storm-tossed darkness of the altered clearing, I could see the world of Elfhame changing around us. What had been a beautiful, healthy forest began to twist and decay before my eyes. It was as though the ravages of time were on fast-forward, like a human DVD.

The leaves, which had been beautiful hues of gold and purple, shriveled into sickly gray-brown clumps, dropping to the ground around us. The shrubs—heavy with vibrantly red flowers and berries only moments ago—wilted and dropped all their fruit, which rotted before our eyes.

I clapped my hand over my nose and mouth as a horrendous stench filled the air. The reek seemed to rise out of the ground as sucking mud and sludge formed under our feet. It was like a foul swamp had bubbled up from somewhere below the forest, engulfing it.

I scrambled upright and let out a sound of terrified disgust, searching frantically for high ground and a dry place to stand. But the sickening muck was spreading even as I watched—transforming the entire forest into a repulsive pit of disease and decay.

I spun on the spot, seeking the only other person here.

"You!" I demanded, pointing my finger at Vale. "What the hell is happening? Are you doing this somehow?"

"Me?" An incredulous look came over his too-handsome face. "What makes you think this is *my* fault?"

"You were the one pitching a fit just a few minutes ago, and then *this* happened!" I threw my arms out wide, gesturing to the destruction spreading all around us.

"*I* don't have the power to destroy a world," he hissed in a low voice.

I gasped. Was that a jab at Ember? *Now*, of all times? Fury overrode my usual meekness. "Oh, no? Then explain this!"

"*I can't.*" The words were a vicious snarl.

"We were standing in a perfectly normal forest, and now everything has changed!" I gestured wildly at our surroundings again, as though he might somehow have failed to notice the storm, and the raven, and the foul muck creeping up around our ankles. "Where is Dianthe? She might be hurt! And what about your friends? *What happened to them?*"

Vale shook his head helplessly, looking dismayed and vulnerable for the first time.

The mingled terror and fury inside me snapped, and I found myself shouting into his face at the top of my lungs.

"You have to know!" I shrieked, like some deranged harpy. "You and your mother are Queen Titania's advisors! You *know* things! You *live* here!"

"And that's supposed to make me an expert on random dark magic in the middle of a fucking forest?" he snapped.

"You're more of an expert than me!" I clenched my fists to hide how badly they were shaking. *I couldn't do this again. I couldn't become a victim of Elfhame's madness. Not a second time.*

Vale's jaw clenched, accentuating his high cheekbones. "I don't know what's happening here."

I took several deep breaths, trying to calm the storm of emotion boiling inside my heart. In that moment, I didn't care if he was fated to be my mate or not. He had rejected me, and I wanted to fly at him in my fury… in my desperation not to be someone's victim yet again.

Calm. I needed to stay calm.

"Surely, if things like this," I gestured around us again, "are happening in her realm, Queen Titania *has* to know about it, right? Surely, she'd consult with you and your mother. You're her closest advisors!"

Vale's expression went stony and blank, as though he was hiding his true response to my words.

"What?" I demanded.

"Nothing." The granite façade didn't crack.

"Oh, no. That look meant *something*," I goaded. The muck around my ankles rose another inch, and I suppressed a shudder. "Since I'm stuck in this mess with you, I think I should know all the facts! What are you hiding?"

In a small corner of my mind, I was shocked at my own daring. Normally, I would never have the courage to speak to a higher-ranking shifter in such a way. Apparently, my terror that I was about to end up in the clutches of some dark fae force was stronger than my fear of a dominant wolf. Who knew?

I stared down the mate who didn't want me, not breaking eye contact as a submissive shifter should. In that moment, I felt as wild as the storm around us—untethered and dangerous.

Yeah, dangerous — sure, whispered my ugly inner voice. *If the stench gets much worse, you might puke on his boots or something. How terrifying.*

I ignored it, continuing to glare.

The moment stretched. Finally, Vale let out a frustrated growl. "There may have been some whispers at Court."

I blinked, part of me shocked that I'd managed to bully him into talking.

"Okay," I said cautiously. "What are these whispers saying?"

He made a sharp, frustrated gesture with the hand that wasn't holding the bow. "It's just unsubstantiated rumblings. People with too much time on their hands, speculating that a mad witch may be trying to raise Oberon from the dead."

SIX

MY ENTIRE BODY froze to ice between one heartbeat and the next. Someone was trying to resurrect my abductor, who had been killed during his apocalyptic battle with Ember?

"What the *actual fuck*?" I rasped. "Is… is that a thing here? Resurrecting dead people?"

Vale glared at me. "No, it's complete nonsense. That's why I didn't want to mention it. He's gone forever. A person can't come back from the dead — it's ridiculous."

Once upon a time, his words might have been comforting. I used to be too preoccupied with my own problems to worry about any realms other than the one I inhabited with the Greystalker pack. I knew nothing of magic, other than the inherent natural magic of my people that allowed us to transform into wolves.

I used to be so naive, but I knew better now. If anyone had the power to raise the dead, surely it would be a magical practitioner from Elfhame.

I pressed the palm of my hand to the center of my forehead, feeling faint from more than the suffocating miasma of rot.

"I said it's nonsense." Vale repeated. "Stop looking like that."

"So you say," I fired back. "But here's what *I* say — Titania had a duty to notify Ember about these rumors, even if she doesn't believe them herself. We needed to know about this!"

My voice rose again; I couldn't help it.

"Typical Earther," Vale muttered, raising his eyes to the heavens as though praying for patience. "Always jumping to the worst conclusion. It's no wonder that everyone here distrusts the people from your realm. How do you live like this, jumping at every shadow?"

My jaw hung open for a long moment. I snapped it shut before the stench gagged me.

"Jumping at…" I trailed off in disbelief. "We are trapped in a bloody *dark dimension*, complete with attack ravens and a death swamp!"

"And your hysteria isn't exactly helping the situation, is it?" he snarled.

White-hot anger flashed through me, and I slogged forward through the muck until we were almost nose to nose.

"You will not speak to me this way," I snarled back. "You will not treat me like I'm dirt under your feet, because surely even *you* couldn't have failed to notice that we're mates!"

His upper lip curled in contempt, baring a white canine. "The fuck we are."

I stared at him in disbelief. Had he failed to recognize the pain in his chest? Or was I somehow mistaken, and the sensation I'd felt was something else?

No, my instincts said, clear as day. *He is your mate. You feel the draw towards him, and you sure as hell felt the rejection.*

"Say that again," I demanded. "Look me in the eye and tell me we aren't mates."

Looking me square in the eye without the slightest hesitation, Vale said, "You are no mate of mine."

I nodded, slow and deliberate. "Oh. Is that so?"

Without warning, my hand whipped out and grabbed the V-shaped opening of his tunic. Before he could stop me, I used all my strength to rip the fabric away from his chest. Lightning flashed in the sky above us, revealing an identical mark to my own, just above his heart.

"Want to try that again, Vale?" I asked.

Vale jerked backwards as though my touch had burned him. His expression was as thunderous as the sky above the forest. "No cruel trick of biology is going to tie me to some craven omega wolf I've never even met before! How *dare* you lay hands on me?"

I opened my mouth, ready to release words like razor blades, when a harsh, unearthly laugh filled the clearing.

There was something vaguely familiar about the sound, and it made the hair on the back of my neck stand straight on end. I had thought I was afraid before, but now clammy sweat broke out on my body, my gut churning queasily.

Despite everything, I shrank towards Vale—hating myself for the deep-rooted instinct pulling me closer to my mate when danger appeared. I spun in place, trying to find the source of the evil cackling.

Vale, too, responded to the sound, raising his bow and nocking another arrow. His hard eyes scanned our surroundings. The echoing laughter seemed to emanate from the dark shadows between two twisted trees. My sharp gaze spied a figure standing there, the hood of a long cloak raised over its head.

As one, Vale and I turned so we were facing the intruder, shoulder to shoulder. I bared my teeth at the figure, while Vale's arrow was pointed directly at the center of its chest. In the darkness, it seemed larger than life, far bigger than any fae or shifter should be.

I squinted hard, trying to discern its features through the darkness. It was impossible; the face was swathed in the hood's shadow.

The high, almost hysterical laughter continued as it stepped slowly into the clearing. With a sudden twang, Vale loosed his shot. The arrow hurtled forward, only to pass straight through the approaching phantasm—landing with a dull *thunk* in the tree behind it.

I stumbled backwards in the mud, not sure whether to be more frightened by the figure's insubstantiality, or less. In the stormy light of the clearing, its outline seemed to shrink to normal size, but it remained faintly blurry around the edges. Pale hands reached up and grasped the edges of the hood obscuring the intruder's face.

My mouth dropped open in shock as the figure's features came into view. A *very familiar* set of features.

"Hello, my pets," said Pavia—the witch who had once betrayed Ember and kidnapped me, delivering me to Elfhame's mad king as a prisoner for torture and execution. Her voice dripped with hatred dipped in poisoned sugar. "Now, you both are going to help me right a wrong. With your assistance, I will finally kill your bitch queen, Titania, and take my rightful place at my beloved king's side!"

SEVEN

"PAVIA," I SNARLED, the hated name emerging from my lips dripping with contempt. I would recognize that woman anywhere. I'd grown up around her as she watched over Ember, plotting for the day she might drag my friend back to her mad father in the fae realm. Her wrinkled face would be forever burned into my mind as the one that had caused all our suffering to begin.

The betrayal that Ember had experienced burned in my heart. This woman, who had pretended to love her like a mother, had tried to facilitate Ember's destruction for her own selfish gain.

Vale glanced back and forth between us, assessing my reaction. I saw the moment when he, too, recognized the crone in front of us.

"You," he said in disbelief, taking a threatening step forward. I could practically hear his teeth grinding together in anger as he realized exactly who had put the two of us in this situation.

Pavia smiled with a mouth full of rotting teeth. My nose wrinkled in disgust. She'd really let herself go during the months since escaping Titania's forces. And now she thought she could be the consort of a king? She must be as mad as Oberon had been.

Clamping my jaw, I mastered the impulse to taunt her with the impossibility of her desires—*barely*. Vale didn't censor himself, however. When he spoke, his voice was thick with anger, and I could feel his temper rising through our mate bond.

"You're the witch that is accused of attempting necromancy! Don't tell me that ridiculous claptrap is true. Are you *delusional*? Why have you trapped us here in this shadow world of decay?"

"What about the others?" I demanded, my thoughts turning once more to Dianthe and Vale's friends. Had Pavia killed them? Were we the only ones left alive? Had her powers increased so much that she could destroy life in an entire forest with such little effort?

Pavia didn't answer. She and Vale were still staring each other down, as if readying for a fight. But how could Vale take on such a powerful witch? Would he try to battle her alone?

Fear clenched in my stomach at the prospect, unlike anything I had ever experienced before that moment. My wolf howled her distress. He was our mate! We couldn't let him take her on by himself.

I could fight. Adrenaline surged through me, lending strength to my shaking limbs. I could shift, and the two of us could attack Pavia as wolves.

Or was I being as delusional as this crazy witch? I had never been a warrior by any stretch, but I had started working with Cai to build my skills in the time since the battle at the palace. Cai had insisted that as an advisor, I needed to be able to defend myself and those around me.

Even though I was hesitant at first, I had to admit that the lessons weren't as bad as I had feared they would be when he first approached me. It turned out that Cai was a wonderful teacher, patient and understanding as he trained me and some of the other young wolves.

At this rate, it looked like I'd have to put my training to the test for the first time.

"Oh, never fear—I have the *perfect* plan," Pavia said, taking a step towards Vale and shaking me free from my thoughts. "*You* will serve as bait for Titania—" She jammed a finger toward Vale's chest. "—and *she* will be bait for that half-breed whelp, Ember." The finger moved toward me.

Despite my best efforts to be brave, a cold sensation settled in my stomach as my last captivity played over and over, running on a continuous loop in my mind's eye.

I shook my head sharply, trying to dispel it. I would *not* be taken hostage again. I'd die first.

"Why Ember?" I demanded, pleased when my voice didn't shake. "What do you want with her? She no longer has the power to harm either realm. She can't be used as a weapon. There's no reason to try to capture her now."

I attempted to keep my voice reasonable, not wanting to betray my desperation over my best friend's safety. She had mated with both Cai and Tamlain specifically so that neither the human world nor the fae world would be in danger from her unbalanced powers.

Pavia gave me a disdainful look. She let out a low, ugly noise, which turned into a shriek of laughter a moment later. Her hysterical braying grew so intense that she leaned over, putting her hands on her knees to regain her self-control.

"Oh, you pathetic little shifter, you were never the brightest sidekick, were you?" Pavia cackled, straightening up to glare at me.

I scowled back at her, anger and fear battling for supremacy inside me.

She shook her head as though I'd disappointed her. "You know so little about the realms, it's a wonder that anyone trusts you to travel back and forth between them as an envoy. It's true that Ember is entirely useless as a weapon now. I'll freely admit that. But! She is highly valuable in other ways."

"What sort of ways?" Vale asked, his eyes narrowing.

"In *every* way," Pavia snarled at him. "Her blood has value."

"Her blood?" I asked, not sure I wanted to know.

Suddenly the swampy ground shuddered beneath us. The clouds tore open, a shaft of brilliant sunlight bursting through the stormy slate gray. Where the ray struck the ground, the blackened leaves and mud began to sizzle, as if burning, revealing healthy ground underneath. I could see glimpses of the purple and gold leaves that had decorated the clearing before Pavia's attack, as though the shadows she'd cloaked us in were melting away.

How was it possible? For a moment I wondered if the sickness of the forest around me had only been a hallucination of my overstressed mind — but if that was the case, Vale wouldn't have shared the same vision.

Unless the fact that he was my mate meant he'd suffered the same delusion I had? Could that be?

I'd given up on the possibility of finding a mate long ago, so I knew very little about what mates experienced together. From everything that I'd heard and Ember's accounts, their bond was incredibly strong and could span realms.

The ground quaked under our feet again with the sound of shifting stones nearby. More holes tore open in the sky, letting in the sun; yet the darkness seemed to grow behind Pavia. It billowed out behind her, dark smoke in tendrils that snaked their way around the trees. Grey, sick bark turned black, as if the forest was burning away without visible flames. I could feel an icy breeze blowing against my face, even as the sun rays warmed the air at my back. The scent of death and decay wafted on the wind, mixing with the fresh, summer scent I remembered from the real Elfhame. My fists clenched, as I willed the world of light and warmth to reappear fully.

EIGHT

LIGHT AND DARK fought for dominance around us, neither one able to take precedence in the tortured clearing. A groan crept up from deep within the soil, the strain of the battle stretching all the way from the core of the world.

The tears in the cloudy sky ripped open like an old garment torn apart at the seams. Brilliant light exploded all around us, temporarily blinding me. I brought my hand up to shield my eyes, trying to see through the actinic glare.

Beside me, Vale let out a dark laugh. "Yes," he said. "It turns out that blood can be powerful, indeed."

Turning towards him, all I could make out was his silhouette, but I could sense the feral smile coming through in his words.

Abruptly, the blinding light dimmed to a tolerable level. I blinked rapidly. When I was able to focus, it was to find that the darkness and disease were gone, as was Pavia's insubstantial specter. Everything had returned to normal, with the warm sun beating down on my face and the gentle, sweet-smelling breeze lifting the hair off my neck.

Glancing around, I sagged in relief to find Dianthe standing nearby, along with Vale's two friends, Aiwin and Edric. All three had their hands raised, casting a dome of magic over our heads. It grew even as I watched, swelling into a huge bubble that would soon encompass the entire forest. I lunged forward and grabbed Dianthe's arm before that bubble could pop, terrified we might be separated again.

Dianthe's eyes settled on me, relief flooding her lovely features. The three fae slowly brought their hands down, letting the magic dissipate into nothing. I held my breath, but the sun continued to shine, and the plants didn't wilt with unnatural decay. The ground under my feet was solid, and no stinking mud clung to my feet.

Dianthe turned and gripped me by the shoulders.

"Darby," she said with relief, giving me a tiny shake. "Are you all right? Have you been harmed at all?"

In my peripheral vision, I could see a similar reunion happening between the others. Edric was gripping Vale's shoulder, looking deeply concerned. Aiwin was wiping sweat off his freckled brow; relief clear on his handsome face.

"Dianthe," I croaked, my voice shaking, "It was Pavia. She's back, and she's as crazy as Oberon was. She's trying to get Ember and kill the queen!"

Dianthe's lips parted in shock. "She's *what*? You must tell me everything that happened, Darby. Quickly!"

In a rush, I told the story, capturing the attention of Aiwin and Edric in the process. All three fae listened intently with expressions gone hard and worried.

When I reached the point of the story where light had flooded the dying clearing, my voice broke, and I shook my head.

Dianthe looked grim, her jaw set. "Well, that's certainly a story I didn't expect to hear today." She didn't elaborate, but continued to stare off into space, her mind obviously racing.

I was silent for a moment, but I had questions that needed answering.

"How did you save us?" I asked. "How were you able to pull us out of that... that... *shadow place*?"

It was Aiwin who answered. "We have a blood bond with Vale," he said. "We used that connection to reach through the barrier of black magic and poke holes in it until it collapsed."

"Black magic?" I breathed. "You were able to smash through some evil spell that Pavia was casting around the two of us?"

He and Edric nodded.

I looked to Dianthe for confirmation. She lifted one shoulder in a resigned shrug. "They were the ones with the connection. I just provided them with a power boost."

My mind spun uselessly in shock. It felt like we had resolved the last major crisis and threat to peace between the realms, only to be thrown back into the fire with this new situation. Really, this had to be the worst luck that either world had ever known. Two major threats in such a short time? How was that possible?

It's the same threat, though, I realized. *It always starts and ends with Pavia.*

This new crisis, on top of the realization that Vale was my mate, was too much for me. Questions were swimming around in my mind, clogging in my throat until one finally broke free and came pouring out in a rush.

"Can Pavia really bring Oberon back from the dead?"

I couldn't keep the quaver out of my voice as four pairs of eyes turned towards me. The memory of my last captivity still haunted me. My body was shaking like a leaf. It was all I could do to keep from collapsing to the ground in hysterics.

I shoved at the unwanted memories, trying to push them down and out of sight.

"Of course she can't," Dianthe said. "Don't be ridiculous."

Her words were firm, but the uncertainty in her eyes betrayed her. She glanced towards Vale for a moment and their gazes met.

"We must report this to Queen Titania," he said, his feud with the fae huntress evidently forgotten, at least for now.

I clenched my jaw. All I wanted was to ask Dianthe to open another portal back to Earth, so I could throw myself through it headfirst and never look back. I had to get away from Elfhame before I lost control.

You can't, a small, unwanted voice inside me insisted. *You have a responsibility to Cai and Ember. You promised to meet with Queen Titania. You must honor that.*

The voice was right. I'd made a commitment, and one didn't stand up the Queen of Elfhame lightly.

"Yes," I agreed with a sigh, "You're right. We need to speak with Titania as soon as we can."

Dianthe put a comforting hand on my arm. "I know you're worried about Ember, but think about it like this. If Pavia were in a position to simply kidnap Ember from Earth, why would she need to capture you as bait?"

I digested that in silence for a moment and then nodded. "Right," I said, trying to take comfort in her words.

With an encouraging smile, Dianthe said, "She's probably not as powerful as all that. I bet she was just being opportunistic since you were already on Elfhame."

I thought that was a bit of a stretch, but I appreciated her effort to cheer me up all the same. "Maybe you're right. I hope so. Either way, we should probably head towards the palace."

As the others made plans to depart, I looked longingly towards the sky, as if I could see Earth from my vantage point in the clearing. It was impossible, though. The two realms were separated by more than distance.

Dianthe cast a portal to the royal quarter, and just as I was about to step through, I looked down at the simple, conjured set of robes I was still wearing.

"I can't speak to the Queen like this," I protested.

Dianthe snorted and gave me a wry look. "You don't really think I'd let us walk into court in these clothes, do you?"

"Oh, of course not," I replied, my voice dripping with sarcasm. "What could I possibly have been thinking?"

54

We both stepped through the portal and appeared near the palace before I was even finished rolling my eyes.

As soon as everyone had followed us through, Dianthe waved her hand across our bodies and conjured two full length gowns suitable for courtly attire.

I combed my long hair out with my fingers and twisted it into a knot at the back of my head. Dianthe reached up, smiling, and twirled some stray hair behind my ears.

"Perfect, as always," she assured me.

"Uh, thanks," I muttered, feeling my face growing red.

With a quick glance, I found Vale's eyes boring into me. He still wore his customary scowl—but his pupils were dilated, and his lips had parted slightly.

I looked away, sighing. I could feel the bond between us burning brightly inside my chest, making my insides twist and ache with longing. Drawing a deep breath, I opened my mouth to speak, my eyes meeting his with difficulty as I fought my omega-wolf's nature.

Before I could get the words out, Vale turned his back to me and stalked away.

The breath left my lungs in a rush.

Fucking brilliant.

NINE

WATCHING MY MATE storm away was a bitter experience. But, hey, on the positive side, it was no longer my main concern now that evil people were once again trying to capture me as a means to get to my best friend. With trembling hands, I smoothed the folds of my gown down. The motion was needless, however. Dianthe's conjured fabric was perfect in every way.

Edric stared after Vale, confusion breaking through the deep lines of worry that had formed on his face ever since the revelation about Pavia. Even as the handsome shifter stormed away, Edric waved his long hand towards Vale's back and transformed his hunting garb into a ceremonial robe that shimmered in the light.

Vale whirled on him with an expression like storm clouds, but after catching the pointed look Edric was giving him, he grudgingly nodded his head in thanks. Edric then magically changed his own attire to something more courtly—dark breeches, shining boots, and a smartly tailored tunic in brilliant emerald green. He turned towards Aiwin, who held up a hand to forestall him.

"No, my friend, the boar will ruin whatever you conjure me," he said. "My offering of fresh meat to her majesty's kitchens will have to suffice."

I noticed for the first time that blood was smeared on the shoulder of his jerkin. Aiwin shifted the kill to a more comfortable position and jerked his head towards the grand entrance.

"My lady," he said in a polite tone. "Would you do us the honor of attending court?"

I glanced towards Dianthe as I opened my mouth in confusion. "Uhh…"

Dianthe waved her hand impatiently. "It's a tradition to invite guests to enter the court. A social protocol."

"Oh," I replied, my face going red. For a moment I'd wondered if the flame-haired fae had taken a shining to me as well.

Ugh. Don't be crazy, girl. One alienated mate is enough.

As if to punctuate my thoughts, Vale let out an irritated growl and stalked over to the guard at the entrance. They exchanged a few hurried sentences before the guard nodded and pushed open the huge double doors.

We trooped through the halls of the Summer Palace, dripping as always with greenery and flowers that seemed to grow directly out of the walls and tree-trunk beams. Birds chirped, insects buzzed, and a heady floral perfume scented the air. No one stopped us as we approached the throne room, though we garnered several curious and wary looks.

"Don't expect a pleasant welcome," Vale muttered. "The queen specifically requested no interruptions this morning."

I scowled at him, swallowing the protest that wanted to break free. Surely Titania would understand. This was a matter of life and death! Even so, fresh worry pricked at me. What would we do if she refused to see us? If she refused to hear our tale of what had happened? Would we have to stand around for hours like idiots, waiting for the allotted time of my existing appointment this afternoon?

Without my conscious volition, my inner wolf reached out towards our mate, instinctually seeking out the comfort of the connection between us.

Vale clenched his jaw and rushed to push open the throne room doors, which reminded me quite effectively that I was not privileged to have that kind of warmth in my life.

My wolf whimpered piteously.

I dropped my gaze to the floor, biting the inside of my cheek to chase away the renewed sting of rejection. Dianthe's fingers cupped my elbow as she steered me forward, brushing past the guards who raised their eyebrows at my presence.

Even here among the court officials, there was stigma between our people. It irked me that I'd held this position of envoy for months now, and they still treated me like an outsider every time.

Did Vale and his mother face the same kind of prejudice? Or were they immune thanks to their close connection to Titania?

Irritated, I shook the thought away. Passing through the door was like stepping into a little slice of heaven. The sweet fragrance and gentle, dappled sunlight magically filtering down through the ceiling eased the crazed sensations that Elfhame forced upon shifters and humans alike.

The beauty of the throne room was more formal than the wild profusion of nature forming the rest of the palace, with high, graceful arches carved out of cool marble. Flowers and vines twisted themselves around each of the beams in intricate braided patterns, creating a colorful drapery that glistened in the light. Carefully manicured trees stood proudly between the pillars, their branches heavy with ripe fruit.

It was, as always, stunning.

Our surroundings were nothing compared to the queen herself, though. Even by fae standards, Queen Titania was breathtakingly beautiful, her clear eyes and sharp cheekbones announcing her royal blood to the world.

As Vale had warned, it was clear she wasn't pleased with the interruption. Her sharp, green-eyed gaze fell upon us as we slowly stepped forward and lowered our heads in respect.

"Your Majesty," Vale said, bowing low. "Please accept our deepest apologies for the interruption. We are here on an errand that cannot wait."

Vale gestured behind Dianthe to where Aiwin stood, still gripping the large boar.

"Accept this boar as a tribute to your patience and generosity," he said as Aiwin dropped the kill on the floor before the queen.

She surveyed it for a moment before nodding to a servant that stood nearby. He rushed forward and removed the carcass, presumably taking it to the kitchens to be processed.

I shot a furtive glance around the throne room, which was nearly empty. Aside from the servants, only the female shifter who I recognized as Vale's mother was present. She stood proud and silent behind Queen Titania, staring at her son with a faintly furrowed brow.

I swallowed convulsively. Could she somehow sense the fate marks that had activated between us when Vale and I met? Did she know what had gone on in the last few hours? Sometimes I felt like my own mother could read my mind. Was it the same for these two?

Vale glanced at his mother, but his gaze did not linger on her.

Had it been my imagination, or did a slight red tinge seem to be forming on his cheeks?

I squinted at him sidelong for a few seconds before deciding it must have been a trick of the light.

"Very well, my young advisor," the queen said, snapping my attention back to her. "What important tale do you have to tell us on this fine morning?"

Vale stepped forward and cleared his throat. "We have reason to believe that necromancy is occurring within the kingdom, Queen Titania."

The queen's perfect, porcelain features gave a startled twitch of alarm. She glanced around at the group of us standing before the throne, her eyes briefly settling on me before moving back to Vale.

"That is a serious allegation," she said. "Against whom do you level this charge of forbidden magic?"

"King Oberon's mad witch, Pavia," he replied darkly.

Complete silence followed his words. After a moment, Vale's mother stepped forward.

"Tell us everything, my son," she said, her own face grown pale.

I didn't want to listen. I didn't want to re-experience the horror in the clearing. The darkness in my mind seemed to form itself into the shape of the rotting swamp that had nearly consumed us.

Staring fixedly at the floor, I tried to block out Vale and Edric's voices as they explained events on both sides of the black magic. Aiwin also chimed in to add his observations. To my relief, Vale left out the ridiculous argument that he and I had about our fate marks.

That would've been just perfect, I thought in disgust. All this situation needed was for him to spill his guts to his mother and the queen, rejecting me publicly in front of the entire fae court.

"Based on what we experienced today," Vale concluded, "the rumors that Pavia is attempting to resurrect King Oberon appear to be correct."

Another heavy silence followed his pronouncement. Queen Titania's face was now chiseled into a look of icy rage.

TEN

WITH A TINGLE shivering up my spine, I glanced around the throne room, noticing for the first time that the birds and the insects, which had been chirping contentedly a moment before, were now silent.

I knew, intellectually, how closely tied the queen was to her realm—but it was still disconcerting to experience firsthand.

The stillness was positively eerie. I shivered and pressed closer to Dianthe, unable to stifle the reaction. My fae friend glanced down at me and gave a reassuring smile, though it was tight around the edges.

We really needed to get word to Ember, Cai, and Tamlain. I tried to communicate this message with my eyes, in hopes that Dianthe would speak up—saving me from having to confront Titania when she was already in a bad mood.

No luck. Dianthe only shot me a confused look in response to my wide, unblinking stare.

Great. Taking two deep breaths, I stepped forward on shaky legs and bowed low to the fae queen.

Wow, I'm getting really courageous these days, I thought, feeling her heavy gaze on the back of my neck. After what seemed like an appropriate interval, I looked up.

"Queen Titania, I must insist that we inform the Greystalker pack leadership of these developments," I said, hating the tremor in my voice. "In fact, I'm very concerned that we have been unaware of this threat up to this point. This information is vital to our survival and the ongoing efforts to bridge understanding and awareness between our two realms."

"I agree," Dianthe piped up dutifully, her voice emerging noticeably stronger than my own. "This rumor about Pavia is something that would have been valuable to know, in our capacity as liaisons between the two worlds. When information such as this comes to light—even if it's couched as hearsay—we need to know about it."

Queen Titania held up a hand for silence. The power in her gesture seemed to strike me dumb for a moment, and I swallowed uncomfortably around a tongue that felt like it had curled up on itself.

"I concur that this information is important for the Greystalker pack," she said after a short pause. "Darby Adalwolf, I grant you leave to return immediately to Earth, that you may give your report to Tamlain and your pack leaders. We will reschedule our planned meeting for another time, child."

I blinked at her in surprise. Okay—that had been easier than I'd thought. Just how worried *was* Titania about this threat?

It struck me all at once that it was her crazy ex-husband Pavia was apparently trying to raise from the dead. So... if Titania was worried, I guess she had good reason.

"We must combine our efforts to stop this new threat to both our worlds," she said, in a tone of finality.

I coughed in an embarrassed sort of way. "Did you, uh, want to reschedule our meeting now, Your Majesty?"

Queen Titania gave me a cool look. "Wouldn't you agree, child, that the current danger of a reincarnated King Oberon far outweighs the less-pressing matter of the educational efforts between our two worlds?"

I could feel myself flushing red with embarrassment. Goddess, I was so bad at this. "Of course it does. Believe me — my priorities from this morning when I left Earth have… shifted somewhat."

"Naturally," the queen agreed, turning towards Vale's mother. "Zara, we must confer on this. You and Vale will remain here with me while the others see to their respective duties."

"Of course, your majesty," Zara replied immediately, bowing.

"The rest of you, leave us now." Titania's voice was soft, but it held a dangerous edge. In a way, her reaction to the news was reassuring. It was obvious she was taking our report very seriously indeed.

The queen's eyes lingered on me for a moment before she turned towards her advisors, clearly dismissing us from her attention. Dianthe wrapped an arm around my shoulders and steered me firmly towards the door, Edric and Aiwin on our heels.

Once we were outside, the two male fae turned to us.

"Well… that was certainly interesting," Edric commented, raising a canted eyebrow.

Aiwin snorted and waved a hand over his soiled clothes. The blood and dirt disappeared from the fabric as though it had never existed. "That, my friend, is an insult to understatement."

Dianthe nodded, thoughtful—her head tilted slightly to the side.

"So, now what?" she finally asked.

The three fae looked at each other, clearly unsure what we were meant to do next.

"I have to return to Earth," I said firmly. "I need to talk to Ember and her mates right away."

Dianthe nodded, but her gaze was still distant, her focus on something I couldn't see.

"*Dianthe*," I prompted again, giving her arm a little shake. "I have to go."

Edric shifted his weight from one foot to another. "Is it wise for you to return to Earth alone?"

I blinked at him. "Why wouldn't it be?"

Reluctantly, I remembered Dianthe's uncertain expression when she'd been reassuring me that Ember would be safe from Pavia on Earth.

Edric sighed and ran a hand through his silky blond hair. "We don't know how powerful Pavia is, truly. This could be another trap. How do we know that she won't follow you and try to abduct you again?"

It was my turn to shuffle uncomfortably. I hadn't really considered the possibility that Pavia might follow me to Earth. It hadn't seemed likely, since she already knew where Ember was. She didn't need to follow me in order to return to the Greystalker lands, where she'd hidden in plain sight for many years.

But the prospect of being used as bait again was deeply unnerving. Horrifying, even.

"I propose that I accompany you on your return journey, to keep you safe," Edric said. "Aiwin can remain here and guard Vale, who might also be considered a target."

I felt my stomach unexpectedly twist itself into a nervous knot at the prospect. I swallowed hard, trying to prevent a blush from rising to my cheeks.

Edric was very handsome. *Incredibly* handsome, if I was being honest. Was he truly that invested in my wellbeing? He'd been kind and courtly toward me, in the way that I had always imagined a male shifter would be towards his... well, his *mate*. Was it possible that he was interested in me in that way? Was he attracted to me in the way my own mate wasn't?

Vale isn't your mate, sneered my ugly internal voice. *He despises you.*

At my shoulder, Dianthe let out a low growl of displeasure, startling me free of my reverie.

"You disapprove of this plan, huntress?" Edric inquired, raising his eyebrows.

"*Yes*, I disapprove," Dianthe shot back. "If anyone is to guard Darby, it should be me."

Taking in the hard look on my friend's face, I considered my options for a moment, willing the nervousness stirring in my stomach to calm down.

I needed to think, not react. I breathed deeply, in and out... in and out. As my head cleared, my thoughts about our predicament began to untangle themselves.

I probably did need protection—but I also needed to know what went on here in my absence. I needed someone who could come and warn me if Pavia made a move or somehow got closer to achieving her goal.

Try as I might, I couldn't even *think* the words 'bring Oberon back from the dead.' The idea was too horrible. That bastard definitely needed to stay six feet under.

Besides, whispered that snide inner voice, *if Edric goes with you, you can always throw it in Vale's face that one of his buddies cares more about the safety of his fated mate than he does.*

That was petty, and I knew it. But the part about needing someone I trusted here in Elfhame to keep on top of events was valid strategy.

Taking Dianthe's hand, I spoke to her softly, but with perfect sincerity. "I appreciate your willingness to protect me, my friend, but I need you here."

Dianthe's eyebrows drew together unhappily.

"I need someone I can trust to make... *subtle inquiries*," I replied in a meaningful tone. "If you catch my drift."

Dianthe had a network of people from all walks of life in the fae city. She could find out more information for me than Edric or Aiwin, whom I'd only just met.

Even though I could tell she understood my decision, Dianthe still seemed reluctant.

"Are you sure?" she asked, squeezing my fingers.

"I'm sure." I injected as much confidence as I could into my tone. It was true I barely knew Edric, but something about him came across as inherently trustworthy. I was an omega wolf who was basically scared of everything... and yet the prospect of trusting myself to his protection didn't frighten me.

Dianthe nodded her assent, resigned. Then she turned towards Edric with narrowed eyes.

"If you let any harm come to her—even a single hair on her lovely head—you will answer to *me*. Have I made myself clear?"

Edric, ever gracious, bowed his head solemnly. "Your concern does you credit, huntress. On my house and my name, I assure you that I will protect your friend with my life, should it come to that."

I quashed the little flutter that bubbled in my stomach and chest at his words.

"I'll remain here at the palace and join up with Vale once the queen dismisses him," Aiwin said, looking with concern towards the massive double doors that were now firmly shut behind us.

I sensed he was fighting the temptation to burst back inside without a summons. The fact that he was so concerned for my mate's safety shouldn't have mattered to me after the way Vale had treated me. And yet, somehow, it did.

"Guard yourself as well, my friend," Edric said, clasping forearms with Aiwin as we took our leave.

The three of us left the red-haired fae behind, returning to the little cottage in the forest that had always been my safe haven on Elfhame. The familiar stone walls and the sweet, earthy smell that permeated the place calmed the storm whirling inside me. I retrieved my backpack from the bedroom and changed from the magicked-up court attire into my own clothing.

Slinging the pack over my shoulder, I walked back outside and stood on the cobbled walkway leading from the front door into the woods. Dianthe was waiting for me. She and I stared at each other for a long moment, reading each other's trepidation in the lingering look.

"I'll see you soon," I said to my dear friend. "Be careful, Dianthe."

With her head held high, she nodded, but I could sense her worry.

"I wish you well, Darby," she replied. "Be safe. Give my regards to the others when you see them."

With those words, she leaned forward and planted a sisterly kiss on my cheek. With a wave of her hand, a portal to Earth opened a few feet in front of me. After a last backward glance at my faithful friend, I stepped through the portal leading to Earth — with Edric following close at my heels.

ELEVEN

MY FEET FOUND the ground in the familiar coastal northwestern forest that contained the Greystalker packlands. Edric's shoulder brushed mine as he, too, stepped out into the human realm. A moment later, Dianthe's portal dissipated behind us.

The fae turned on the spot, taking everything in with wide, glinting eyes. "This is *fascinating*," he said.

We had appeared well within the boundary of the pack's territory, just close enough to the village that I could smell wood smoke drifting lazily through the trees. The sun overhead proclaimed that it was nearly the lunch hour, and many families were busy preparing their midday meals.

"This way," I said, heading toward the scents of cooking meat.

As we walked among the trees, Edric's fingers brushed over the bark of a massive fir. Here, the trunks were painted in rich, earthy browns. It was nothing like the vivid colors of the plant life on Elfhame.

"Your trees are so strange," he observed, still clearly entranced by the differences between our worlds. "The leaves are so tiny, like little green needles. Not at all like the trees at home."

I made a non-committal humming noise and shot him a sidelong look, trying not to be obvious about my observation of him. His beautiful features were enraptured, his attention fully immersed in the unfamiliar landscape. He exclaimed over the small flowers that grew up through the underbrush, running his fingers through the seed heads of the tall grasses flanking the main path through the village as we walked.

"Do all the shifters on Earth reside here?" he asked, examining the dwellings lining the path as we entered the settlement.

"No, just the Greystalker pack," I replied. "There are many other packs scattered around the human realm—but aside from our nearest neighbors, we don't have much to do with them as a whole."

Unbidden, I recalled my whispered plans with Ember to sneak away to a different pack so we could both find mates and, hopefully, a better life.

I snorted softly, reflecting on how much had changed in the last year.

"What is it, my lady?" Edric asked. He placed a light hand on my arm, bringing us to a stop on the trail. "You seem rather distracted. Are you not glad to be home?"

I suppressed a shiver in response to the warmth of his touch. My inner wolf perked up in interest.

"I'm fine," I said, ignoring his second question. I could feel heat rising to my cheeks despite my best efforts.

And… he wasn't going to let it go, apparently. His slanted eyebrows drew together. "You look flushed. Have you taken a fever?"

"No," I shook my head, too rapidly to be casual. "Nothing like that. It's just the walk. I told you, I'm fine."

Edric nodded solemnly and then gestured around as we continued. "Tell me about your life here. Your village appears quite charming."

I laughed, aware of the bitter edge behind the sound. "Honestly, I've never *had* much of a life here—at least, not until recently. I'm a nobody, really."

He turned towards me with a genuinely surprised expression. "How can you say that?"

"It's the simple truth. My family is low status. I've always been at the bottom of the pack."

His head tilted in curiosity. "I don't understand. How can you be a nobody when your closest friend is the alpha's mate, and you regularly attend audiences with the queen of Elfhame?"

I opened my mouth for a moment, then shut it. He had a point. Why was it so hard for me to truly internalize the changes that had occurred over the past few seasons? I lifted one shoulder and made another noncommittal noise in my throat. I really wasn't sure how to answer his question.

After a few quiet moments, Edric broke my thoughtful silence by asking, "Then perhaps you can tell me what your current role is, within the Greystalker pack? Formally speaking, I mean."

I sheepishly rubbed my neck. "Well… Ember and I set up an exchange program, of sorts, between Earth and Elfhame. Not just for shifters or fae, either. We take humans, too. It's open to anyone who is unwanted in their world, offering them a place where they can belong and get an education."

"Indeed?" Edric asked, his full attention pinned on me. "That sounds like quite an ambitious undertaking."

I nodded. "I suppose it is, yes. Before she mated Cai and Tamlain, Ember was exiled from the pack. It was a difficult life for her, to put it mildly. We don't believe anyone else should have to experience what she did as an outcast. It's been a complicated process, and it's going quite a bit slower than we'd like. Especially finding locations where these individuals can stay. Some are housed with families in the pack—especially the children. But others prefer to keep their own lodgings."

Without realizing it, I'd grown animated as I explained the work about which Ember and I had become so passionate. Edric's eyes sparkled as he watched me. I blanched, suddenly self-conscious.

"Sorry… am I talking too much?" I asked. "I, uh, tend to do that sometimes."

He scoffed. "Not at all. This work of yours is fascinating. As it happens, this is my first time on Earth. It's nothing like what I was told as a child. Noble bloodlines or not, I suspect I would've benefited from a program like yours."

Warmth blossomed in my chest at his words.

"We want everyone to feel welcome, not just those that are disadvantaged," I told him. "We don't have the resources we need yet, but I think that's the best way to soften the rhetoric between our two worlds and start breaking down the barriers between our peoples. Actually, I had an update to deliver to the queen regarding our progress. That's why I was supposed to meet with her this afternoon, before... well..."

My voice trailed away, and Edric sighed.

"Indeed. An unfortunate turn of events, to put it mildly."

That was a gross understatement when it came to the prospect of a madwoman bringing the scariest fae bastard in the entire kingdom back from the dead.

I glanced up to see Edric regarding me solemnly. When he saw me looking, he offered a wry smile. It threatened to steal my breath away.

What was *wrong* with me? And yet, this gentle regard felt so much better than the rejection and vitriol I'd received from Vale. Maybe my reaction wasn't so surprising—I'd never really been the object of a male's attention before. Not like this.

It was a nice change.

Abruptly, I was grateful that no one else knew about the mate bond. Grateful that I wouldn't have to answer any awkward questions.

I'll never tell a soul, I decided, as I led the way towards Cai, Ember, and Tamlain's home. *If Vale wants to be a complete asshat to me, then he doesn't deserve another moment of my time or energy. So what if I'm enjoying the attention and kindness of an attractive fae?*

Walking alongside this gorgeous male of noble birth, I wondered for a moment if Vale and I would ever be forced to publicly acknowledge that we were fated mates. I couldn't think of any instances where a fate-bond had simply been ignored by both parties. I'd only ever heard horror stories of marks being burned away after a public rejection—and then I'd seen it happen firsthand with my best friend.

Even though it had turned out all right in the end for Ember, I wouldn't wish that kind of trauma on anyone. But to simply disregard the bond's existence? As far as I knew, that wasn't even the stuff of legends in our pack history.

Turning past the town center square, I led Edric up the western slope towards the alphas' den—effortlessly picking my way through the maze of paths that crisscrossed the village.

As we approached, I could see flickering firelight through one of the front windows of the dwelling. Relieved that someone was apparently home, I knocked on the solid oak door.

"This news isn't going to go over well," I warned Edric grimly.

The door opened, and I found myself face to face with Tamlain. He smiled one of his faint, crooked half-smiles at me, but when his gaze shifted to Edric, it faded, his stern brow furrowing in confusion.

"Darby," he greeted. "I infer that your visit to Elfhame did not go as planned."

"You could say that. Sorry, but I need to speak with you guys and Ember right away," I said, throwing a quick, nervous glance over my shoulder. All of the sudden, I had the strangest feeling that we were being watched by unfriendly eyes.

There was no one there, of course. Then again, I supposed a bit of anxiety was perfectly normal after the morning I'd had. There was nothing to fear in the heart of the Greystalker lands, surrounded by my packmates and secure in the alphas' dwelling. Ember was probably in the next room, safe and well.

Tamlain waved us over the threshold and into the living room of the leaders' luxurious den. As I'd guessed, my friend was sitting comfortably curled up in a chair, a book splayed open on her lap. She looked up as we entered, and a smile split her face. Her familiar half-black, half-platinum-blond hair glinted in the light from the hearth.

"Darby," she greeted warmly, putting her book aside. "I didn't expect you back for hours!"

Her words cut off as she took in the expression on my face. Her eyes flickered to Edric and back to me, growing guarded.

"What's wrong? What happened?" she demanded, drawing Cai to the gathering with her sharp tone of voice.

The Greystalker clan leader poked his head in, and immediately frowned as he took in the strange fae in his sitting room.

"Hello," he greeted. "Have a seat, Darby. You look as pale as a ghost."

I sank into my usual chair across from Ember's, scrubbing my hands over my face as though to brush away cobwebs. There was no way to sugar-coat this, as much as I might wish there was.

"Pavia's back," I said.

Ember and her two co-mates exchanged glances laden with unspoken meaning.

"Go on," Ember said. "You'd better tell us everything."

TWELVE

I RELAYED THE story of Pavia's attack and our subsequent meeting with Titania as succinctly as I could. It took only a few minutes to pass on the relevant details. "Based on how everyone in Elfhame is reacting to the news, I get the impression there's a good chance the crazy bitch can succeed in bringing him back to life," I concluded.

Tamlain had listened to my report with tightly crossed arms, his expression growing increasingly thunderous as the tale unfolded. By the time I was finished, he looked like he wanted to mount someone's head on a pike, and I had a sneaking suspicion who might be his preferred candidate.

"It appears I will need to have a word with Her Majesty," he said, his tone deadly quiet.

"Umm… hey, lover?" Ember asked. "Could we maybe not start by alienating any powerful people who are currently on our side in this mess?"

She was the only one of the three who looked even remotely calm. Still, there was something eerily dead-eyed about her expression. Which made sense—of everyone here, she had the most to fear from Oberon's return.

Tamlain let out a disgusted snarl. "Titania knows better than to withhold that kind of information from us. It undermines the very trust we've been trying to build between Earth and Elfhame! Her reticence has also given Pavia space and time to strengthen her powers."

Ember sighed wearily. "Look… I'm sure she was doing what she thought was best for everyone."

"And yet, here we are," Tamlain continued, not mollified in the least. "How are we to combine our efforts to stop this new threat, when we've only just discovered the threat exists?"

"We still have time," Cai said, though he didn't look any happier than Tamlain. "We'll start planning for contingencies at once."

"I must go to Elfhame immediately," Tamlain stated, in a tone that brooked no dissent. "I still intend to speak to the queen."

"Speak to her, or lecture her?" Edric asked wryly.

For the first time, it occurred to me to wonder if the two fae knew each other personally, and if so, how well. Edric and Dianthe had appeared to be strangers, for all that Dianthe kept an ear to Titania's court. Tamlain was Dianthe's cousin, so perhaps he didn't know Edric either.

Whatever the case, Tamlain didn't acknowledge Edric's quip. Instead, he strode to a row of hooks in the corner of the room and retrieved his cloak, swinging it over his shoulders in a single, smooth movement. He returned to Ember's chair, leaning over it to tip her chin up with a gentle touch of his fingers.

"Be careful," Ember told him, her forehead creasing in worry.

"I will return shortly, beloved," he said. "Do not fear."

I looked away as the pair kissed, aware of the faint burn of unworthy jealousy growing in my chest.

Tamlain straightened with a rustle of clothing. Raising his hand in a brusque, circular gesture, he cast a portal to Elfhame as though it were no more difficult than opening a wooden door.

He turned, his severe expression landing on Cai. "Guard her," he said.

At that, Tamlain disappeared through the portal, which collapsed to a point and vanished soon afterward.

"Yes, *sir*," Cai murmured wryly to the empty space where his co-mate had stood moments before, although there was no heat in his tone.

A low sound of frustration echoed around the room. Still seated in her chair, Ember was gently slapping her closed fist against her forehead.

"What is it?" I asked, crossing to crouch at her side.

"It's *me*," she said. "I don't have super-strong magical powers now that I've mated. That means we're even more vulnerable than the first time we battled Oberon and Pavia."

She huffed out a breath, turning her full attention to me. "Cai can assign guards for you and your family, Darby. We'll make sure you're all safe."

Looking deep into my best friend's eyes, I marveled that she would be thinking about my safety before her own. To almost everyone else in the pack, I was still the worthless omega whelp they'd known for years—despite my wolfbirth ceremony and my new role as envoy. Only Ember and her mates treated me as important.

I smiled, though it felt strained. "I already have a guard," I reminded her, jerking my chin toward Edric. The fae was standing silently near the window, staring outside — presumably to give us the illusion of privacy.

"And while I won't say no to having a couple of guards outside my parents' place," I continued, "I think Dianthe's assessment was right. Pavia doesn't really need me. I was a target of opportunity because I was visiting Elfhame. But now I'm back on Earth. She already knows where you are and how to reach you. If there was an easy way for her to get here, she'd have already come, knocked on your door, and grabbed you."

Cai let out a low rumble of discontent.

"So, umm, maybe don't answer the door anytime soon?" I added dryly, trying to lighten the atmosphere. "Just in case."

Ember smiled a little at my half-hearted attempt at humor, but her face fell a moment later. "*Gods*. This is all my fault."

I scowled at her. "No, it's not! How can you say that?"

"Ember," Cai said firmly. "Let's try to remember that if I hadn't let Pavia influence me with magic, I wouldn't have rejected our bond when it first activated. And if I'd mated you when I should have, your powers would never have been a danger to Earth in the first place. You wouldn't have been any use to Oberon's crazy plans."

Ember shook her head. "But if it weren't for my hybrid blood, then Pavia—"

"*Pavia*," I interrupted firmly, "is an absolute psychopath. She's obsessed with Oberon, and she probably would've done everything in her power to bring him back regardless."

My best friend let out a gusty sigh, slumping back in her chair. "I guess you're right."

"Damn straight I'm right," I said. We gripped hands. To my relief, Ember looked at least slightly reassured. "I'm going to go home now, if that's okay," I told her, glancing across the room at Edric. "I guess I'll have to introduce my family to my new bodyguard, huh?"

"I guess you will. Have fun with that, by the way," Ember murmured. She raised a suggestive eyebrow at me, and I struggled mightily not to blush.

Instead, I turned to Cai. "Please keep her safe," I begged him. "You know how she gets when she thinks other people are in danger."

Usually, I wouldn't have the guts to speak to an alpha that way—not even Cai.

"With my life," he promised. "And, yes, I do know how she gets. I'll send guards for your family shortly, Darby."

"Thank you," I murmured, before Edric and I took our leave and departed.

After a few minutes' walk, we turned onto the path leading to my family's modest dwelling. As we grew nearer, I smelled my mother's cooking wafting out from the narrow windows.

Breathing the familiar scent in deeply, I could feel my spirit begin to calm. The village was safe. Ember was safe. I'd delivered my important message to the people who could—hopefully—do something about it.

"Mother!" I called out, as we reached the front door of my family's small den. "I'm home!"

"Darby!" she exclaimed, her familiar plump, dark-haired form appearing in the kitchen doorway. She briskly dried her hands on her apron, a smile creasing her face as she saw us standing in the entryway. "You're back early! And who is this?"

"This is Edric, Mama," I said, gesturing to our guest. "He's a fae, from Elfhame."

Blinking in surprise for a moment, my mother quickly recovered and replied, "I see. Well, Edric, it's wonderful to meet you. Please, come inside and make yourself at home."

I ushered my fae bodyguard further into the dwelling, to the area we used for company.

"Edric, please do have a seat and warm yourself by the fire," my mother told him. "Darby, would you help me prepare some drinks for our guest?"

"A drink would be wonderful," Edric replied, smiling at her pleasantly. "Thank you for your hospitality."

Not for the first time, I wondered if all fae nobility were such gentlemen, or only him. I followed my mother into the kitchen, well aware that making drinks was just a pretext to get me alone. For this reason, I was unsurprised when she rounded on me.

"You need to remember yourself, Darby." Her tone and expression were worried.

And… okay. That wasn't what I'd been expecting. "Remember myself?" I echoed, confused.

"Yes," she whispered urgently, gesturing toward my sternum. "You have a *fate mark*."

My shoulders sank. So did my stomach. "Yes. I know. It's not as if I could forget."

Her gaze sharpened, but she turned and began stacking cups on a tray. "You need to be careful about how affectionate you are with such a handsome stranger, child. There's someone out there waiting for you, and he definitely isn't a fae."

THIRTEEN

THE IRONY OF the situation wasn't lost on me. I grimaced, remembering the look on my mate's face as he, too, felt the burn of the mark on his chest as we connected.

"Don't worry, Mama," I assured her. "I promise I haven't forgotten my mate's existence for one second."

She narrowed her eyes at me, as though suspecting me of sass, and pushed the tray into my arms. "See that you don't. The last thing this family needs is that kind of a scandal."

Chastened, I returned to the fireside and offered Edric a cup of herbal tea. He took it graciously. I quickly relayed the news that there might be more trouble coming from Elfhame, and that Cai would be sending guards to watch over things.

My mother's expression grew drawn. "Is that why you're here as well, Edric?" she asked.

He nodded solemnly. "I'm pledged to act as bodyguard for Darby until those in power are able to deal with the threat. However, I hasten to add that no one believes the threat extends to Earth — not at the present time."

That seemed to reassure my mother, at least. It also provided a reasonable explanation for Edric's presence here; one that wouldn't ping my mother's scandal radar. The fae sipped his drink, making pleasant small talk with my mother while I stared restlessly into the flickering flames.

Why couldn't Edric have been my mate? Obviously, it was rare, but it *did* happen that fae and shifters could be compatible—just look at Ember and Tamlain. Suddenly, I couldn't stand to be in this tiny den, under my mother's watchful and vaguely disapproving eye, for a moment longer.

"Edric, if you're finished with your tea, can I show you around the Greystalker village?" I asked.

He set his cup back down on the tray with a delicate clink of china. "Of course," he replied easily. "I would love to learn more about your culture. Madame Adalwolf, thank you once again for your generous hospitality."

My mother's cheeks pinked, as she stammered something appropriately polite. Apparently not even she was completely immune to his charms.

I led Edric outside and turned towards the town square. But instead of lingering in the center of the village, I headed south, up a path that went deeper into the mountains.

The breeze that lifted the hair off my neck seemed to be calling to my inner wolf, and she stirred in my heart, as restless as I was. The air was fresh and clear, making me want to run and run until I left the world behind, shedding all the rejection, pain, and fear that lived within my human skin. As a wolf, I could give myself over to my base instincts and just... *be*.

Did I dare indulge that desire, with Edric here? I took my courage in both hands and drew breath to speak.

"Do you mind if I shift form?" I asked him, hating how tentative I sounded. "It's such a beautiful day."

His eyebrows rose. "Not at all," he said. "In fact, that sounds like a rather lovely idea."

Before I could puzzle out his meaning, he waved a hand over himself. The air twisted improbably, and a tall grey wolf stood before me. Edric blinked at me with deep, golden eyes.

I gaped in surprise, feeling like an idiot. Edric was a fae. He was *magic*. *Of course* he could shift into various animal forms. Unaccustomed glee stole over me, despite the grim events from earlier in the day.

With a mischievous grin, I ducked behind a large tree trunk and shed my clothes in record time, leaving them in a pile among the gnarled roots. Once naked, I let the shift overtake me, padding back out in my wolf form to join my companion.

I stretched my front legs long and low in a play-bow, feeling energy tingle through my paws. With an excited yip, I bolted and took off running, heading deeper into the forest.

Edric loped behind me, following my lead. We ran for a time along a ridge, climbing higher and higher toward the upper elevations. Dappled patches of sunlight reflected off my companion's sleek fur as we ran silently through the trees, keeping pace with each other.

The fae growled playfully at me and bumped my shoulder with his. Looking over at him, I saw his mouth open wide, tongue lolling out to the side. The impish glint in his eyes made my wolfish heart flutter as I nudged him back.

We wrestled playfully, my wolf's glee spilling over to the human part of my mind. I laughed internally, colliding hard against him and forcing him off the path. We bounded around each other; our run forgotten in the joy of the playful battle. Inevitably, as the larger and far more dominant wolf, Edric quickly got the upper hand on me.

That was when I realized this might have been a serious miscalculation on my part.

The butterflies in my stomach hadn't gone away, simply because I wasn't human anymore. I could barely tear my eyes from the long muscles rippling under Edric's soft pelt as he covered my body with his, pinning me on my back.

I had no idea what insane impulse made me shift form, but a heartbeat later, I was a naked human lying on the soft ground, pinned beneath a fully clothed and painfully attractive male fae as he, too, shifted back.

"Er…" he said, a bit uncertainly — the sound cut abruptly off when I grabbed him by the tunic and pulled him down for a kiss.

I'd never kissed anyone before. Not like this. Edric smelled like loam and green plants and sunlight. His lips tasted like spice and musk.

He was so *warm*.

My body sought his like a flower turning toward the sun. For a long moment, he returned the kiss, our lips brushing and sliding together sensuously. Then, he made a reluctant noise and cupped my cheek with one hand, easing me away until a bare inch separated us.

"My lady," he murmured, and I could feel the words against my lips—a bare puff of air.

Abruptly, mortification at my own foolishness flooded me like cold, brackish water. What had I been thinking? Of *course* this beautiful male wouldn't want me in such a way. Not even my own *mate* wanted me! I was *such an idiot*—

"I'm sorry," I blurted, too flustered to do the obvious thing and shift back to wolf form so I could run the hell away and live in a cave for the rest of my life. "I'm so sorry! I shouldn't have—"

"No, please. Let me speak," he said, cutting across me. "That wasn't a complaint. You merely took me by surprise."

My heart was pounding with adrenaline, but I forced myself to stay still and not to panic. My naked skin tingled where we were still pressed together, Edric's heat combating the horrible chill that had stolen over me.

"Oh," I managed.

"Perhaps you could tell me exactly what you wish of me?" he said. "Because I would hate for there to be any misunderstanding."

There was no mockery in his voice, and yet the idea of simply blurting out that I wanted him to touch me, to kiss me and make me feel the things I would never feel from my asshole of a mate, felt unthinkable.

I swallowed hard.

"You're very handsome," was all I could come up with.

His mouth quirked in a way that said this wasn't the first time he'd heard the compliment. One

90

of his slanted eyebrows rose. "And you are very beautiful."

My face felt like it might spontaneously combust, and I seriously doubted whatever bright red color was currently suffusing my cheeks could be classified as beautiful.

"I'm really not," I said.

A small frown furrowed his high forehead. He tilted his head at me as though perplexed. "Are you implying I have poor taste?"

My cheeks burned hotter, but even in my flustered state, I could see the glint of gentle humor in his gaze. If only he weren't so *close*...

I swallowed again, a graceless gulp.

Did I dare ask for this? What would be the repercussions if I did?

I tried to knock enough brain cells together to *think*. What if I just... told him the truth? Not about Vale, obviously—but about what I wanted. Could I really do that? Open my mouth, and say what I felt?

"I've... uh... never really been with someone like this before," I said, and licked my lips.

Surprise flitted over his finely sculpted features. "Truly?" he asked, with the tiniest hint of skepticism.

I shook my head. "Never."

He gave me that look again, like he was trying to see inside my head.

"Now, *that* is an absolute travesty, if you'll forgive me saying so," he said. "I don't suppose you'd allow me the honor of rectifying such a terrible waste of potential?"

My heart, if anything, pounded faster. "Well," I began hesitantly. "I mean… if you're offering…"

"Oh," he replied with relish, "I most *certainly* am. Now, my fair lady—since I am already pledged to you for the duration, in what way may I be of service?"

FOURTEEN

CLEARLY, I WAS hallucinating. This had to be some kind of fever dream brought on by years of sexual frustration. Here I was, too low status to have ever merited the offer of more than a perfunctory pity-fuck from any of my age-mates. Too closely watched by my family to ever consider accepting those rare offers.

Obviously, I'd succumbed to some sort of weird fae illness on Elfhame, and even now I was writhing fever-struck in my bed, dreaming of a gorgeous male offering to be *'at my service.'* In which case, the way forward was obvious.

"I want you to make me come," I blurted. "Lots."

A smile that could only be described as *devilish* slid over Edric's fair features. "I'd assumed we might take that part as a given," he said, mock-solemnly. "But if you have any specific preferences—?"

I didn't, of course, because I was a clueless virgin who'd just had my first kiss about thirty seconds ago. Rather than say any of that aloud, I channeled my inner Titania and raised a languid hand, waving it at him vaguely in a sort of *'go on, then'* motion.

"Surprise me," I said, trying to inject a suitable amount of regal carelessness into my tone.

Edric's left eyebrow quirked upward. "Ah," he teased. "This is to be a test of my abilities, then. Very well, my lady. But you must inform me immediately if something is not to your taste. Are we agreed?"

I tried not to feel patronized, because in truth, that seemed like both a thoughtful and a reasonable request for him to make, under the circumstances. It *was* just a bit unusual from a shifter perspective, where dominance and the mindlessness of sexual heats tended to monopolize people's views of sex. I reminded myself firmly that Edric wasn't a shifter.

"Agreed," I said, a bit breathlessly.

Another pleased smile crinkled the fine skin at the corner of his eyes. I wondered, not for the first time, how old he was. He *looked* young, but for fae, that didn't mean much. For all I knew, he could have lived hundreds of years, despite his youthful demeanor.

All thoughts of Edric's age fled as he leaned down and kissed me again. Indeed, all thoughts of any kind fled… because this time, he took control. And it quickly became apparent that just because he wanted me to speak up if I didn't like something, that didn't mean my body wasn't about to be thoroughly and deliciously dominated—starting with my mouth.

I whimpered as he teased my lips open and licked his way inside, sharing his rich, spicy taste with me once more. The fact that I was on my back already was handy, since my inner wolf wasted no time in rolling over to show her metaphorical belly.

Were you supposed to be able to breathe while being kissed like this? And… did I really care?

After a few moments' breathless possession, I decided that I did not, in fact, care.

Only when gray fog began to swirl at the edges of my vision did Edric reluctantly let me up for air. I panted helplessly as he tilted that devilish smile at me once more, and promptly began to kiss his way downward, starting from the hinge of my jaw.

My omega instinct to show throat was immediately rewarded when those soft, demanding lips sucked a tingling line down the tendon at the side of my neck, punctuated by sly nips too gentle to leave a mark—but only barely.

A whine rose in my throat, completely unbidden. Edric only chuckled against my overheated skin and kept sliding further down my body by achingly slow degrees. He lavished attention on my clavicle, flicking his tongue into the dip at the base of my throat and making me shiver. Then he kissed his way down my cleavage, such as it was. Honestly, without some creative breast-binding or the odd, shelf-like construction of the gowns Dianthe conjured for me when we visited Titania's Court, it had always felt more like *flattage* than cleavage.

I was, therefore, rather surprised when Edric seemed fascinated by my substandard breasts. Then I forgot to be surprised, because he lifted a hand and stroked his fingertips along the underside of one, spiraling inward until my nipple snapped to attention. The delicious sensation seemed to have a direct line to my pussy, which pulsed and ached with sudden fullness.

"Your breasts are divine, Darby Adalwolf," Edric murmured. "Selfishly, I find myself hoping I'm the first one to ever tell you that—although I'm quite certain I won't be the last. Were we on Elfhame, I would commission a silk gown to be made in the exact dusky shade of these beautiful rosebuds."

The part of me that had seldom heard compliments of any kind—much less ones so lavish—wanted to squirm away and hide in a hole. But Edric's fingers closed around my left nipple, pinching it lightly, and I arched instead, gasping.

"So responsive," he said, and replaced his fingers with his lips.

My surprised squeak at the new sensation of gentle suction turned into a low moan. My inner thighs were growing slippery with excitement, and he hadn't come anyplace near them yet. Somehow, it still felt like he was touching me there—a phantom caress that only made me want more.

He shifted his hips to the side, not relinquishing my breast, but rolling to lie next to me rather than straddle me. I missed his warmth immediately—at least, until his elegant, sword-callused hand slid hot and possessive over my stomach... moving down, down, down, his fingers delving into my soaking wet folds with sure precision.

I cried out, because this was nothing at all like my occasional fumbling attempts to pleasure myself in the dark, my parents only a room away in our crowded den with its flimsy interior walls. Edric's slow, confident touch took away all my higher brain functions, leaving only the wolf and the woman behind.

My hips arched mindlessly, driving the rhythm my body needed from him. He followed my lead as effortlessly as a dance partner, melding his movements seamlessly to mine. His slick fingers slid forward to circle my clit, and back, to tease my untried entrance.

It was so good… *so good.* I never wanted it to stop, but I could feel it building to something inexorable and unavoidable. This was completely different from the frustrating feeling of not quite being able to scale the peak. Under Edric's expert touch, the peak was about to crash down on my head without any input from me; an unstoppable avalanche.

Teeth scraped delicately over my pebbled nipple, and just like that I was gone, my back curving like a bow as I came. Edric nursed me through my orgasm, drawing aftershocks until my muscles trembled and went limp, every bit of tension wrung from me.

His lips drew away from my nipple with a soft pop, and he rested his chin lightly on my breastbone. I couldn't seem to drag my unfocused gaze from the sky above us, but I could sense him smiling up at me from his vantage point.

"You are a joy to pleasure, Darby," he said, solemn as a vow. "And now, I believe my instructions included the words, 'Make me come, *lots.*' So, you might want to hold onto something."

I made a sort of questioning '*Guh*?' noise, which cut off when he kissed his way down my stomach and attacked my sex like a starving man set before a banquet. I bit back a yelp, too sensitive after my first climax, but before I could form a protest, *too much* became *oh gods, please never stop this ever.*

How could anything feel like this? Why did anyone anywhere ever do anything that *wasn't this*? I would live here in this clearing, lying on my back and being eaten out by a beautiful fae until I perished from hunger or thirst... no doubt with a huge, sappy grin still plastered on my face.

Edric made me come.

Lots.

I probably should have paid more attention to the phantom sound of a male wolf howling in fury and agony within the depths of my mind, lost somewhere to time and distance.

I did not pay more attention. See above, regarding the beautiful fae cradled between my legs, introducing me to a higher plane of existence with his mouth. For this reason, I felt my lapse was understandable and would probably hold up in a human court of law.

When I finally came down from my endorphin high, I was curled against Edric's side, wrapped in a blanket that had the strange, ozone-and-thunderstorm smell I'd come to associate with magically conjured items.

Edric, for some unfathomable reason, was still fully dressed. His arm rested around my shoulders, his thumb caressing my upper arm idly. I hummed and stretched, feeling a combination of slight soreness and utter, uncomplicated wellbeing that felt completely alien to my experience.

Edric smiled down at me in the slanted afternoon light. A beam of it haloed his blond hair from behind. "Well, my lady? Has your devoted servant performed his duty adequately?"

My inhibitions had clearly fled right along with the tension in my muscles, because I smiled back and said, "Hmm. Yes and no. Full marks for the orgasms. Seriously, A-plus work there… but you do appear to have *far* too many clothes on."

Edric's smile widened. In the distance, the spectral male wolf snarled and lifted his muzzle to the sky, howling out his rage in the depths of my soul.

FIFTEEN

DESPITE HIS RESERVED and courtly nature, Edric wasn't shy about his body. And why should he be? He was gorgeous. Where so many shifter males were broad and muscular, he was lithe and graceful, like one of the humans' marble statues that Ember and I had been fascinated by in the pages of old books.

Naked, he sprawled back against the bole of a tree with his corded arms stretched wide, his fingers entwined behind his head as a cushion against the rough bark.

"Look your fill, my lady," he said. "Touch anywhere you like. I will tell you if something isn't pleasing."

Only a fool laid a banquet before a hungry wolf and expected her not to devour it. So, devour it I did. I started with his delectable lips, but quickly indulged my desire to taste every other part of him for comparison's sake. When instinct got the better of me, leading me to bite a mark into the tender flesh above his left hipbone, I froze.

That had been wrong, hadn't it? Would he be angry, after he'd taken such care to be gentle with me?

But instead of chastising me or pushing me away, he groaned, his hips flexing beneath my hands.

"Marking me as yours already?" he asked. "I suppose you should add a few more bites for good measure. Fae heal devilishly fast, after all."

My tension faded, and my inner wolf dove back in for another taste, and another. I was fascinated by the way his member twitched with every fresh nip of my teeth. And he *had* said I could touch him everywhere…

His hard shaft was slightly salty, the smell of musk more prevalent here. I licked a stripe up his length, drawing a shuddering moan from him.

"Will you take me in your mouth?" he asked, his voice gratifyingly hoarse. "Threaten me with those sharp teeth as you swallow me down, Darby Adalwolf of the Greystalker Clan?"

I smiled up at him, showing off my pearly white canines. What was it about this fae that made my nervousness and inhibitions flow away like the water receding after high tide?

"All the better to eat you with, my dear," I teased, quoting one of my favorite human stories from childhood.

Suiting action to word, I slid my lips over the head of his cock and down. It was long and slender like the rest of him, but it made a pleasing weight against my tongue. The tip tasted saltier than the rest, with a slight bitter kick. Eager to please him as well as he'd pleased me, I experimented with how much I could take without gagging, as well as what kind of pressure and movement drew the best reactions from him.

After a blissful few minutes of this, a hand cupped my jaw and gently drew my lips away. I let go with a wet pop, looking up the length of his body in concern.

"Am I doing it wrong?" I asked. "Did you not like that thing I did with my tongue just now?"

His laugh was breathless. "Rather the opposite. You have a wicked mouth indeed, but I am not such an oaf as to spill my seed down your throat with no warning. That sort of thing is more Aiwin's department."

Something in my lower belly stirred to life again, despite the fact that I was still completely wrung out from my earlier orgasms. Why should the mention of Edric's flame-haired friend excite me so, when I had Edric himself right here? Then the rest of his words registered properly.

"You're going to spill?" I asked, intrigued. "Can I watch?"

"It does seem rather inevitable at this point," Edric replied with humor. "And if that would please you, then by all means. Perhaps your hand?"

That made sense. Eagerly, I propped myself on an elbow next to him and teased the velvety flesh of his cock — still slightly damp from my saliva — with my fingertips. It twitched hard, pulsing. A small dribble of the salty-bitter fluid I'd enjoyed earlier dripped onto his stomach.

He made a punched-out noise. "A wicked tongue *and* wicked fingers."

"Was... that it?" I asked hesitantly. "Did you come?"

He laughed again, a single, amused huff. "Hardly, my lady. Wrap your fingers around me. Stroke up and down."

I did as he'd requested, watching with fascination as he threw his head back and arched, driving his length into my loose fist the same way I'd rolled my hips to control the rhythm when he'd pleasured me earlier. I tried to follow his movements as he'd followed mine, and before long he let out a stifled cry, his body bowing.

His seed spurted satisfyingly, covering my hand and his stomach in thick, ropy jets. I kept stroking him until he gave a final shudder and went limp, sprawling boneless against the tree. In my hand, the flesh that had been hard and throbbing moments before softened and began to shrink. It didn't seem like it would be comfortable for me to keep pumping him, so after a couple of light, caressing touches, I let him go.

His spent cock lay sweetly against his thigh. Curiously, I licked his spend from my fingers, taking in the texture.

He made an appreciative humming noise and opened an arm, inviting me to curl against his side once more.

"I'll clean us up in a moment, but for now you've quite reduced me to helplessness," he said.

I took the invitation, sighing as I settled in next to him. Now that my attention wasn't so focused on what we were doing, the mournful howling of my mate's inner wolf once again tickled the edges of my awareness.

I must have been too quiet, because Edric gazed down at me with a worried furrow in his brow. "Are you all right, my lady? You seem suddenly very pensive."

I hardened my heart toward the shifter who'd publicly spurned me. If Vale was upset about me being with another male, he shouldn't have thrown me away like trash.

"I'm fine," I said. "Better than fine. Thank you for that, Edric."

"You are a beautiful woman and a beautiful wolf, Darby," Edric said. "Don't thank me for what any male in his right mind would dearly enjoy offering you."

The contrast of his kindness and my mate's cruelty brought the burn of tears to my eyes. I blinked them back. "You know, you're not so bad yourself." I nudged him playfully with my elbow.

It was getting late. We would need to leave soon in order to get back to the village before nightfall. I would have to give up this moment of connection… pretend it hadn't happened. I should also bathe in the river before going home, so there would be no chance of my parents smelling Edric's scent all over me.

He'd been kind to me. Paid me compliments and shown me that I had worth. Even so, this could never work long-term. I needed to ignore my growing feelings for this beautiful fae.

But what if I didn't want to?

SIXTEEN

UNFORTUNATELY, THE walk back down the ridge gave me plenty of time to second-guess myself. I'd cheated on my mate, knowing that he—or at least his wolf—would have felt every moment of my time with Edric.

The hot shame flaring in my cheeks had more to do with the fact that Edric and Vale were friends than any guilt about rejecting my mate the way he'd rejected me. Had I done that specifically because it would hurt Vale even more if he somehow found out who I'd been with?

Before I could tumble too far down that rabbit hole, a cold breeze flowed up the mountain and lifted the hair off my face, making me shiver. This seemed to shock some sense back into me.

Vale wasn't my mate. He'd rejected me first, and then he'd treated me like dirt. Why should I feel guilty for cheating on someone who hadn't honored our bond in the first place?

I tried to convince myself that he deserved everything he got. He'd had his opportunity, and he'd blown it.

That much was certainly true. Vale had recognized our fate mark at the same moment I had, and he'd acted terrible about it.

A sudden thought struck me, and I felt my stomach plummet. What if he really *could* tell who I'd been with? What if he was so in-tune to our little activities that he knew it was Edric? I wanted to punish Vale, but I didn't want to punish the fae who'd been so kind and caring toward me.

I spent a few minutes fretting over the possibility, trying to convince myself that Vale wouldn't be angry with his friend. After all, Edric clearly knew nothing about fate marks. In no world had this been his fault.

The innocent fae in question walked next to me, blissfully ignorant of the storm of worry that was currently wreaking havoc in my brain. We'd made part of the return journey as wolves, retracing our steps to where I'd left my clothing folded at the base of a tree. Once I'd changed form and dressed, we'd continued on two legs.

He bumped against me so that our shoulders brushed gently. It was a friendly gesture, but I couldn't help wondering if he, too, felt something more after what we had just done.

"I can understand why your pack settled here," he observed, looking out over the glorious view. "It's beautiful."

I tried to smile, but the familiar scene was hardly enough to distract me. I shivered again, trying to banish my thoughts and exist in this moment... the simple moment before everything got way more complicated.

I wondered if this was what Ember would've done in the same circumstances.

"Are you cold, Darby?" Edric asked, frowning down at me.

I nodded, glancing down at the goose bumps that had risen on my arms. My teeth chattered together for a moment. "A b-bit," I admitted.

With a wave of his elegant hand, Edric conjured a heavy coat that draped smoothly across my shoulders.

"Thank you," I said, wrapping it around myself.

Edric's thoughtfulness was something totally alien to me. Not only had he magicked me a heavy, fur lined leather coat, but it was warm as if it had been hanging in front of a fire for a few hours. Instantly I could feel my body relaxing; I hadn't realized just how tense I had been until my shoulders fell away from my ears.

"This is lovely," I told him, running my fingers up the supple leather.

He smiled at me, his wolf showing through for a moment. "Anything for a beautiful lady wolf."

I could feel myself blushing again, and I turned towards the scenery. The sky was growing darker in the east as the light began to fade.

"We should hurry," I whispered, aware that my disappointment was evident in my voice.

Edric seemed hesitant to move, our arms still brushing against one another. He didn't speak, but he looked down on me with a reluctant expression.

"Must we?" he asked eventually.

I let out a rueful huff of laughter. "Unless you want to explain to my mother what we were doing up on a mountain all night."

"Ah," he said, looking equally wry. "I see your point. Parents can be rather vexing, can they not?"

"You don't know the half of it," I said.

We walked briskly towards the village, and I filled the silence by telling him about some of the customs of my people. Edric seemed particularly fascinated by the wolfbirth ceremony.

"So, you don't have the power to transform yourselves before that moment?" he asked.

"No. We do," I explained, "but it solidifies our bond with the pack when an elder guides us through the process to shift the first time."

"What happens if someone shifts on their own?"

I looked away and shook my head.

"Taboo?" he asked.

"Let's just not discuss it," I muttered. "I need to get cleaned up before we get back to my family's den."

Nodding respectfully, Edric leaned against a tree as I proceeded through the forest to the river. Taking off the heavy coat that was becoming a little too warm, I stripped down and washed myself as best I could, scrubbing away the scent of sex.

I knew if my mom smelled him on me, I'd never, ever hear the end of it. It was a nightmare scenario that I was *not* willing to explore.

By the time I returned, the scent of our lovemaking had been washed away. All I could detect in the air around me was the fresh forest smell that always accompanied a good swim in the river.

I shook out my hair and tossed it messily over my shoulder.

"Will your mother ask about your swim?" Edric asked, looking at my wet hair.

"No," I assured him. "Of all my packmates, I think I probably bathe the most. Easily double the amount of some of the males—that's for sure."

He smirked at the way my nose wrinkled, following me down the mountain to the town.

My attitude, as it turned out, was far too cavalier. I had not properly taken into consideration the suspiciousness of a nervous mother. By the time we returned, she was outwardly agitated, making it clear that we'd been gone too long.

"Darby Adalwolf! Where in the two realms have you been?" she demanded—her eyes narrowed, and her cheeks flushed with outrage.

SEVENTEEN

"IT'S NOT EVEN dark yet," I pointed out, gesturing towards the purpling sky overhead. Some deep orange beams of light from the sunset were still penetrating the thick trees around our village.

Her tense lips twitched, but she didn't speak. I let out a longsuffering sigh and went to set the table. My mother was in the process of stewing a deer that my father had hunted down, the pot bubbling over a crackling fire. The heat from the hearth sank into my skin, warming my bones that had seemed to grow cold after the magic on the ridge had faded to shame.

We sat around the small wood table, eating in silence. Edric complimented my mother's cooking and thanked her for the hospitality.

"I had not expected my guard duty to include such delicious meals," he said, bowing his head in her direction.

"It's no trouble," my mother replied in a terse tone.

Edric shot a mildly questioning glance in my direction, as though silently asking how he had offended her. All I could do was give him a tiny shake of my head and try to smile reassuringly. It came out feeling more like a grimace.

The rest of the meal was quiet. Eager to leave the awkward situation, I downed my bowl of broth in three large swallows, generating another look of disapproval from my mother.

"Edric?" I asked, rising from my seat. "Would you like me to make you up a bed in the sitting room?"

"Please, don't go to any trouble for me. A chair will be fine."

"It's no trouble at all," I assured him. I gathered spare blankets and pillows, laying them in a neat stack on the edge of the decrepit couch.

I couldn't take the tension in the room any longer. It was setting my nerves on edge.

"I'm really tired after all that walking," I informed the room at large. "I'm going to bed."

"Good night," Edric said in a polite voice. "Sleep well, and do not fear. I'll be keeping watch."

I gave him a small smile and shuffled down the dark hallway towards my room. I wondered if I should feel more nervous than I did, with Pavia still on the loose. She was the one that had instituted my kidnapping the first time, after all.

There was a part of me that was *terrified* by the idea of Oberon being raised from the dead. That was only natural. But here, now, I couldn't seem to focus on the bigger picture.

Crawling into bed wasn't nearly as relaxing as I'd hoped it would be. My mind raced in ten different directions, making me toss and turn uncomfortably for what seemed like the entire night.

There were times that I would replay the events on the ridge, feeling my heart race and warmth pool in my body. During others I would wonder how I managed to get myself into a mess with the fae world yet again. Those thoughts would inevitably lead me back to Edric, and the longing for his presence would once again distract me from my fear.

Of all the times to wish for a bedmate, was now really the moment? I groaned aloud and rolled over again. I tried to adjust my pillow to get comfortable, but Edric's presence elsewhere in the house only seemed to intensify my sleeplessness.

The night passed painfully slowly, with no sign of Pavia or, thank the gods, Oberon. Morning brought no relief to my self-inflicted torment, since the moment I stepped from my room my eyes landed on a perfectly groomed Edric. Infuriatingly, he looked as fresh as ever, with not a single hair out of place.

"Good morning, my lady," he greeted me formally.

I winced inwardly, knowing that my hair was an insane tangle, standing up on one side and smashed against my face on the other. *Of course* he'd be the most beautiful thing to walk the freaking planet, even first thing in the morning. I gritted my teeth against the thought and tried to rub the sleep from my eyes.

"Hi," I rasped, glancing through one of the front windows to see that a light frost had fallen overnight.

"Was your sleep disturbed?" Edric asked, coming to my side but standing at a respectful distance.

How could I answer that? Like hell I was going to tell him the truth, that I'd wanted his body wrapped around mine the entire night.

"Oh," I replied, searching frantically for a logical reason for my insomnia. "You know, a bit. Lots to think about."

"I swear to you, I will not allow Pavia to harm you again."

Seizing on this ready-made answer, I chewed on my lip. "It's just hard knowing that she's out there, still trying to hurt the ones I love."

Edric nodded in understanding. "I'm sure this brings up many unpleasant memories for you. I am very sorry that you have to go through it again."

"Darby? Please come help me prepare breakfast," my mother called from the kitchen, derailing my train of thought. For once, the distraction was a welcome one.

The morning meal passed much in the same manner as dinner the night before, and before I knew it, the four of us headed to the alpha's den to meet with Ember for an update. The cool morning air at least managed to shake me free from my exhausted stupor, and I breathed deeply to enjoy the mountain breeze.

As we walked, I turned towards Edric and asked the question that had been nibbling at the edges of my thoughts.

"Do you think my family is also at risk?"

He looked thoughtful for a moment, tilting his head side to side in consideration. "It's possible. However, I believe that you are more likely to be the target, as you have a direct connection to Oberon's daughter. Although Ember is protective of your family, it's nothing in comparison to her protectiveness toward you."

He'd made no attempt to keep his voice low, and I threw an apologetic look towards my father. He simply shrugged, though. He and my mother already knew the risks, after what had happened before. As ever, they were more worried about my safety than their own.

"It could be revenge, though, right?" I asked, unable to let it go.

"Revenge certainly was Oberon's style," Edric mused. "I suppose we may assume that his puppet would have similar tendencies."

I growled in frustration. "This keeps getting worse and worse! Why can't Oberon just *stay dead*?"

Edric laid a warm hand on my shoulder. "We are endeavoring to keep him that way."

As we passed through the town square, almost to Ember and Cai's den, the sound of a fae portal opening nearby made me jump.

Of course, everything was making me jump these days — but in this, I wasn't alone. Edric whirled toward the flaming oval, a wicked dagger appearing in his hand as though by magic.

I spun toward the noise as well, only to find Dianthe and Aiwin stepping into our world. Both of them looked decidedly harried.

"What is it?" I demanded, rushing to Dianthe and grabbing her wrist. "Dianthe! What's happened?"

"It's a *royal mess*, that's what it is!" she snapped, looking both angry and worried. "Is everything all right on this side of the veil?"

I nodded, wide-eyed. "As far as I know."

"Aiwin," Edric called, coming forward to greet his friend. "I thought you intended to stay with Vale and protect him."

"I did," the red-haired fae replied, his tone dark. "But Vale fled my presence last night, an hour before sundown. He was furious about something, but he wouldn't say what."

A cold fist gripped my stomach. He'd grown angry shortly before sundown? I winced. My romp in the grass with Edric definitely hadn't gone unnoticed, then.

My convulsive swallow felt like sandpaper against my throat.

Edric, unaware that our actions had likely been the cause of his friend's volatile behavior, let out a frustrated huff.

"He needs to work on his self-control! *How many times* have we had to deal with him disappearing without an explanation?" he said plaintively.

I stared at Edric's worried expression. This was the most candid I'd ever seen him, and I could only imagine that his friend's disappearance was a source of more worry than he was letting on.

"Just wait. That's not the worst of it," Dianthe interrupted.

"No," Aiwin agreed. "It isn't. Sometime after he disappeared, the palace was infiltrated."

"Oh, *no*. Not the queen?" I asked in horror. If our most powerful ally in Elfhame had been captured or even killed, then we were in real trouble.

But Dianthe shook her head. "No, not the queen. It's almost as bad, though. Someone broke into Vale's chambers and kidnapped his mother. Titania is in a rage — Zara is her dearest advisor, and probably the closest thing she has to a friend."

"If it wasn't a war before, it certainly will be now," Aiwin agreed. "Titania will tear Elfhame apart to get the Lady Zara back."

A chill that had nothing to do with Titania's anger shivered down my spine. Vale's mother was gone. Taken. And Vale hadn't been there to protect her... because I'd slept with his best friend, and he'd been too upset to stay.

EIGHTEEN

"THIS IS A DISASTER." I said blankly. "If Titania flies off the handle, it could tear Elfhame apart."

Dianthe nodded, her face pinched with displeasure. "She's furious, and I can't really blame her. It's quite something that they managed to get into the castle and snatch her advisor right out from under her nose."

By 'they,' I assumed she meant Pavia and any allies she might be working with. I sincerely hoped Dianthe didn't mean that Oberon—or his ghost—was somehow involved.

Was he a ghost? Or was he just dead? Could you resurrect someone who *wasn't* a ghost?

I wasn't sure, but Edric's voice drew me out of my circling thoughts. He was pacing, the light glinting off his shiny platinum hair.

"What are the queen's orders for us?" he asked.

"Like I said, she's in a towering rage. Unfortunately, her commands didn't make a lot of sense." Dianthe huffed in frustration. "But she did keep Tamlain and Vale in the palace with her, to help with the investigation. Then she sent us here to warn you."

I wanted so badly to ask about Vale. How was he? Would Titania be able to keep him safe when she couldn't protect Zara? Just the sound of Vale's name made my stomach squirm with discomfort and guilt. Biting my lower lip to keep my questions from spilling out, I stared hard at my feet.

"Dianthe knew the way here, so she was able to portal us directly into the square," Aiwin said, looking around with interest. "This place has very strange trees. Is it all like this?"

The calm expression on his face told me that very little ever got to this fae. Right now, I knew that was the kind of equanimity all of us needed.

"Uh, sort of," I answered, glancing at a nearby tree. "We don't have vibrantly colored plant life like Elfhame. Not except for the flowers."

"*Anyway*," Dianthe interrupted sharply, "we need to regroup and figure out what we can do about Vale's mother."

"We'll need someone to monitor events on both worlds who can serve as a messenger between the rulers here and Queen Titania," Edric offered, rubbing his chin.

"I'll do that," Dianthe said. "I'm used to portaling back and forth between the two worlds on a regular basis, and I know all the parties involved."

"In that case, I will remain here to help Edric guard Darby," Aiwin said, meeting his friend's gaze with an eyebrow raised in question. "Titania is already watching over Vale like a hawk, so I'm not much help there."

Edric, his expression more concerned than his counterpart's, gave me a worried look. "That would be useful, yes. We'll need to stay close to her. Pavia has used her as bait in the past. It's safe to assume she'll try to do so again."

Dianthe let out a low growl of warning. "Protect her well, or you'll both answer to me."

My parents had been hanging back, watching these new developments. But at that, my father cleared his throat. "I'm afraid you'll have to stand in line."

"We will protect her," Edric told them without rancor. "No harm will come to you under our watch, Darby. Or to your family, if we can possibly help it."

Dianthe gave a reluctant nod and caught my eye to make sure I was all right with the plan. I gave her a tiny nod in reply.

"In that case, I'm going to return to the palace and speak to Queen Titania again," she said. "We didn't really get a chance to learn all the details about what happened. I'll be back shortly with a report."

Before I could reply, she waved her hand and slipped through an open portal, disappearing back to Elfhame.

My questions died in my throat as the portal crackled out of existence, leaving only empty space behind.

Sighing, I returned my attention to my parents and my fae companions, who were glancing around at the trees surrounding the edge of the town square.

"Perhaps we should not linger in the open like this," Aiwin said. For the first time, his expression had grown grim and focused. "This isn't a strategic location."

"We were headed to Cai and Ember's den," I told him. "They're the pack's leaders, along with Tamlain."

Aiwin let out a low breath of wry amusement. "How odd to think of a fae general living with shifters."

I winced internally at the reminder of how rare it was for fae and shifters to mix in such a way.

"We're nearly there," I said instead. "Let's go tell them what's happening."

"Yes. They definitely need to know about this," said my mother.

The alpha's den wasn't far—just a short way up the slope beyond the square. I knocked on Ember's door for the second time in two days and was greeted by her welcoming smile. She must have seen something in my expression, though, because hers fell immediately.

"Oh, shit," she said. "What's happened now?"

◆

After Cai and Ember heard our report of the newest developments happening back in Elfhame, Ember let out another heartfelt curse and threw her hands up in frustration. "I *hate* how Titania just assumes she can order Tamlain around the moment she needs him for something."

"Well," Cai said dryly. "She *is* his queen. And on the positive side, this way we have someone right in the middle of the investigation who can keep us updated."

"Dianthe is keeping her ear to the ground as well," I said. "But for now, it sounds like we're stuck waiting on an update from them."

Ember sighed. "I guess you're right." She eyed Aiwin. "I expect your den is getting a bit crowded at this point. There's also the matter of Pavia knowing the layout of the town—something I'm not at all happy about. If she does come looking for you, she knows exactly where to find you."

"It wasn't as though she ever took much interest in me back when she lived here," I said. "But you're right that in this place, everyone pretty much knows everyone. I guess Pavia was no exception."

Ember tapped her lips, thinking. "How about this? You could use the new student dens that we're building on the edge of the settlement for a few days—just until this mess blows over. Edric, Aiwin, you are our honored guests, and we'd like to be able to make you as comfortable as possible."

"That is very kind of you," Edric said, tipping his head in a polite bow.

"Sounds good," Aiwin put in. "Not that I'm picky about accommodations." He nudged Edric. "Not all of us grew up in fine, noble houses."

Ember dredged up a smile for him. "It's the least we can do. They're small, but comfortable. You could stay in one, with Darby and her family staying in another next door. Cai can order some extra guards to watch over the place, as well."

A frown formed on Edric's attractive face. "No—with all due respect, I'm afraid that simply will not work. Aiwin and I are honor-bound to protect Darby, with our lives, should it come to that."

Ember blinked, her penetrating gaze moving back and forth between Edric and me. "I… *see*."

I could feel myself going red. Ember had been my friend for too long for her to fail to notice something brewing between myself and Edric. If she knew that I was growing more and more attached to a fae who was not my mate, would she be disappointed with me?

Surely not, given her own history.

"In that case, Darby should stay with you and Aiwin," she said, turning towards me as though for confirmation. "Would that work for you, Darby?"

I had let my brain zoom into overdrive for a moment before my father's voice brought me crashing back to reality.

"With respect, alphas, I do not believe that would be in the best interest of my daughter." He looked distinctly uncomfortable. Not surprising, since I could count the number of times I'd seen him disagree with a higher-ranking wolf on one hand, and still have fingers left over.

"Mr. Adalwolf, I understand your hesitation," Cai chimed in, having remained silent through this part of the conversation. "And if this were under any less extraordinary circumstances, I would agree with you."

My father shifted his feet, clearly uncomfortable that the alpha was speaking to him.

"However, Darby is an adult," Cai continued, "and this way she will be protected by two fae trained in magic and combat, while also making you and your mate less of a target. Ember's right. I'll put guards on both of the dens where you're staying, and we'll make sure everyone is safe."

While Cai didn't put the full weight of his alpha power into his voice, he did make it entirely clear that the arrangement was not up for debate. My mother looked like she was in danger of expiring on the spot due to apoplexy, but neither of them were in a position to argue with the pack leader. Meanwhile, Ember subtly caught my eye and gave me the barest flutter of a wink, making my cheeks flame even hotter.

NINETEEN

WITH HIS JAW set, my father dropped his eyes to the ground in submission and nodded. "As long as Darby is safe, that's all that matters."

I reached out and gripped his hand with my own, touched by his words. I knew how unhappy he was with Cai and Ember's plan for me to stay with the two male fae, so it meant a lot that he would say something like that.

"She will be perfectly safe with us, sir." Edric's voice was deadly serious.

I tried to catch his eye, but my new fae companion had drawn himself up to his fullest height and looked prepared to do battle on my behalf on the spot.

"Darby," my father said, a note of pleading in his tone, "please conduct yourself as a wolf of your standing should."

Just like that, fresh frustration swirled together with my warm feelings from a moment ago. Because what the hell was *that* supposed to mean?

Not only was our standing about as low as it could get in the Greystalker pack, but I'd never given either of my parents a reason to doubt me. I wondered why now, all of the sudden, they didn't seem to trust me.

Maybe because you haven't been acting very trustworthy with Edric? The snide little inner voice was unwelcome. I did my best to quash it.

Edric and Aiwin shared a brief look full of meaning, and I felt my insides trying to shrivel up in embarrassment. Would Edric tell Aiwin what we'd done together? Looking down at my feet, I let my hair fall around my face, hiding my shining red cheeks.

"Perhaps we should go to these student accommodations now?" Edric suggested, rescuing me from my burning self-consciousness. "I do not like this new development at all, and I would prefer to get Darby and her family to a position of better cover."

Cai nodded his approval and ushered us outside, turning toward the path leading to the dens that we would be inhabiting for the night—and possibly longer.

"Wait, can I pack a bag?" I asked, looking back in the direction of my family's den. "My parents could probably use some of their things as well."

Cai hesitated, looking at each of the fae in turn, both of whom nodded warily. "We'll all go together," said the alpha.

We returned to the modest structure. I rushed through the front door with Ember on my heels and didn't pause until I was in my bedroom, where I began throwing clothes towards a bag in the corner while the two fae and Cai lingered in the cramped sitting room.

"It's going to be okay, you know," Ember said. "We got through this once before, we can do it again."

"Yeah," I hedged, not taking my eyes off my disorganized packing.

Ember wasn't done, though. "Try not to worry. We won't let anything happen to you."

I paused in my efforts to stuff clothing into the bag. "But what about you? She went for you before. She'll probably do it again. What if she tries to use me as bait like Oberon did the first time?"

Ember's expression was as serious as I'd ever seen it. "That's what we're going to prevent. We have more help this time, and we're way ahead of her. Even if she wants revenge, she doesn't have the same resources now as when Oberon was alive."

I sighed. My friend did have a point, but it didn't ease the knot of fear in my chest. Pavia was unpredictable, even unhinged. How could we be sure that we were even on the right track when it came to anticipating her plans?

By the time we returned to the town square with our hastily packed bags, more than half an hour had passed.

As a group, we proceeded towards the vacant dens, the smell of freshly dug earth pungent in the air. We were lucky that the construction, only recently completed, was done on the new quarters. In some ways, it would give us a much more comfortable space than the tense and awkward night we'd had with my parents. In other ways, it was going to be just as uncomfortable—for me, at least.

Cai unlocked the door and pushed it open, allowing us all to go inside. Ember touched my hand and gave me a reassuring smile as we passed through the front door.

My father's eyes lingered on me for a moment, and I could tell by the tightness in his lips that he still disapproved of the situation. He would never defy his alpha, though.

"I'll see you later," I told him and my mother, giving each of them a swift hug. Then, echoing Ember, I added, "It will be all right. You'll see."

When Cai had delivered additional promises for the imminent arrival of guards, and everyone had finally left, I looked around the living space. It was chilly and a little musty from lack of use.

"We should block all the light," Aiwin said, drawing the heavy curtains in front of the windows. "Perhaps anyone up to mischief will think this is an unused den."

"Or one that still needs more work or something," I agreed, relaxing a bit as dimness fell over the room.

Using a block of flint and some kindling, I started building a fire in the hearth, hoping to take the chill from the air.

"Darby, may I ask you something?" Edric asked, uncharacteristically hesitant.

"Sure," I replied, brushing bits of crumbling bark off my fingers.

The blond fae leaned against the wall nearby, watching me. "Why does your father seek to control you so? You have come of age in your culture, have you not?"

Aiwin let out a strangled sound. "Edric! You know you're supposed to be the one with manners, right?"

I felt my face heat up again and tried to tell myself it was from the warmth of the flames. "No, no, it's okay."

Aiwin raised a skeptical ginger eyebrow at me.

"He has the right to ask," I told him.

Taking a deep breath, I brushed my hair back, looking at both of the beautiful fae sharing this intimate space with me.

"In shifter society, when we come of age, sometimes a—a mark appears."

"A… mark? What kind of mark?" Edric asked, his eyebrows drawing together.

I looked at the ceiling, thinking. I wasn't sure how to explain it to them without showing them. But that wasn't something I was ready to do—even though Edric had seen it already. He just hadn't known what he was looking at.

"It looks something like an old scar, or maybe a human birth mark?" I hedged. "They're called fate marks."

Aiwin snorted. "How could such a thing appear out of nowhere when you come of age?"

I swallowed and replied, "They're to show that you have a mate out there somewhere. They will develop the same mark when they come of age. That's one of the ways that you recognize your mate. I suppose it's a form of magic, though we don't think of it as such."

Edric's eyebrows shot up. "And you have one of these marks? You have a mate that you're fated to be with?"

I nodded, chewing on my lower lip. "Apparently so."

His naturally pale complexion went paler. "Then I fear I must apologize. I believe I may have stepped out of line yesterday. I was not aware of this... tradition."

"No, no," I answered quickly, taking a step forward, "you didn't, I promise. My mate isn't here. I'm not with anyone. Why shouldn't I enjoy myself now? I can't cheat on someone who is not in my life, after all."

Something deep in my stomach squirmed uncomfortably at my own words. That had been dangerously close to a lie.

A look of concession passed across Edric's face, and he gave a slow nod. "I suppose that's fair."

Aiwin looked back and forth between us before his green gaze landed on his comrade. "Wait, am I to understand that you've been *enjoying yourself* without me?"

Edric scowled. "Now who needs a lesson in manners, you oaf?"

Aiwin pasted on an innocent look that sat poorly with the impish gleam in his eyes. "Not at all, my friend." His teasing gaze moved to me. "I merely thought it polite to let our fair shifter know she was missing out on the more entertaining half of the full package."

I gaped at him in a way that probably resembled nothing so much as a landed fish. "You mean... you usually enjoy yourselves... *together*?"

Had that been my voice? It didn't sound like my voice.

Aiwin shrugged, a half-smile tilting up one corner of his full mouth. "Let's just say, it has been known. But my companion is right—it wasn't my intention to make you uncomfortable. I apologize for that, Darby. Though I do hope Edric treated you right, absent mate or no."

I continued to gape. *He didn't want to make me uncomfortable?*

It was all I could do not to let out a bark of hysterical laughter. He'd just as good as told me that I could have both of them if I wanted, and now I was going to spend the next who-knew-how-long stuck in hiding with them in this tiny den?

There was uncomfortable, and then there was *uncomfortable*. This, I thought as I did my best not to squirm against the heat building inside me, definitely fell under the latter.

TWENTY

BEFORE LONG, CAI'S promised guards showed up with bags of provisions for our stay. After dropping the food off, they disappeared back outside to patrol the perimeter. Edric and I had enjoyed a simple breakfast earlier that morning, but in the mad scramble to find out what was going on in the palace and deliver the news to Earth, Aiwin hadn't.

The red-haired fae eyed a pair of dressed hares curiously. "They're quite small. Are they kitlings?"

I glanced at the carcasses, which were good-sized adult rabbits, at least a couple of pounds apiece. "Er... no?"

"Much of the wildlife on Earth is modestly sized compared to the game back home," Edric said. "I saw an adult deer that barely weighed more than I do."

"Huh," Aiwin mused. "Well, give them here. I think we have the makings for a stew, even if I don't recognize all of the ingredients."

"No!" I said quickly. "I'll do it. You're both guests here, and you're already tasked with protecting me. Cooking is the least I can do."

Edric chuckled. "Too late. We've dangled unfamiliar ingredients in front of him. He won't be happy until he's experimented with them."

Aiwin rolled his eyes. "Compromise, then. Show me how you'd cook a stew, and I'll help you chop and stir while Edric keeps watch."

That sounded fair, if he really was so interested in Earth foods.

"Okay, if you're sure," I said, looking over the simple fare inside the burlap sack. "Let's see... ramps, Jerusalem artichoke, wild carrots, and... turnips. Definitely a stew. Help me bone these rabbits, and we'll use the trimmings to make a stock. The meat will turn into inedible lumps if it simmers that long."

"Not so different from how I'd make a stew, it sounds like," Aiwin said with a smile, and we both got started.

It felt odd to work so seamlessly with a near stranger. We cut and chopped and simmered and seasoned, Aiwin chatting easily with me as the time passed. Stews couldn't be hurried, but the hours slipped by surprisingly pleasantly given all the horrible things hanging over our heads.

At least when I was focused on food preparation, I wasn't as focused on what might happen when darkness fell, leaving me alone in this cozy den with two handsome fae who seemed—for whatever bizarre reason—to be attracted to me. And just like that, I was blushing again. I quickly leaned over the bubbling pot to stir it, so I could blame my reddened cheeks on the heat.

It was mid-afternoon when the stew was finally ready, and by that time, Aiwin was sheepishly apologizing every time his stomach rumbled.

"You have to feed him at least twice a day, or his stomach gurgles so loudly it scares the game away," Edric said solemnly.

Aiwin gave him an unimpressed look, but he accepted the steaming bowl I handed him eagerly. It really *did* smell good. He'd suggested some changes to my recipe after tasting the simple spices Ember and Cai had included in the care package, and from the small sips I'd tasted, it was a noticeable improvement over my mother's recipe.

I brought flatbread from the supplies and cups of water from the pump to the table. Aiwin and I sat and ate the delicious fare with gusto, while Edric took his bowl to his post by the small window to eat standing up.

Curiosity had been gnawing at me the more I saw the two fae interact. "How did you two meet?" I asked, after swallowing a bite of bread dipped in the hearty broth.

Edric gave a small laugh, not looking away from the edge of the window, where he was watching our surroundings through a gap in the curtains. "Oh, dear. My most embarrassing moment."

"Not at all," Aiwin said. "I can think of quite a few that were more embarrassing, actually. There was the time you and Vale tried to climb the tapestries in the palace chapel and got caught by the—"

"Yes, *thank you*," Edric said peevishly. "Anyway, the answer to your question, Darby, is that I'd snuck away from my parents to go on a solo hunt, even though I was far too young. A unicorn cornered me in front of some thick underbrush, and I couldn't get away."

I drew in a breath, picturing the scene. I'd seen unicorns from a distance on Elfhame, and they were *terrifying*.

Aiwin took up the story. "I was out foraging for berries when I heard the cries. The beast had already struck him several times with its front hooves by the time I followed the commotion to its source, and Edric was nearly unconscious on the ground. It was lowering its horn to gore him when I burst into the clearing."

"You fought it?" I asked, my eyes as wide as dinner plates. From the way he and Edric interacted, I was pretty sure they were about the same age. That meant Aiwin would have been just a boy as well.

He snorted derisively. "No, absolutely not. Unlike *some* people I could name, I'm not an idiot. I used magic to distract it—cast a spell to make it think there was a female unicorn in distress nearby, and when it ran off to check on her, I cast another spell to cloak both of us from view."

"He carried my unconscious body all the way back to his family's cottage," Edric said. "Then he and his parents worked healing magic on me, and his father followed my tracks back to the city. He had to ask around for hours before he found out who my family was—"

"*Minor nobility*," Aiwin stage-whispered, hiding the words behind his hand.

"My parents were so grateful for Aiwin's bravery and quick thinking in saving me that they didn't try to discourage our friendship afterward," Edric finished.

"Even though I'm common as mud," Aiwin added with a crooked grin.

Now it was Edric's turn to snort in amusement. "Don't let the self-deprecating act fool you. He may not have noble blood, but he has strong magic."

"I guess he must," I said, "if he fooled a unicorn with it."

I was almost certain a slight flush of embarrassment colored Aiwin's face at that, and it made a refreshing change to be the one making other people blush, rather than the one doing the blushing.

"Oh, yes." Edric's tone turned teasing. "The only reason I pursued the friendship was because he also helped tutor me in warding and spellwork."

"Well, you *were* fairly useless at it," Aiwin muttered around a bite of stew. Then he winked at me, his gaze twinkling, and my heart gave an involuntary little flutter. "He got better eventually," Aiwin finished.

From what I'd seen, he certainly had.

A new question niggled at me. *Don't ask, don't ask, don't ask,* I coached myself. It worked for about ten seconds, then I blurted, "How do you two know Vale?"

Aaargh. I was such an idiot.

They looked at each other as though I'd asked a much more complicated question. After a moment, Aiwin shrugged.

"Not exactly a secret anymore, is it?" he said.

Edric made a noncommittal noise, but then he turned to me. "Since you've spent time in Elfhame's Court, I'm sure you've already heard the story of Zara and Titania."

"Some of it," I said. "I know Zara was exiled from her pack here on Earth, and she became a friend and confidante of Titania. But she was pregnant with a pup, and Oberon wanted a shifter slave of his own. Titania helped Zara hide Vale from her husband as a favor because they were friends."

And, as a result, Oberon had taken revenge on Titania by siring a hybrid shifter pup of his own—Ember. I didn't bother mentioning that part, since it probably wasn't relevant. Everyone here already knew that Oberon had been an asshole.

"Just so," Edric agreed. "The part you don't know is that Titania hid Vale with Aiwin's family. They grew up together. We all did, once Aiwin and I became friends."

"Oh," I said quietly, freshly struck by just how much trouble I might be bringing by having feelings for Edric, and maybe for Aiwin as well.

I knew I should confess that Vale was my mate. Did the others even know about Vale's fate-mark? They must have seen it at some point, just as Edric must have seen mine when we were together in the woods. They just had no cultural frame of reference for it.

Edric frowned. "I still don't know why Vale acted so boorish toward you, Darby," he said, driving the invisible knife deeper. "I suppose I could be a good friend and assure you that he isn't usually like that, but it's hardly an excuse."

Aiwin grunted. "He's a moody bastard at the best of times, but that was beyond the pale."

I swallowed hard and pushed the topic away. "It's not important. Tell me more about growing up on Elfhame. It's so very different than Earth."

The rest of the afternoon passed in companionable enough conversation and shared work, as we cleaned up after the cooking and stored the leftover stew for later. I learned more about Elfhame and the interesting pair in front of me, and in turn, they pried a bit about my life out of me.

When I started to yawn, my eyelids growing heavy, Aiwin rose and threw some more wood onto the hearth fire.

"You should rest," he said. "Do you want company tonight?"

I glanced nervously at Edric. The aristocratic fae seemed interested in my reply, but not upset. I'd realized earlier, though, that as angry as I was with Vale, I couldn't be the kind of person who would torture his wolf when he was frantic with worry for his poor mother. Add to that the fact that we were in hiding from a mad witch and my disapproving parents were in a den not twenty feet away from this one, and the answer had to be no.

"I don't think we should… do that tonight," I said awkwardly.

But Aiwin only gave me a rueful smile and shook his head. "I didn't mean for lovemaking, lass—not that I'd have said no if you asked. It's going to be a cold night, you're rightfully frightened of what's going on, and I was given to understand that shifters liked to pile up in a bed together for companionship and comfort. But I can bed down on the floor or the settle if you'd rather."

My eyes flew to Edric, who only raised an eyebrow. "Don't look at me. I'll be on watch for the first half of the night. Aiwin will spell me later."

I licked my lips, reminding myself that I was allowed to have this—for now, at least.

"Okay," I whispered. "You're right. I really don't want to be alone."

TWENTY-ONE

MAYBE I WAS getting better at asking for what I wanted, but I wasn't making much progress when it came to being mortified about it immediately afterward. It was true that shifters didn't have a lot of use for personal space when it came to piling into a den to sleep.

Other shifters.

Not me, the omega outcast from my age group. The closest experience I could draw on was occasionally cuddling up to Ember when one or both of us had suffered a particularly rough time of it. Sharing a bed with Aiwin… didn't feel very much like that.

"You'll pardon me if I keep my boots on," he said. "Edric already warned you that my company manners are terrible, but I can't abide sword-fighting in stocking feet."

Despite myself, I snorted. "Fair enough. What do I care? It's not my bed; not my sheets and blankets."

"That's the spirit," he replied.

Which was how I found myself fully clothed in a strange bed with a fully clothed, red-haired fae. On the one hand, I felt like I should try to disappear through the floor in mortification over my neediness. On the other hand, now that I'd had a tiny taste of lying in a male's protective embrace with Edric, I wanted it *all the time*.

Aiwin didn't wait for me to dither. He reached out a hand and tugged me down next to him, dragging a blanket up with his booted foot so he could cover us.

"Nothing's more exhausting than being on high alert for danger for days on end, is there?" he said, positioning me the way he wanted me, with my head resting in the crook of his shoulder.

I felt hyperaware of all the places my body pressed against his through our clothing. He was so different from Edric, who was all lithe, elegant lines. Aiwin was heavily muscled with a soft layer of padding over his chest and stomach that said he seldom went hungry.

Once, when we were young, Ember had run away to the nearest human city and come back with what she called a *teddy bear*—a brown, stuffed thing with buttons for eyes and some of the stitching coming loose. She'd given it to me as a gift, and I'd adored it so much that it was still sitting on a shelf in my room, threadbare and missing a button-eye.

Cuddling up to Aiwin gave me a similar feeling of security. A huge breath gusted out of me in a relieved sigh.

Callused fingers stroked through my hair. "That's it. Might as well rest up while things are quiet. Edric will watch out for danger."

"*Sure I will… if any of it manages to get past the dozen or so fine shifter lads standing out front with spears and crossbows.*" The wry words filtered back to us from the front room.

"Oy! They don't have magic, though, do they?" Aiwin called in return, sounding amused. "Don't think I tutored you in spells for all those years so you could stand around looking pretty during a fight!"

I couldn't help myself from descending into giggles, burying my face against Aiwin's neck to stifle them.

"Seriously, lass, get some sleep," Aiwin said, poking me in the side. "Everything'll be fine."

I didn't think I'd be able to, but I nodded anyway. My giggles faded away, and I focused on the warmth of a body next to mine and the thick, woolen blanket. Five minutes later, my awareness slid away like a fish darting into the depths of a murky pond.

❖

When I woke up, the gray of predawn rendered the cozy room in shadows, and I was curled up against Edric rather than Aiwin.

"Whu—?" I mumbled, still only half aware. How on *earth* had they managed to switch places without waking me up?

"Oh, good, you're awake," Edric said in a teasing tone. "I was about to lose feeling in my sword arm. Did you sleep well? You were out like a snuffed candle all night long."

I still felt like the woolen blanket was tangled around my brain—fuzzy and stifling.

"I guess I must have." I scrubbed at my eyes, which were gritty with sleep-sand. "Did anything happen?"

"Two of the guards got into an argument around midnight because one of them wouldn't share his flask," Edric said dryly. "That was about the extent of the excitement. Now, if you'll let me have my arm back, I should probably go help Aiwin with breakfast. I try to tell him that nobles don't cook, but he never buys it."

"*If you can wield a dagger, you can wield a kitchen knife, you posh twat,*" Aiwin called from elsewhere in the den.

Edric heaved a put-upon sigh. "You see what I have to deal with? Get some more rest if you can. We'll wake you when the food is ready."

"Thanks." I shuffled around until Edric could extricate himself and flopped down again once he'd left. A little voice that sounded like my mother insisted I should be up and about, doing the cooking so they didn't have to. But just this once, it felt nice to be waited on.

Without the veil of sleep and a comforting male presence next to me, it didn't take long for my worries to start creeping in again. Had Tamlain and Dianthe found anything useful on Elfhame? What did Pavia want with Vale's mother? How was Vale doing?

I stifled the last question.

Vale would be upset. *Duh.* He'd be *frantic,* because he cared about his mother in a way that he obviously *didn't* care about me. I couldn't do anything to help from here, and he probably didn't want my help anyway.

A brisk knock sounded at the front door, startling me upright in the bed.

"*Ah, Madame Adalwolf. Mister Adalwolf.*" Edric sounded pleasant and unconcerned, even as my heartbeat rabbited. "*Good morning. Won't you come in? We were just about to break our fast, but there's plenty of food to go around."*

There was a bit of low murmuring as familiar footsteps entered and the door closed. I consciously tried to calm myself. There was nothing incriminating to be seen. Everyone was fully dressed, and I was alone in the bed. Also, I wasn't a child.

Damn it.

My mother bustled into the bedroom as though she owned the place, giving a little gasp of disapproval when she found me clumsily trying to untangle myself from the bedding.

"*Darby.* What on earth are you still doing in bed!"

I fumbled mentally for a second. "Sleeping?" I offered.

"And letting guests do the work of making breakfast?" she asked, clearly scandalized.

I could see her examining the room for any evidence of indecorous behavior, and I couldn't stop myself from holding my breath.

"Hmph," she said after a moment. "I know we didn't raise you to be a layabout. Get yourself together and come to the kitchen."

This wasn't the first time I'd thought about moving out on my own—not by a long shot. It might have been the deepest yearning I'd ever felt for the idea, though.

"I'll be right there," I said meekly.

Breakfast with my family was every bit as awkward as dinner had been when Edric had first arrived. It was almost a relief when another knock at the door interrupted us.

I leapt up to answer it and found Ember outside with Tamlain standing at her shoulder. The forbidding fae general looked even grimmer than usual, and I wondered when he'd returned from Elfhame.

"Hi, Darby," Ember said. "More bad news, I'm afraid. Can we come in?"

My heart sank. "Sure. We're eating, do you want to join us?"

It was Tamlain who answered. "Thank you, but that won't be necessary. I fear there is much to do."

By now, Aiwin and Edric had come to see what was going on.

"General," Edric greeted. "What's happened now? Is there any word on the Lady Zara?"

Tamlain's stony expression grew stonier. "After a fashion."

I gestured the pair to enter, making the modest student den feel badly overcrowded. Edric waved them toward the chairs he and Aiwin had abandoned, but again, Tamlain shook his head.

"There has been another development," he said, addressing all of us. "As far as we can piece together, last night the young shifter, Vale, received a missive directing him to meet with Pavia. She offered to allow him to trade himself for his mother as a hostage. He elected to act without informing anyone directly, only leaving behind a note in his quarters briefly explaining what he planned to do."

"*No*," I breathed, suddenly unable to move — not so much as a blink.

Ember took up the thread. "Neither he nor his mother returned. We can only assume that the whole thing was a trick to get him into Pavia's clutches right along with Zara."

My wolf howled, breaking free of our joint paralysis. Panic thrummed along my nerves. The floor suddenly seemed very far away, as though my head was floating up toward the ceiling.

"We have to get him back!" I choked out. My fingers clenched the back of my chair like claws, the knuckles white as bone.

Every eye was abruptly on me.

"Darby?" Ember sounded tentative. "We'll try to get both of them back, of course…"

I shook my head frantically. "No! We have to go, *right now*, and get him free of Pavia!"

Aiwin was looking at me very strangely. "Lass, don't get me wrong. Vale and I have been friends most of my life, and I'd damn well step in front of a sword or a spell to save him. But I didn't get the impression there was any love lost between the two of you. Why the urgency? We need a plan before we bumble in ham-fisted."

I shivered violently, suddenly realizing what my outburst must look like. All at once, the stupid secret I'd been keeping reared up like an angry unicorn, looming over the scene.

I tried to swallow, nearly choking on my own spit. "Vale is…" The words were a pitiful croak.

Ember looked at me with open concern. "Darby," she began. "What is it? Talk to me."

I steeled myself, meeting her eyes and nobody else's. "He's my mate. Vale is my fated mate."

TWENTY-TWO

THE ROOM SEEMED to have gone very quiet. I forced myself to glance around, my stomach feeling like it was about to flip over. Edric and Aiwin exchanged a look. Surprise was apparent on Aiwin's face, while Edric's expression was quickly morphing into outrage.

I couldn't blame either of them. They must feel like they had betrayed their friend by engaging in intimacy with me, and I'd encouraged that betrayal by keeping my mouth shut about my mate bond with Vale.

"He rejected me," I said in a tiny voice, as though that excused it. "You saw how he acted around me."

"It's true, he *was* particularly asinine toward you," Aiwin muttered, although he still looked decidedly disgruntled.

Edric's expression had hardened to marble, unreadable.

I turned back to Ember, my eyes pleading with my best friend to understand. After the shock cleared from her face, she gave me a grim little smile that said she knew exactly what I was feeling. My breath gusted out in relief. Part of me had feared that she would judge me for my actions.

Stepping close to me, she murmured in my ear. "I've been there, sweetheart. I understand that pain, and also the conflict in your heart."

She gripped my hand and gave my fingers a light squeeze. Her voice had been so low that only I heard her words.

I fought back tears and tried to hide them, though my attempt at a smile of thanks felt like a sad and twisted thing. Ember had always been my best friend, my champion. Her support meant everything to me as we navigated this crazy world together.

"Please," I said in a cracked voice, "we *have* to save him. Even if he doesn't want me, I can't stand the thought of something happening to him."

"Yes. We must do something," Edric spoke in a clipped tone.

Ember paced back and forth, glancing between me and my parents, who had stayed frozen in shock throughout the latter part of the exchange.

"Vale can take care of himself, don't forget that," Aiwin said. "I'm not at all surprised he went charging off to save his mother, even if it meant defying the Queen's orders."

"Stupid," Edric hissed between clenched teeth. "He's an impulsive idiot, and he always has been."

"No," I said. "He did it for love. He loves her more than anything, of course he'd want to save her."

My words seemed to hang in the air, suspended as if by the thread barely holding Vale and I together. *He loves her more than anything.*

"Darby must remain here and safe," Edric said. "That's even more imperative, given this new development."

"What?" I asked, turning towards him. "Why?"

"It's obvious, lass," Aiwin said, giving me an uncharacteristically impatient look. "You are even more of a target now than before."

I swallowed. "Why would you say that?"

Ember caught up with their thinking faster than I did and swore under her breath.

"*Shit*. Pavia has more leverage now to control Titania," she snarled, clapping a hand to her head and pacing faster. "But..."

"Still no leverage to control you," Tamlain finished.

"We need to travel to Elfhame and find out what's going on," I insisted. "We can't just stand around here talking!"

Several pairs of eyes abruptly pinned me in place.

"You're not going anywhere," Edric said.

I squared my shoulders and lifted my chin defiantly, feeling for a moment like I wasn't at the bottom of the pack. "You can't stop me."

"No," Cai retorted, "but I could."

He had a point. I turned towards him with burning eyes.

"*Alpha*." I hated the instinctual whine that crept into my voice. "You're my pack's leader, but he's my *mate*. I must try and save him."

Our eyes met. I managed to hold the contact for a moment before I had to drop my gaze. Staring into an alpha's eyes was like trying to stare into the sun. It made your soul feel scorched.

Cai looked thoughtfully down at me and nodded his head. "Very well. I can't ask you to forsake your soul's other half, when I know full well that no one could keep me from Ember if she were in danger. You are to remain with your bodyguards, though, and listen to their counsel."

Relief flooded me. "Of course!"

"Darby," Cai said heavily, "I'm serious."

Wilting under the weight of his alpha tone, I stared hard at the ground again. I wanted so badly to vanish into the floor, but unfortunately for me, that had never been a practical option.

I nodded, needing his attention to shift elsewhere.

"If I may make a recommendation," Edric said, stepping forward.

"Of course," Cai answered.

"I believe we would have a better chance all going to Elfhame together, rather than splitting our forces. We need to confer with the Queen, and there is no benefit to splitting up."

Tamlain gave a thoughtful nod. "That is sound strategy."

Ember and Cai nodded agreement.

"Any objections?" Ember asked, turning her attention to my mother and father.

My father looked pained. "As a parent, I object to Darby running head-first into greater danger."

My mother's eyes flashed as she met my gaze. "A mate bond can't be ignored. Darby, we both want you safe, but I know why you need to do this. Go with my blessing. Bring this ungrateful whelp of yours back here, and I'll tell him in no uncertain terms what an idiot he is for rejecting my beautiful, perfect daughter."

Father sighed. "You heard your mother. I'll want a word with him as well. Be safe, Darby."

My throat was too thick and tight to reply in words, but I darted forward and hugged them both, trying not to let them feel me trembling with fear.

"Mr. Adalwolf," Cai said, once I'd reluctantly let go. "I rely on you and your wife to let the rest of the pack council know what's happening." He unclipped the beaten copper pin fastened to the shoulder of his cloak and handed it over. "Show them this, and they'll listen to what you have to say."

"Yes, alpha," my father replied, closing his fingers tightly around the token, which was in the form of a running wolf's silhouette.

"In that case," said Tamlain, "I suppose there's no time like the present.

He brought his hand down in a long swooping motion, opening a portal to the vibrant realm of Elfhame. One after another we piled through, Edric and Aiwin on either side of me. I'd barely swept through into the forest when I felt the two brush up against my sides, almost pinning me between them.

For a moment my heart raced, and my head swam, but then I looked at their faces and found no playfulness or romance present. Their eyes were sweeping the clearing where we landed, hands gripping the hilts of their weapons.

I cringed, not having taken into account that we might come under attack the moment we arrived.

"Clear," Edric said in a gruff voice, straightening from his battle stance but losing none of his vigilance. "We must stick close together. There is security with many."

"You could just say there's safety in numbers," I muttered.

"'*In numbers*'?" Aiwin echoed, a wry smile spreading across his face as we started walking towards the summer palace. "How can you be safe in a number?"

I shrugged. "That's just the way the saying goes. At least on Earth."

"Earthers are strange," he replied.

"Yes," Ember agreed, looking around as she spoke. "We are. But we really need to get moving. I don't like staying in one place for too long."

"Where's Dianthe?" I asked, hoping for news of my friend.

As if my words summoned her, she stepped from behind a tree and into the clearing.

"Ask and ye shall receive," she teased me, giving me a small pinch on the arm. "I can't miss out on all the excitement."

"I requested she rendezvous with us here," Tamlain said, shooting his cousin a quelling look.

"What excitement?" Ember asked her. "What have you learned, Dianthe?"

The smile slid off of Dianthe's face as she took a breath. "Titania received the ransom demand shortly after Tamlain left."

A hush fell over the clearing, everyone going still and silent. The leaves on the trees no longer whispered in the wind, and everyone listened eagerly.

Ember cleared her throat. "What does Pavia want?"

Dianthe's usually bright face was troubled. "Ember, you need to understand…"

"*What does she want?*" Ember repeated, her tone growing sharp.

The fae huntress sighed. "She wants you, Ember. You in exchange for Vale and Zara. This has always been about you."

TWENTY-THREE

MY STOMACH TURNED over. A buzzing filled my ears as sounds of dismay erupted around the clearing. I couldn't bear the thought of exchanging my best friend for the mate who'd scorned me. The idea was vile.

"We can't just give this crazy witch whatever — *whomever* — she wants," Aiwin said. Edric murmured something to him in such a low voice that I couldn't catch his words, but whatever he said made Aiwin shake his head violently.

A red haze had dropped over the clearing, swirling inward from the edges of my vision. Or maybe not. Maybe that was just me, since none of the others were reacting. It felt like the mental protections Ember had given me against the madness of Elfhame had been ripped away. Swallowing a whimper of distress, I transformed in an instant, four paws hitting the ground. I shrugged off my human clothing and rubbed my face against the inside of my front leg, a whine escaping my throat as I tried to clear the haze of distress.

"Easy, Darby," Dianthe said, coming to my side and laying a soft hand against my shoulder. "What is it?"

Even through my wolf form I could tell she correctly interpreted my look of total incredulity at the question.

"Yes, fine, you're right," she said, raising her hands and giving me a grim smile. "Sorry. It's a terrible situation. What do you earthers say, again? A *shitty* situation?"

Ember laughed—but in a tired, sad sort of way. "Yeah, that's about right. It seems like there's only one option."

"*No.*" The others spoke in unison, making me jump, my hackles rising.

God, in that moment I *hated* Elfhame. Hated what it did to me, hated who I became when things inevitably started going wrong around me.

Ember shook her head stubbornly. "Stop and think, people. I'm tired of everyone I care about being hurt just so that this bitch can try to get to me. It's time to stand up to her."

"We don't even have a good understanding of her power," Cai interrupted, sounding unnerved. "We can't risk you in a direct confrontation."

"*Definitely* not." Tamlain's tone was severe.

"And yet, as we stand here, Vale and Zara's lives hang in the balance," she retorted, glancing in my direction. "He's Darby's *mate*, Tamlain."

Our eyes met, and I knew she understood the conflicting feelings roiling through me like poison. I shook my head, but dropped my gaze to my paws, sighing heavily.

The human inside me was crying, yet wolves had no ability to produce tears. I wanted to howl in frustration, though. Why did life have to be so cruel to us?

"We need to meet with the Queen first," Edric said. "We must know her thoughts before we act. Otherwise, we risk working at cross purposes." He shot me a fleeting, sidelong glance. I still couldn't read his expression.

The others nodded in reluctant agreement, although Ember still looked angry enough to rip someone's throat out. After a bit more unproductive discussion, we headed through the forest towards the path that would take us to the summer palace, where Queen Titania was holding court.

I transformed myself back into human form, even though I really didn't want to. Dianthe waved her hand, cladding me in a formal gown as the transformation settled. With another wave, she replaced the casual breeches and tunics the others were wearing with dresses and robes suitable for an audience with a monarch.

"Not really my style, but I suppose it'll do," Aiwin said, looking down at his emerald-green formal robes. "Thank you... I think."

Dianthe only rolled her eyes at him as she twisted her hair into an elegant knot at the back of her head.

The sound of trumpets greeted us as we approached an arched gate made of living trees. The guards, recognizing us, made way—massive branches swinging to the side to allow us entrance.

"Her Majesty is expecting you," one of them stated.

The palace was as enchanted as ever, nature melding with the architecture until it was impossible to tell where one ended and the other began. Tamlain led the way through the massive corridors like a man on a mission. He barely nodded to the guards flanking the entrance to the throne room before pushing the large double doors open. Inside, sunlight filtered through the leaves that made a canopy overhead. The sweet smell of flowers filled the air.

Even so, a grim air hung over the queen's domain. No birds chirped and warbled among the greenery. No murmur of voices filled the hall. Very few of Titania's subjects were present, and those that were stood tense and silent around the edges of the room, as though fearful to approach the throne.

I couldn't blame them. Queen Titania paced restlessly on her dais, anger flashing in her eyes. As soon as she spotted us, she halted, drawing herself up to her fullest height.

"*How did this happen?*" she demanded, her shrill tone making me flinch in fear yet again.

"Your Majesty," Edric began, dropping to one knee and bowing his head, but he was cut off by Titania's sharp gesture.

"No! This was careless and impulsive! Despite our best efforts, this old woman—this witch—has been free to stroll into the heart of my kingdom and walk away with everything I hold most dear! She has threatened the peace we've been working so carefully to build, using *exactly the same gambit as last time*. What have we learned? Nothing!"

No one dared to speak up. Certainly not me. I dipped my head, hoping my loose hair would hide my face. I wanted nothing more than to transform back into a wolf, despite the terrible pain of my mate missing. Despite the fact that I'd been rejected.

"Dianthe!" Queen Titania snapped.

Dianthe strode forward to flank Edric, also dropping to her knee and bowing her head. "Yes, Your Majesty?"

"We must launch a rescue mission at once!"

Dianthe hesitated, bringing her face up slightly.

"That will be complicated by the fact that we do not know where Pavia is holding her hostages," she replied in a careful tone.

"That is unacceptable! We must discover where she is keeping them!" the queen raged.

Again, no one dared contradict her openly when she was in such a mood. She seemed to gather the truth from our silence, however, and began pacing in agitation again. Edric and Dianthe remained where they were on the floor, shooting wary glances at each other. Cai leaned over to Ember and whispered quietly in her ear. She murmured something back to him, barely moving her lips.

It was all I could do to keep breathing when Titania stopped pacing abruptly and whirled on us.

"Well, then. It seems that we have no other choice," she said regally, as though issuing a royal decree.

I looked up quickly, fresh misgivings threatening to squeeze the air from my lungs.

"It appears we must pay the ransom," she said, her expression growing hard. "We will exchange Ember for Vale and Zara."

All around me, the others tensed. I didn't think my heart—which had been racing before—was beating at all now. This had been my worst fear, from the moment Dianthe told us of Pavia's ransom demand—that Titania would do *anything* to get her advisors back, no matter how outrageous the demand.

Anything—including giving Pavia exactly what she wanted.

TWENTY-FOUR

AN EXPLOSION OF voices followed the Queen's pronouncement, echoing off the walls of the throne room despite their muffling layer of flowering vines.

"Your Majesty!" Dianthe exclaimed in dismay.

"Queen Titania, I have grave concerns—" That was Edric, who had half-risen from his courtly bow.

"Absolutely not," Cai snapped.

Ember sighed in exasperation, pinching the bridge of her nose with her thumb and forefinger as she exchanged a glance with me. The people in attendance were all talking over one another.

I felt a shameful whine rising in my throat as I stared hopelessly at my best friend. I could barely stand this feeling of being torn in two. It wasn't fair! I couldn't risk my best friend to save Vale and his mother, even if Vale *was* my fated mate.

"Silence!" Queen Titania proclaimed loudly, her power rising like a windstorm inside the hall.

My hair whipped around me as everyone stopped talking and looked up at the monarch, and then settled into place on my shoulders as quiet fell, the wind dying down.

"I realize this is not an ideal scenario," she said when every eye was fixed on her. "Yet, I do not believe there is much choice. I will not leave my closest advisors in the grips of a dark witch—not with their deep knowledge of the realm and its defenses. All of Elfhame is at stake."

"We have a choice," Cai snarled, stepping in front of Ember with the light of battle shining fiercely in his eyes. "We'll leave right now." He spun towards Dianthe. "Open a portal."

The Queen's guards sprang forward in an instant, pointing swords and lances in Dianthe's face.

"Think carefully about your next move, Titania," Cai growled. "Because your treaty with Earth hangs in the balance." He fell to all fours, transforming into his towering wolf form. The clothing Dianthe had conjured for him earlier dissipated in a cascade of colorful sparks.

Guards rushed toward the center of the throne room from every direction, weapons drawn. I cowered back, certain that open fighting would break out at any moment.

Tamlain had been silent during the heated exchange, one hand held protectively around Ember's upper arm. Now, he took a step forward, placing himself between the queen and Cai's wolf.

"Your Majesty," he said, his deep voice cutting through the confusion.

Titania's gaze fell on him and narrowed. She raised a hand. The guards slowed to a stop, the clatter of their boots falling silent.

"Cai," Tamlain said. "This discussion would be more productive if you would rejoin us in your human form."

Cai huffed and transformed back; Dianthe's magicked clothes reforming around him as he rose from his crouch. His pleasant features were creased into a dark scowl.

"Perhaps there is another way." Edric, who had been hovering at the edge of the incipient melee with Aiwin, removed his hand from the hilt of his sword. "A compromise, so to speak."

I straightened slowly from my defensive hunch, eager to hear Edric's idea, but terrified of what Titania might ultimately decide.

Queen Titania surveyed our motley group imperiously, one eyebrow raised. "A compromise, you say?"

Tamlain, apparently reassured that his co-mate wasn't about to tear anyone's throat out, spoke. "You speak of the danger to the realm inherent in leaving your advisors in Pavia's grasp, but do not discount the danger that would come from allowing Ember to fall under her power. Ember has been her primary target for a reason."

An uncomfortable pause settled over the room as Titania considered this. The guards shifted restlessly.

"If I may speak?" Edric asked.

"Proceed," the Queen commanded, turning and seating herself regally on her throne. Dianthe, no longer held at sword point, backed away a few steps—allowing Edric to command the assembled audience alone.

"Perhaps we can use this ransom demand to our advantage, Your Majesty," he began.

I blinked. How could any of this mess be to our advantage?

Queen Titania did not answer, but she continued to survey Edric thoughtfully.

"We have control of at least some of the variables in a ransom delivery," he said. "At this time, we don't know where Pavia is. We don't know who—if anyone—is helping her, or how she's controlling Zara and Vale, or what her ultimate plan may be. We can't expect her to keep her word; not after she tricked Vale. So, I propose we take back what control we do have. Let *her* spring *our* trap for a change."

I glanced at Dianthe and Ember. Dianthe looked intrigued. Ember crossed her arms.

"I'm listening," she said.

The Queen laced her hands together in her lap, clearly considering it. Aiwin and Dianthe began whispering quietly together. By the tone of their low voices, I could tell they liked the idea and were already deep in scheming something. Dianthe, in particular, was looking at Edric with new respect.

"An interesting proposal. Could you put such a plan together quickly?" the Queen asked, interrupting their quiet conversation.

"Now, wait just a minute—" Cai took an aggressive step forward.

Tamlain moved in front of him. "We reserve the right to overrule any scheme that endangers Ember," he said, holding his hand out toward the alpha shifter in a quelling gesture.

Ember sounded tart. "If it traps Pavia and puts a stop to her madness, I'm all for it."

Dianthe glanced back at us. Edric looked confident and Aiwin was nodding enthusiastically.

"Yes, Your Majesty," Dianthe said. "To answer your question, I believe we can come up with something workable in a short amount of time."

Titania considered them all for several moments, her expression cold and haughty. "Very well. I will release Pavia's messenger and bid him to return with my reply. The exchange will take place at midnight in the clearing south of Oberon's ruined castle. If you position yourselves well, you may gain a slight tactical advantage. Inform me of the details as soon as they are in place."

Edric bowed gracefully. "It will be as you say, Your Majesty. Rest assured that we, too, desire the safe return of Vale and Lady Zara."

Queen Titania nodded brusquely before waving an imperious hand at one of her ladies in waiting. The young fae looked barely old enough to attend court, but she curtsied and immediately hurried away. After a few moments, she returned to whisper in her queen's ear.

Queen Titania straightened in her throne. "The messenger to Pavia is dispatched." Then she rose, dismissing everyone from the throne room. "Now, begone, all of you. I would have solitude to think."

Good for you, I thought. *Thinking about any part of this disastrous mess is the last thing I want to do right now.*

TWENTY-FIVE

WE TROOPED OUT of the palace under the fading light of Elfhame's sun, the rays glinting off gold leaves high in the tops of the trees. I allowed my eyes to linger on the strange colors blending together, forcing a calm I did not feel.

Cai, Tamlain, Edric, Aiwin, and Dianthe were discussing strategy in urgent tones. I moved silently to Ember's side and spoke in her ear, my voice too low to interrupt the others. "I'm going with you."

She shot a dark look in my direction, her long, bi-colored hair falling over her shoulder. "Darby, you shouldn't. This isn't going to be pretty."

"I have to, he's my…" My voice trailed away, and I cleared my throat awkwardly. "You'll need all the help you can get."

Ember turned, taking my hands in hers. "Darby. Pavia has already tried to capture you once, simply because she knows she can use you as a weapon against me. I couldn't bear that. Not again. Not after last time."

I squeezed her fingers, but I couldn't let her back me down. "I'll fight as my wolf. She won't even recognize me."

Skepticism creased Ember's brow.

"Okay," Dianthe called, "we think we've got a plan nailed down. Ember, you need to be a part of this. Get your arse over here."

Ember rolled her eyes at me and dragged me over to the rest of the group, where I stood close to her, braced for whatever crazy plan they'd come up with.

"It's fairly straightforward," Dianthe began. "We use magic to conjure a cage that has a rigged panel, which will be easy for you to control from the inside, Ember. Aiwin and Edric are Vale's closest friends, so they'll deliver you in the cage to Pavia, since it's plausible that they want Vale back badly enough to capture you and turn you over."

"Is it really, though?" Aiwin asked wryly, earning him an annoyed look from Edric. "What? He can be irritatingly moody sometimes."

"I'll tell him you said so," Edric muttered.

"Yes," Dianthe said firmly. "You *do* want him back — a fact which you'll make very clear when you deliver Ember inside the rigged cage. You'll need to sell it to Pavia, or this won't work. You'll make the trade, and once Vale and Zara are safe in our hands, Ember releases herself from the cage. Then we attack and take out Pavia once and for all."

There was too much that could go wrong. I looked appealingly at Cai and Tamlain. "Are you two seriously all right with this?"

"Not particularly," Tamlain said, in his characteristic dry tones. "However, it is true that the danger to Ember — not to mention Elfhame — will remain until Pavia is stopped. There is also the small matter that the queen may try to force the issue of the ransom unless we offer her a better option."

Cai gave a disgusted snarl, then turned to his mate. "Ember, this is your call, not anyone else's."

My friend didn't even hesitate. "Yeah, I'm in. Let's put this bitch down once and for all, before she really *does* figure out a way to resurrect my deadbeat sperm donor and make everything a thousand times worse."

There were times when I really hated my own cowardice, and this was one of them. I'd surrounded myself with noble, fearless people, and at times like this, the contrast was particularly painful.

I swallowed the urge to tell them it was too dangerous, that we couldn't risk it.

"Okay," I managed. "If you're sure, Ember."

She squeezed my hand in wordless reply.

<hr>

Our midnight deadline didn't leave us much time to plan and implement everything. After some discussion, Tamlain left to inform the queen of what was happening, on the theory that as a respected former general, she might be more inclined to listen to him and give weight to his words. Whereas Cai would probably lose his temper and start a battle in the throne room.

As one, Edric, Aiwin, and Dianthe moved to face each other in the quiet courtyard where we'd retreated after our royal audience. They held their arms outstretched, fingers touching.

"What are you doing?" I asked, moving to stand with Ember and Cai so I could see better.

"Making the cage," Dianthe explained, her eyebrows furrowed in concentration. "Bit of quiet, please—this is tricky."

I watched in fascination as bright silver light exploded from their hands. As one, they swept their arms forward toward the center of the circle. The beams of silver light combined at the center and grew, bars stretching up and out until they formed a large cage.

When it was complete, all three dropped their hands. The newly conjured cage glowed molten red for a moment before gradually cooling into solidity. Ember stepped forward and examined the bars, careful not to touch it yet. She grimaced at Cai, who wrapped a comforting arm around her.

"You guys couldn't have made it any bigger?" she said in exasperation.

Dianthe patted her arm. "These two do have to carry it around, you know. Don't worry, you won't be in there for long." She touched the bars quickly, testing the temperature, then pointed to the floor. "See? Here's the rigged panel. You can open it anytime."

We couldn't actually see anything, since it was so well hidden… but we all watched as she touched a nearly invisible pressure plate on the floor of the cage. The front panel immediately popped open, free to swing outward from hinges at the top. A wolf or human could easily crawl through the opening and escape in seconds.

"As soon as Tamlain gets back, we should leave for the rendezvous," Cai said, looking up at the sky. "It's nearly nightfall."

He was right. It was already dusk, and the brightest stars were visible in the eastern sky. We only had a handful of hours left to put our plan into action.

Tamlain reappeared a few minutes later. He'd ditched his courtly attire for practical fighting leathers, and his sword hung ready at his side. "We have Her Majesty's blessing to make the attempt. However, should it go wrong, she will disavow all knowledge in hopes of preventing retribution against her advisors."

Frustration welled in my chest. "Why can't she see how important it is that we stop this?" I asked plaintively.

We should have had Titania's forces at our backs, ready to support us—not a warning that the ruler of Elfhame would happily throw us under the proverbial human bus if things went to hell.

Ember's smile wasn't a pleasant expression. "The thing about people with power, is that they tend to react badly when someone threatens to take that power away."

"Well put," Aiwin muttered.

"You're certain you still want to go through with this?" Cai asked, his tone grim.

Ember sighed. "I'm not sure 'want' is the right word, but I'm not backing out now. Let's go get this bitch."

The rest of us turned to look at the cage, gleaming silver in the last hints of the day's light.

TWENTY-SIX

AFTER ANOTHER brief portal trip, I found myself looking at a familiar scene of devastation. Just the sight of Oberon's destroyed castle across the clearing made it feel like a hand was gripping my throat. This was where I had been captured. Tormented. Abused. With the rubble of the once-proud towers in the distance, it might as well have happened yesterday.

And now, Pavia sought to resurrect my tormentor… to start the whole thing up again like a wheel, turning and turning, grinding the rest of us beneath it.

Was my mate undergoing the same pain and terror I had experienced? I didn't want to imagine what horrors Pavia could inflict with Vale's mother as a weapon to use against him, and vice versa. Vale had already sacrificed himself in a doomed attempt to save her. What else would he endure on her behalf?

Choking, I whirled away from the sight of the castle. Against my better judgment, I tried to turn inward, seeking the connection my wolf held to Vale's soul. There was nothing, just a blank hum of mental white noise. I wrapped my arms around myself, trying to rub some life back into them. My fingers had gone numb.

"Darby?" Ember asked tentatively. "Are you all right?"

Damn my best friend for always knowing. I should be reassuring her, not the other way around.

She was the one about to climb into a cage and offer herself up as bait for our enemy. She was, as ever, the hero. I was, as ever, the sidekick.

"Yes, just nervous," I replied, evasive.

I knew she wouldn't believe me. At least not fully, so I added, "There are so many things that can go wrong with this plan."

That had the benefit of being true. It was also about as unhelpful as it was possible to get.

Her look was knowing. "We'll get through this. We always do."

I managed a nod and an unconvincing smile for her.

"Ember?" Dianthe called. "It's time."

Everyone except Edric and Aiwin found a place to hide at the edge of the forest. I laid on my belly behind a tall clump of grass, trusting the darkness to obscure my presence from view. If I parted the grass slightly, I was able to see Edric, Aiwin, and Ember's distinctive bi-colored wolf form. As I watched, she crawled into the silver cage beneath the light of the moon.

Over the rustle of the breeze in the grass, I could hear their voices.

"We'll need her to be completely visible," Edric muttered glancing in all directions. "We don't know which direction they'll be coming from."

Aiwin jerked his chin toward the ruins. "Look over there. I'd say the old witch is laying out the welcome mat for us."

I peered in the direction he indicated, where a raised stone plinth stood in the middle of the clearing that had once been the palace courtyard. It was made of some smooth stone that glittered slightly, like the distant stars. Some kind of heavy cloth lay over it, cushioning the top.

I squinted as the moon emerged from behind wispy clouds, illuminating the scene more clearly. The fabric was trimmed with gold thread and edged with ermine, rich white fur with dark speckles. I shuddered. A sudden memory of Oberon, clad in his gold-trimmed, ermine-edged cloak, rose in my mind like a vision.

With difficulty, I blinked it away—but not before the specter sent my heartbeat into a fast gallop.

Get a grip, Darby. Being afraid of an empty robe isn't going to help. It might not even be Oberon's. It might just be coincidence.

"Do you think they're hiding in the old city?" Aiwin asked.

"Impossible to say," Edric replied. "Whatever the case, it's clear we're intended to put the cage on this stone. I don't sense any magic coming from it or the cloak, do you?"

"No," Aiwin said. "I suppose we ought to play along, and it's as good a place as anywhere, when it comes to letting her be seen."

Despite my best attempts, the images in my mind were coming faster and faster. There seemed to be nothing I could do to stop them. I could feel the pain across my shoulders and back again, phantom whip marks from the torture I'd sustained at Oberon's hands.

Shaking, I raised my head in time to see Aiwin and Edric carefully set the cage on top of the plinth and robe. Ember, in her wolf form, stirred around in the silver cage, growling at the two fae in a convincing display of frustrated rage.

"Sorry," Aiwin said, having jostled her around somewhat during the transfer. "Promise not to bite me?"

Ember huffed and laid her ears back, holding her performance until she had an audience.

The two fae stepped away, waiting with the rest of us for something to happen. The seconds stretched to minutes, which turned into nearly an hour. I was beginning to lose patience with Pavia. Wasn't this trade what she wanted? She'd sent the messenger, after all. Why leave us hanging like this?

Maybe she'd changed her mind? Or maybe it was some kind of a trap. We'd half-suspected it, after all. The question was, did she suspect *our* trap in turn?

The sound of footsteps swishing through grass made me perk up. Ember raised her head off her paws, looking to the west of the castle. Two figures appeared from the shadow of the rubble, moving slowly with a shuffling gate.

Light broke over the faces of the newcomers. It was all I could do not to gasp aloud and give away our position. Zara and Vale made their painfully slow way toward us, both of them wearing shapeless gray smocks. Zara's hands were bound behind her back, and a cloth gag was shoved deep in her mouth.

She wouldn't have the power to fight off a fly, I realized, horrified.

What had Pavia done to them?

Vale's eyes were dark and cast towards the ground, yet he guided his mother forward with a firm hand hooked in her arm.

I stared hard at Zara, who I knew to be one of Queen Titania's most trusted advisors. Her eyes were blank and vacant, as if Vale was simply pulling a shell of a person along with him.

"Vale," Aiwin said in relief. "We've come to make a trade for you and Zara. Look, we've captured your wolf. Where is Pavia? I'm sure she'll want to take charge of her new prisoner personally."

My heart gave a painful spasm at his words, even though I knew this was all a part of the ruse. Regardless, it was hard to hear the words 'your wolf' in connection to anyone else but me.

Stupid, I berated myself. *Stupid, stupid. You're not his wolf. He rejected you. We'll free him and his mother, and if we're lucky, capture Pavia when she shows her hateful face to take Ember away. Then I'll forget about Vale and go on with my life. After all, it's exactly what he's going to do.*

Vale and his mother came to a stumbling halt next to Ember and the two fae. He didn't reply to Aiwin. In fact, he didn't even seem to acknowledge that he'd heard the words. I frowned. Had Pavia drugged them? It might explain why Zara looked so unsteady.

Around me, the others waited in hiding, tense and searching the surroundings for Pavia. It couldn't be this easy. Aiwin and Edric would be able to grab Vale and Zara, while Ember freed herself, and Tamlain cast a portal so we could all flee to safety. We could get away in moments, even if it meant we missed our chance to capture our enemy.

Edric ducked his head, placing a hand on Vale's arm as he tried to catch his friend's eye. "Vale?" he asked. "What is it? What's wrong?"

With no warning, Vale wrenched his arm free and shoved both Edric and Zara away with vicious strength. Edric staggered back, taken utterly by surprise, while Zara crumpled to the ground and lay still.

A sudden burst of adrenaline had me lunging from cover, shifting form as I went. I was dimly aware of Cai, Tamlain, and Dianthe following suit behind me, weapons drawn.

Before I'd gone two strides, Vale darted a hand into the folds of his shapeless smock and came out with a wicked dagger clutched in his grip. The blade flashed in the moonlight — arcing up, then down. He stabbed through the silver bars of the cage with a feral snarl, and blood spurted as the vicious point embedded itself in Ember's body.

TWENTY-SEVEN

SEVERAL THINGS seemed to happen at once as Vale jerked the dagger free of Ember's flesh. Cai shouted a vicious curse. Ember exploded out of the hidden hatch in the cage, snarling in rage and pain as blood poured down her shoulder. A burst of crackling magic whizzed past me from behind — Tamlain or Dianthe letting fly with an attack meant to drop Vale where he stood.

But Vale only lifted his free arm, swiping it across the front of his body like someone batting away an insect. The magical blast dissipated in a cascade of sparks, leaving him standing unharmed. Vale reached for Oberon's blood-soaked cloak, yanking it free from the plinth and toppling the empty cage to the ground.

I lunged for him, clamping my jaws around my mate's forearm with the intention of dragging him to the ground and subduing him before the others killed him. I expected him to shift into his wolf form to meet my attack, like to like. Instead, an electric jolt burned through me from the point of contact, hurling me backward. I tumbled to the ground in a heap, my limbs twitching, unable to make my wolfish body comply with my brain's demands.

In my peripheral vision, light flared.

"Quickly!" snapped a familiar voice, tense with shock and anger. *Edric.* "Get everyone away from here!"

I blinked, the blurriness of my surroundings resolving. Edric stood in front of the portal he'd just cast, his hands raised in front of himself to hold it open. Tamlain and Cai descended on Ember, flanking her protectively. Dianthe ran to Zara, pulling her upright and dragging her toward the portal. Meanwhile, Aiwin lunged for Vale as I managed to roll onto my belly and get my front legs under me.

"Darby!" Edric called, still holding the portal open. "Someone grab Darby!"

I whirled back to see Aiwin wrestling with Vale. My breath caught as the dagger flashed a second time and Aiwin fell to the ground with a cry.

"*No!*" Edric cried, but before anyone could do anything, Vale tucked the bloody ermine cloak under his arm and drew a complicated sigil in the air with his free hand.

Light burst outward from his fingertips, expanding with the same crackle as a portal opening. The light enveloped first him, then Aiwin's crumpled form, and finally me. My vision shorted out, going white. When the dazzling brilliance faded, leaving me with flashbulb pops going off in front of my eyes, everything around me had changed.

The air was dank and musty. Filthy straw crunched beneath me instead of tall grass. Flickering torchlight replaced the dim silver illumination of the moon and stars.

The thin, vertical lines in front of me resolved into floor-to-ceiling metal bars.

Metal bars.

I knew this place. I was in a cell. A *dungeon*. I was in *Oberon's* dungeon—the scene of the worst experience of my life; my deepest fear made real. A strange sort of distance settled over me, separating me from my roiling emotions like one watching a dream unfold without truly being a part of it.

Aiwin lay curled just inside the bars, one arm clamped around his side, blood dripping onto the straw beneath him. Vale stood outside the cell, Oberon's cloak still clutched under his arm, sneering down at us with utter contempt.

"Pathetic fools," he said. "Could you have made this any easier for me?"

A tiny rustle of sound came from behind me, followed by the scent of another person in the cell with us. I turned clumsily, my body still weak and out of sorts. Vale sat at the back of the cell, on the narrow bench that functioned as both seating and a sleeping cot, staring blankly into the middle distance.

I blinked, jerking my head back to the Vale standing *outside* the cell, and then around to stare at the Vale inside the cell again.

What the... *what*?

The second Vale wore torn and stained Court clothing, not the shapeless gray smock that Vale-outside-the-cell was wearing. He hadn't reacted in any way to the sudden appearance of three people in the half-ruined dungeon with him.

Vale-outside-the-cell laughed, the sound like rusty gate hinges.

"Idiot creatures," he said. "How you ever managed to best such a ruler as Oberon..."

The pitch of the last few words rose, transforming into a familiar and much-despised harpyish tone. Vale's face twisted, his body shimmering strangely. I blinked rapidly, and the witch Pavia stood outside the cell where my mate had stood seconds earlier.

Glamour. She'd used fae glamour to disguise herself so she could stroll past all our defenses. We hadn't even considered the possibility.

"*You,*" Aiwin rasped, still clutching his wound. "Don't be so quick to gloat, witch. We're no use to you, and the others got away."

Pavia looked down at him, a twisted smirk pulling at her thin lips. My utter terror at once again being a prisoner in this horrible place was still a distant and shadowed thing. I knew it was there, but it was as though the reality of my recapture by Oberon's servant was somehow less overwhelming than the long months of fear I'd suffered over the hypothetical prospect that it *might* happen to me again.

I finally got my legs underneath me and staggered forward to squeeze my body between Aiwin and the bars, placing myself between the injured fae and this madwoman who'd imprisoned us. A low growl rumbled in my chest, my hackles rising to stand on end.

Pavia snorted at my pitiful show of defiance. She lifted the bloody cloak, examining the dark stains drying on the fur and fabric.

"Oh, believe me. I have exactly what I wanted, *peasant,*" she said, turning the cloak this way and that as though appreciating every nuance of a piece of art. "Blood of the child, spilled by violence. Why would I bother to capture the ungrateful brat when it was so simple to collect her lifeblood? Combined with the magical essence of my beloved liege, absorbed into an item kept close to him for years."

A sharp indrawn breath drew my gaze to Aiwin. His already pallid face had gone gray.

"You foul creature," he said hoarsely. "There's a reason that kind of dark magic is forbidden."

Pavia scoffed. "Forbidden by the small-minded—those who can't wrap their tiny minds around the possibilities." She tilted her head, once more admiring the stained cloak. "With this final item, I have everything I need to resurrect the greatest monarch Elfhame has ever known. And once he is returned, I will rule at his side. Together, we will crush anyone who stands in our way."

TWENTY-EIGHT

"YOU'RE MAD," AIWIN said weakly, still sounding as though Pavia's crazy plan to resurrect Oberon with Ember's blood had shocked him more than getting stabbed had done. I stood over him protectively, wishing he'd just shut up and stop provoking our captor when he was too weak to even rise.

"I don't take criticism from common creatures like you, worm," Pavia said. A cruel smile twisted her mouth. She lifted a hand and waved it at Vale, still sitting in the back of the cell staring blankly at nothing. "A bleeding peasant locked in a cage with two hungry wolves. This should be amusing."

Vale drew in a sharp breath. I could see him taking in my presence, Aiwin's presence, and Zara's absence in quick succession. His eyes grew wide, murderous rage kindling behind them. He leapt to his feet, only to stagger and catch himself against the stone wall as weakness took him.

"*Where is my mother, you soulless cow?*" he snarled.

Pavia laughed gaily. "Oh, don't fret, little wolf cub," she crooned. "You should be thanking me! Doubtless the bitch who whelped you is once more fawning at Titania's side. Wasn't that what you wanted? Isn't that why you came here in the first place?"

Vale's wild gaze flew to me, then to Aiwin.

"It's true, as far as I know," Aiwin rasped. "Zara seemed like she was under some kind of confusion spell, but the others got her away safely. Titania will help her."

Seeming to realize that Aiwin wasn't lying on the filthy floor for his health, Vale stumbled forward and fell to his knees at his friend's side. He couldn't seem to look at me directly.

I turned my wolfish gaze back to Pavia, glaring at her with as much threat as I could muster—not that I had any way to back it up.

She sniffed, looking down her nose at me. "Perhaps Titania has delivered me another weapon to use as well. You were useful as bait once before, girl. You can be useful again when Oberon has need of you."

Despite my strange numbness, her words sent a chill of fear through me. I peeled back my lips, baring sharp teeth, all my fur standing on end to make me look bigger and scarier than I was. Pavia let out a dismissive snort of amusement at my pathetic display of defiance. Then, she turned and walked away as though we were of no further interest to her, once more gazing at the bloody cloak in her hands as she wandered off.

Vale stared after her, open mouthed. Aiwin seemed mostly concerned with the steady stream of blood he was losing. Frankly, that needed to be my first priority as well. When I was sure Pavia wasn't coming back, I shifted form. Unsurprisingly, Dianthe's magic trick to reform my conjured clothing when I shifted was long gone.

I didn't care. In fact, I took a kind of vicious satisfaction in the way Vale's eyes widened as I rose to my feet in front of him, totally naked.

Stare all you want, I thought, narrowing my eyes at him. *You could have had this for the taking, and you threw it all away.*

For most shifters, nudity was nothing. It was part of life. As an omega wolf, I was more self-conscious than most, simply because being naked meant another layer of vulnerability that I couldn't always afford to display.

Here and now, one of the males in this cage had rejected me, and the other one had sheltered me in his arms at night, the perfect gentleman for all that he was apparently a lowly peasant.

"Stop staring at me like a gormless pup," I snarled at Vale. "Your friend is bleeding out from a dagger wound, and we need to help him!"

Vale's head snapped back as though I'd slapped him. He blinked, his gaze flying from my exposed boobs down to Aiwin. I dropped to my knees across from him, fingers scrabbling at the laces holding Aiwin's jerkin and linen shirt closed.

"Where is it?" Vale demanded. "Old friend, where is the wound?"

"Left side," Aiwin gritted out. "Don't think it hit anything vital."

"You're losing too much blood," I said tightly, pulling the soaked fabric out of the way.

"Dagger wounds'll do that," Aiwin muttered.

"We need to put pressure on it," Vale said, and started stripping off his torn jacket and shirt.

Now it was my turn to stare, as my would-be mate bared what seemed like acres of smooth, tanned skin. The inflamed mark on his chest drew my eye—a figure-eight lying on its side, the symbol of infinity in human culture, a perfect mirror of my own fate mark.

Gritting my teeth, I dragged my eyes away in favor of trying to see the details of Aiwin's wound. Between the flickering dimness of the torchlight and the blood welling from it, I couldn't make out anything useful except that none of his guts were poking out through the slash.

"It doesn't look like it penetrated the abdominal cavity," I said, as though the others couldn't figure out the same thing just by looking.

Vale grunted—in agreement, maybe. He positioned his balled up linen shirt above the wound. "Sorry," he said. "This is going to hurt."

"Probably no worse than being gored by an angry unicorn," Aiwin retorted, only to cry out when Vale placed the wad of fabric over the wound and pressed down hard.

I grabbed Aiwin's hand and held it, ignoring the way my knuckles ground together as he squeezed my fingers like a lifeline.

"Hold on," I told him. "Aiwin, hold on. You're going to be okay."

Fae were tough. I'd seen Ember's mate Tamlain hurt far worse than a human or even a shifter could have survived. But it still pained me to watch Aiwin suffer so. Vale's square jaw was clenched, the tendons standing out as he kept pressure on the wound, ignoring the way Aiwin gasped and writhed.

Unable to help myself, I stroked Aiwin's sweaty forehead with the fingers of my free hand. Vale's attention flew to the small movement, his brow furrowing. Overcoming my natural omega reluctance to make eye contact with a stronger wolf, I lifted my chin and glared at him, *daring* him to make a comment about it.

We stayed locked in that tableau for what felt like an age, until Aiwin finally cleared his throat. I looked down at him, finding him pale and clammy but no longer writhing. His hand squeezed mine weakly, his bone-grinding grip from earlier having slackened.

"I, uh, think the bleeding has slowed," he said. "And if you two could refrain from punching each other while I'm stuck here between you, I'd appreciate it."

Vale's hard, glowing blue gaze broke away from me as though he'd just remembered that he was staunching his friend's wound. He looked down, easing up on the pressure he was applying.

"Don't take the cloth away," I said quickly. "You'll start the bleeding again."

"I know that," he snapped.

"At the risk of being forward," Aiwin said weakly, "if you can get my belt free, lass, you can use it to hold the cloth in place over the wound."

I nodded, unable to hide my blush as I unbuckled the strip of leather and eased it free of his belt loops. Passing it under his back, I arranged it so it encircled Vale's wadded up shirt and tightened it down, wincing as Aiwin hissed in discomfort.

"That'll do for now," said the fae. "Thanks."

"Can you use your magic to heal it?" I asked, figuring that if it was possible, he would have done so already. I knew Ember could do it in a limited way, but Ember was a bit of a special case when it came to magic.

He gave a little huff. "What a much simpler world this would be if we could all heal ourselves. I'm afraid not, lass." Then his bleary green gaze turned to Vale. "What about you, my friend? Are you all right? She obviously did something to you earlier. You didn't even react when she portaled us here."

Vale sat back, his bloodstained hands hovering as though he wasn't sure what to do with them now that he was no longer pressing the cloth to Aiwin's wound.

"I'm not sure what she did," he said gruffly. "But I feel normal enough now. You're confident my mother got away?"

Aiwin nodded, and I said, "Yes, a friend of mine portaled her out. They would have gone straight back to Titania at the Summer Palace, I'm sure."

Vale still wouldn't look at me, but he nodded to show he'd heard. I wasn't proud of how badly I wanted to grab him by the shoulders and shake him. The connection between us, which had been a dull, monotone hum of nothing when he was under Pavia's spell, was now locked down tight. A steel door slammed in my face.

My wolf whimpered her discontent.

Vale rolled up his fine, embroidered jacket and eased it under Aiwin's head to act as a pillow. The fae looked between us and sighed.

"Right, then," he said. "Since we're stuck here, I suppose there's another conversation we should be having while we wait for something to happen.

What's this shifter blather about fate marks and mates, old friend?"

TWENTY-NINE

VALE STRAIGHTENED away from his fae comrade, rising to put distance between us as though he'd been burned by the words. "What is there to talk about?" he growled. "A quirk of biology — a bad joke that's been played on both of us. Nothing more."

I bristled, not sure where he got off talking about an 'us.'

"A bad joke played on *me*," I snapped back, "since I'm apparently fated to a cruel asshole who wouldn't know empathy if he tripped over it!"

Aiwin, weakened though he was, pinned his friend with a bloodshot green gaze. "She's got a point, mate. You've been a right arse to the girl since the moment you met. Why is that, exactly?"

Vale shot him a look of combined anger and betrayal. "Because I'm not in the market for a chain to wear around my neck, just because some random female happens to have a scar that looks like mine!" His eyes narrowed. "And I'm not sure why you're complaining, *friend*. It seems you were quick enough to move in, based on the way she was fussing over you earlier."

Aiwin's russet brows drew together, although he appeared more confused than angry. "Let me get this straight. You don't want her — and seem intent on behaving as cruelly as possible toward her — but you're angry that she's friendly with someone else?"

"I'm not angry!" Vale shot back angrily.

"Yes, I can see that," Aiwin told him.

I wasn't proud of it, but an answering anger at the injustice of Vale's treatment of me rose up in my chest, taking control of my tongue. "I slept with Edric," I blurted. "And if the chance arose, I'd sleep with Aiwin, too. You know why? Because they both treat me like a person instead of an inconvenience! So, you can take any opinions you might have about that fact and shove them right up your—"

A sudden surge of jealous rage that wasn't my own slammed through the bond, choking off my words. I took a startled step back, as though the emotion was a physical shove.

Just as quickly, a heavy door slammed shut against the rage, silence echoing through the bond as though it had never been.

"Good for you," Vale said without inflection. "And since you ask, I have no opinion on the matter. I wish you joy of her, Aiwin."

I gaped at the blatant lie; the statement transparently ridiculous after the surge of emotion that had just slammed into me through the bond.

Aiwin, too, was looking at his friend oddly. "Mate, no offense—but what the actual fuck is going on in your head right now?" He frowned. "Is this whole thing because of your... *you know*..." He gestured at Vale in an ambiguous circular motion with the hand that wasn't pressing the wadded-up fabric of Vale's shirt against his wound.

Vale's eyes flashed blue fire. "*Do not speak of that.*"

I stared between them, completely confused and suddenly so tired of this conversation that I could have wept.

"Maybe this shouldn't be our first concern, under the circumstances," I said, my exhaustion coming through clearly in my tone.

"You're right there, lass," Aiwin said, sounding equally tired. "Look. I'm sure the others will be trying to come up with some sort of rescue plan for us."

I nodded, accepting the change of subject gratefully. "Of course they will. Titania was desperate before, but now that she's got Zara back, Tamlain and Ember will be able to talk sense into her, surely. Dianthe, too."

Vale hesitated for a moment before giving a stiff nod, wordlessly accepting the unspoken truce, at least for now.

"Help me get Aiwin onto the cot," he said gruffly. "He'll be more comfortable there."

Some of the tension eased from my shoulders. "Good idea. Goddess only knows how long we'll be stuck here before something else happens."

After checking that the bleeding had stopped and the makeshift bandage was firmly in place, Vale took Aiwin's upper body, and I took his legs. The injured fae stifled a groan as we carefully lifted him and carried him across to the cot. Once he was settled, I fussed over the wound, making sure we hadn't started it bleeding again.

"It's fine, Darby," Aiwin said breathlessly. "Just leave it be for now."

"How was the witch able to do this to you?" Vale asked, obviously freaked out by his friend's weakness. "Why did you let her get so close?"

"She was masquerading as you," I said sharply. "*That's* how she got so close."

Vale's blue eyes shot up to meet mine. "*What?*"

"It was some of the best glamour I've ever seen," Aiwin rasped. "If she weren't a dangerous madwoman, I'd love to pick her brain regarding magical technique."

"She stabbed you while *wearing my face*?" Vale demanded, sounding appalled.

A slight flush reddened Aiwin's cheeks. "Should've known it was a trick, even though it was a good one," he muttered.

"None of us knew," I told him. "Even after she stabbed Ember, I thought it was you, Vale, and you were acting under some kind of mind control or… *something*. How could you have possibly guessed, Aiwin?"

But Aiwin didn't answer. Instead, he stiffened abruptly on the cot. The two spots of high color that had been decorating his cheeks fled, leaving him as pale as a ghost. I leaned over him in concern; one hand outstretched. "Aiwin! What's wrong? Is it your wound?" Visions of the bleeding starting again jostled for space in my head… of infection taking root in this filthy place.

"No," he said, his lips gray. "It's magic. Dark magic. Whatever Pavia was planning on doing with your friend's blood… she's just done it. And it was powerful enough for me to feel it at a distance."

My stomach dropped. "You think her crazy plan might have worked? You mean she might have resurrected Oberon?"

Aiwin licked dry lips, shifting restlessly on the cot. "I think she may have, lass."

Vale rose abruptly and turned toward the front of the cell, glaring through the bars as though he could see past the crumbling stone walls of the palace to wherever Pavia had worked her foul sorcery.

"I'll kill her," he growled, hatred burning behind his blue eyes. "I will kill that bitch for everything she's done."

"Think you might have to stand in line, mate," Aiwin said.

I stared through the bars as well, unwilling to contemplate a world where Oberon once more existed, and I was his prisoner.

THIRTY

THE DAY PASSED, followed by the night. Or at least, I assumed it did. The inside of the dungeon was a murky, undifferentiated twilight lit only by the torches Pavia had spelled to burn perpetually. I remembered that disconcerting timelessness from my last imprisonment.

Aiwin slept a lot. He probably needed it, but it still worried me. He seemed to be getting weaker, not stronger. Of course, that wasn't helped by the lack of food and water. Hunger and thirst prickled at me, just as it did for the others.

After tossing his finely embroidered jacket in my direction and snapping at me to cover myself, Vale seemed content to stew in silence while Aiwin was asleep. I'd resisted the urge to throw the jacket back in Vale's face, mostly because it was damp and chilly within the thick stone walls. The fact that my inner wolf was unashamedly wallowing in Vale's scent as I shrugged it over my shoulders didn't improve matters.

Even arguing with him would have been better than being stuck inside my own head, reliving nightmarish scenarios from the past. But the last thing Aiwin needed was the two of us waking him with shouted epithets... so I bit the inside of my cheek and stayed quiet.

I was curled up in the straw next to the cot, watching the rise and fall of Aiwin's chest with my back facing toward the cell bars when the stench hit me. The tiny hairs on the back of my neck rose to attention, and my inner wolf growled as a horrible sense of wrongness hit me. A sharp inhaled breath came from Vale, who'd been leaning against the far wall with his arms crossed, radiating irritation.

Stumbling to my feet, I whirled to look outside the cell, my mind frozen with apprehension at what I would find.

What I saw there sent ice crashing through my veins. I wasn't sure exactly what I'd expected when it came to Oberon's resurrection. Mostly, I'd tried to convince myself that it was impossible — that such a thing could never truly happen. Beyond that, I'd pictured him returning in more or less the same condition he'd been in before.

It was so much worse than that.

The creature before me stank of the grave. Wrapped in the bloodied cloak, Oberon's gray skin was sagging and loose in places. His eyes were milky white; his hair, patchy and dull.

There was a hole in his left cheek, showing rotting teeth through the gap — as though it had been chewed by rodents.

A terrible sense of dread settled in my stomach. Oberon had been monstrous before. Now, Pavia had brought him back as a *literal* monster. Numb dissociation settled over me, separating me from my body… from my emotions. Cold practicality washed in. I had to keep this horrible creature's attention away from Aiwin. Chancing a quick glance at him, I found the injured fae blinking awake with bleary green eyes.

I stepped forward to the front of the cell, blocking Oberon's view of the cot as much as I was able. A thin thread of surprise pierced the low buzzing hum in my mind as Vale stepped up to stand next to me.

Apparently, Oberon could still see us with his dead, milky eyes—or perhaps he could sense us some other way. Cracked lips pulled back in a sneer. Pavia was here, too, cowering a few paces behind her sick creation. Her *king*. A livid bruise decorated her cheek, I noted distantly.

Oberon waved a skeletal hand, and the air around me solidified, rendering me instantly immobile. This, too, I remembered. Oberon's effortless magical power, rendering me helpless for whatever horror he wanted to inflict.

A low snarl came from Vale, but I could have told him that fighting it was useless.

"*Animals*," Oberon spat, the word faintly slurred thanks to his ruined cheek. "My servant is a fool, capturing you when it is my deceitful daughter that I need."

Pavia cringed, hunching her shoulders and staring down at the floor. "I beg your forgiveness, my king."

"You bring me mindless beasts when I need my ungrateful offspring and her two abominable consorts," hissed the resurrected corpse. "She may still be my greatest weapon. I will kill her shifter mate and hold Tamlain hostage against her. Her power will once more be mine to wield against Earth, while her bond with Tamlain protects this realm from the madness she will unleash for me."

"Yes, my king," Pavia blathered. "It will be exactly as you say, my king!"

I got the impression that Pavia's mad plan to become Oberon's new queen wasn't going so well for her. Somehow, I couldn't dredge up any sympathy for her plight.

She shuffled forward, making herself as small as possible as she pointed at me. "This female is the same one you used before as bait for your daughter, sire. She can be bait again. Send the other one with a message for the others to turn themselves over to you if they don't want to receive her head in a basket," she wheedled.

Oberon seemed to consider this for a long moment.

"Yes," he mused. "Perhaps you are not totally useless to me, witch." His blind gaze fastened on Vale, still bound motionless beside me. "You. *Creature*. Tell my daughter and her two mates to present themselves here before the sun goes down tonight, or I will torture this female and send them her body parts, one by one, until she dies in a puddle of her own vomit and feces."

I could feel Vale vibrating with tension beside me, but aside from that one brief growl, he was as unable to speak as I was. My own tension ached in my frozen muscles. Did Oberon not realize that Vale was the same shifter boy that he'd coveted for so long? The one his wife Titania had hidden away from him?

How could he not know? It wasn't as though there were all that many shifters on Elfhame...

Oberon flicked his fingers dismissively. "Begone with you."

Vale twitched hard, but a portal appeared around him, swallowing him before it contracted to a single, flaming point and disappeared with a whoosh of equalizing pressure.

He was gone, leaving Aiwin and me alone in the cell.

Another wave of Oberon's hand and the heavy lock on the cell door clicked. The barred gate swung open, and Elfhame's corpse-king strode through. He circled me with slow steps, my skin prickling as he passed out of my field of vision and reappeared on my other side.

"Oh, my little plaything," he said. "I remember you now. What fun I shall have with you while we're waiting for my thankless offspring to arrive. Perhaps I will take some fingers or toes first, so I will have body parts ready to send, should my daughter and her concubines drag their feet."

I continued to float somewhere outside my body, watching things from a slight remove… right up until the same dead hand that had banished Vale from the cell rose to stroke my cheek, the scent of rotting flesh overpowering. My wolf yipped in alarm, slamming me back into my physical form. I wanted to cringe away with every fiber of my being, but I was still pinned by Oberon's power.

A weak blast of magic swirled past me from the back of the cell, impacting the corpse in a shower of sparks.

Aiwin.

"Keep your filthy hands off her, you unnatural fiend," he rasped, sounding frighteningly weak.

I couldn't turn to look. Couldn't even move my eyes as Oberon sneered, unmoved by the feeble attack. With a flinging motion, he sent a much stronger attack in reprisal, the magic searing my hip as it passed close to me. Aiwin cried out and went silent.

My sluggish heart thundered into galloping life. Was he unconscious? Dead?

Oberon grasped my chin harshly, his repulsive breath wafting in my face. "I will return soon, little toy. And then our amusements shall begin."

His rough thumb swiped over my lower lip, leaving its foul residue of rot behind as he stepped away — turning to sweep through the cell door, which slammed shut and locked itself behind him. Pavia scurried in his wake, leaving me alone and still frozen… unable to rush to Aiwin's side and render aid.

Unable to even know if he still drew breath.

THIRTY-ONE

THE NEXT FEW MINUTES were some of the longest of my life. My eyes were the first part of me to break free of Oberon's paralysis, but try as I might, I couldn't turn them far enough to see the cot behind me.

Next came my vocal cords. I pushed air past them, but I could only produce animal grunting noises until my tongue and lips came back under my control.

"Aiwin?" I whispered as soon as I was able to, no strength behind the word. Then, louder, "*Aiwin!*"

There was no reply.

He has to be alive, I told myself — trying to hold panic at bay. He *has* to be.

I focused every bit of willpower I had left on getting my fingers and toes to twitch. When my muscles finally started to respond to my mind's desperate commands, I forced each joint to move in turn. My first attempt at a step sent me collapsing to the hard floor. I dragged myself around on shaky hands and knees.

Aiwin lay half-on and half-off the cot, one arm and one leg dangling over the side. *Unmoving.*

I crawled toward him, scrabbling across the thin covering of damp straw. "Aiwin!" I croaked again.

There was no response.

When I reached his side, I darted a hand up to hover over his nose and mouth, holding my own breath as I waited for any sign of his. After several interminable seconds, a puff of warm, moist air tickled my skin. I collapsed backward onto my ass, slumping with relief.

When I'd regained a tiny bit of my composure, I carefully rearranged his body to lie fully on the cot again. Pressing two fingers under his jaw, I felt the thrum of his pulse — too fast and too weak, but *there*.

"Oh, Aiwin," I whispered, moving to stroke the messy tangle of red hair away from his temple. "Why did you attack him when you're already so weak?"

But I knew why. He'd been trying to protect me from the half-dead monster that Oberon had become. He'd cared more for my safety than his own.

I sat there, stroking Aiwin's hair mindlessly, until a low moan slipped free of the fae's lips. My breath caught, and I rolled onto my knees, leaning forward.

"Ah, *fuck*," he rasped, his green eyes blinking open and staring blankly at the cracked stone ceiling. "Wha' happened?"

"Oberon happened," I said, working hard to keep my voice from shaking.

His eyes snapped into focus, zeroing in on my face. "You're here. Are you hurt, lass?"

I swallowed an ugly laugh that was trying way too hard to be a sob. "No, I'm fine. You're the one who's apparently trying to get himself killed. *Don't ever do something like that again.* What would I tell Edric?"

He held my gaze. "Tell him I died bravely and that he should kill the bastard who did it. And also — no promises."

I shook my head, despairing, and gave in to the impulse to lean down and kiss him. At the last moment, I shifted my aim from his mouth to his cheek, unwilling to sully his lips with the foul residue of Oberon's touch. Leaning back to sit on my heels, I took his hand in mine, tangling our fingers together.

"Vale's gone," I said, not sure how much he remembered about that part.

Aiwin's eyes grew alarmed. "You mean—"

I realized my mistake and quickly shook my head. "No! No, not that. He's alive. Oberon portaled him back to the others with a new ransom message. Ember, Tamlain, and Cai are to present themselves here before the sun goes down tonight.

Red brows drew together. "Or else?" he asked.

I looked away, unable to hold his gaze. "Or else Oberon will torture me to death and send my body to Ember in pieces."

The callused fingers entwined with mine gave a weak squeeze.

"He'll have to get through me first."

Aiwin knew as well as I did that trying to protect me would only result in there being two bodies rather than one. The dead feeling of hopeless numbness crept over me once again. In many ways, it was a relief from the terror.

"Will Ember and her mates come?" Aiwin asked soberly. Then he made a frustrated noise. "What am I saying? Of course they'll come. That woman loves you like a sister."

"I don't know," I said, even though it was a lie. "Probably," I admitted, after a pause.

Aiwin nodded. "Don't despair, lass. They won't just show up and hand themselves over. Vale and Edric will come up with a plan to get us out."

At that, I looked at him incredulously. "*Vale*? He hates my guts. I imagine he'd be happy to leave me here to Oberon's tender mercies."

Aiwin's eyes slipped closed. "Oh, you are so wrong, Darby." He opened them again. "Vale may be acting like a horse's arse, but he doesn't hate you."

I raised a skeptical eyebrow.

Aiwin shook his head, wincing as his injuries reminded him that moving was a bad idea. "It's not you. If anything, he hates himself."

I stared at him. *Vale, hating himself? That self-absorbed prick?* "What are you talking about?"

He gave a heavy sigh, letting his head roll back on the cot. "He wouldn't thank me for telling you any of this."

Against my will, curiosity prickled. "Telling me what?"

Aiwin hesitated, as though fighting some silent, internal argument with himself. "Ah, what's the harm?" he muttered, before meeting my gaze and holding it. "Vale can't shift form, lass. He never could."

My mouth opened. "I..." I snapped it shut, thought for a minute, and tried again. "He *what*?"

"He can't transform into a wolf," Aiwin said very slowly and clearly. "Or anything else. He's just a man."

I shook my head back and forth. "No, but that's…" I tried. "He's… he's a shifter. He's my *mate*, we share a fate-mark."

"None of which means he can shift," Aiwin replied patiently.

"This doesn't make any sense, though!" I gestured around myself vaguely. "He's the shifter child that Oberon wanted to take as a slave!"

"Exactly," Aiwin said. "When Titania hid him as a baby to keep him safe from Oberon, she took away his shifting abilities first, so he'd be harder to find among all the fae on Elfhame. She used her magic to make him as unremarkable as possible."

My mouth was hanging open. I couldn't seem to close it.

"When Oberon died, Zara begged Titania to return his shifting abilities," Aiwin went on. "But Titania said it was impossible. Zara tried to do some kind of ceremony on her own to reverse the magic. It didn't work."

"The wolfbirth ceremony," I whispered. Zara had been the only other shifter in the fae realm. There had been no clan alpha to perform it for them. "I wonder if that's when his fate-mark appeared…"

Aiwin shrugged a shoulder and winced again, frighteningly weak. "Maybe. It's true he used to go without a shirt sometimes when we were younger. He stopped after that ceremony. When he used his shirt to staunch my bleeding, it was the first time I'd seen his bare chest in quite a while."

Goddess. I couldn't seem to think—

"Why would any of that make him reject me?" I blurted.

Aiwin looked at me kindly, his green eyes soft in his pale, gray-tinged face. "Maybe he didn't want you to find out. Maybe he feels like he isn't good enough for a beautiful female shifter who can change into a wolf with barely a thought."

I was still gaping at him. After a long moment, I finally snapped my jaw shut.

"I'm going to thump him upside the head," I said. "I mean, don't get me wrong. I *already* wanted to thump him upside the head. It's just that now, I want to thump him for an entirely different reason."

Aiwin closed his eyes, exhaustion overtaking him. "That's fair, lass," he murmured. "Tell you what—Edric and me'll be in line right behind you."

I brought his hand up, still wrapped in mine, and cradled it against the mark over my heart. We just had to survive that long, which was going to be easier said than done.

THIRTY-TWO

AIWIN WAS GETTING weaker before my eyes. As the hours passed, dragging us both closer to Oberon's sunset deadline, he was having a harder and harder time keeping his eyes open.

Part of me wanted to let him sleep… let him slip into unconsciousness so he wouldn't be able to get in Oberon's way when the corpse king came to collect me. But it wasn't just our lives at stake. There were countless others who'd suffer if Oberon and Pavia weren't stopped.

"We have to figure out a way to destroy him for good," I said, leaning my elbows on my knees and tangling my fingers in my hair in an attempt to hold back despair. "What do we know about his weaknesses? Do we even know how Pavia brought him back to life in the first place?"

"If you can really call it life," Aiwin muttered breathlessly. He shifted on the narrow cot, trying and failing to find a more comfortable position. "He's still a corpse. That much was obvious the moment he walked in. He's a dead man animated by magic."

I wracked my brain. "What about the cloak? Ember's blood? Could that be the key to defeating him?"

Aiwin seemed to ponder that for a long moment, his eyes slipping closed before he blinked them open again, scowling at himself. "Maybe so. Pavia needed some way to funnel life force into him. Your friend Ember is half his—"

"You'd better not let her hear you say that," I interrupted darkly.

He lifted a shaking hand in a dismissive wave. "You know what I mean, Darby. He's her father. His seed got her mother pregnant. That germ of him is still inside her, just like her mother's essence is."

"And the cloak was important because it had been close to Oberon for years," I said, putting the puzzle pieces together in my head. "So… what if we destroyed the cloak? He was wearing it when he came here. That must mean something."

Thinking would have been a lot easier if I wasn't so hungry and thirsty, not to mention exhausted and terrified. But Aiwin gave a thoughtful nod in response to my words.

"You might be onto something there, Darby," he said. "I'm not sure anything done directly to Oberon's body could stop him. He's already dead. How do you kill a dead man?"

"But if the cloak and the blood were gone," I continued. "If we, I dunno, burned it or something…"

"Then the magic binding life to his form might snap," Aiwin concluded. "It's not a sure thing—"

"But it's all we have," I said, finishing his thought.

I didn't add that our chances of overcoming Oberon and Pavia's magic long enough to rip the king's cloak away so we could destroy it were essentially zero. We both knew that. Numbly, I watched Aiwin drift off into a restless slumber again, wondering if the sun had set yet.

My answer came a few minutes later. Sick dread settled over me as footsteps approached from the torchlit corridor, Pavia and Oberon appearing a few moments later. My time was up. Maybe my life, too. Silently, I vowed to take the two of them with me if I could, no matter the consequences.

Aiwin regained consciousness with a gasp. Perhaps he'd felt Oberon's darkness, even through the veil of slumber. The injured fae scrambled into a seated position on the bunk, his already pale face growing bone white as the blood drained from it.

"You don't need her," he rasped, his voice sounding like sandpaper. "Take me instead."

I watched in amazement as he pushed to his feet despite his terrible weakness. "Aiwin, no!" I gasped, appalled.

It was too late. Oberon snarled and lifted a hand, magic streaking from his fingers. Aiwin dropped as though pole-axed, before he'd even taken a single step. Pavia, battered and cowed, murmured words I couldn't understand, waving her fingers at me in a complicated sign. I'd been prepared to lunge forward, to try and fight them no matter how poor the odds, but I was too slow.

Apathy settled over my emotions like a smothering blanket, draining the strength from my muscles and the will from my mind. Why had I wanted to fight? There was no point. It was too difficult, and my captors were too powerful. Better to go along with what they wanted.

I blinked at the pair stupidly as the cell door swung open, creaking on rusted hinges.

"That's right, worm," Oberon crooned, the words slurred through his decomposed cheek. "You are mine to play with now. Come along. Time to suffer for your faithless *friend*." The final word sounded like a curse.

They didn't consider me a threat, that much was obvious. And why should they? I was no threat to them. I followed meekly as Oberon turned and strode off, his cloak sweeping dramatically behind him. Pavia fell in behind me.

Best not to make a fuss.

Oberon led the way out of the dungeon, through the ruins of his former palace and up, up, into the slanting light of evening and the fresh air. I knew this place, for all that it was overgrown with nature rather than paved with cobblestones— Elfhame trying to reclaim its own. This was the palace square where I'd been taken for torture and public execution the first time Oberon and Pavia had decided to use me as a pawn.

The realization wafted through my mind without any particular emotion attached to it, Pavia's spell of compliance still holding me tightly in its grip. I knew I should be worrying about whether Aiwin was dead or alive. I knew I should be worrying about whether Ember and her mates would come. I knew I should be worrying about Edric, about Vale. Would they risk themselves in some sort of half-baked rescue attempt?

None of it penetrated the greasy pall of Pavia's mind control.

Despite the damage to the old square, torches had been set up by the hundreds, illuminating the scene in eerie, flickering light as the sun sank low, touching the western horizon. Dozens of armed guards stood at attention around the area, and that was enough to send a pinprick of worry through my apathetic pall.

I'd pictured Pavia and Oberon being on their own—a rogue witch and her horrific undead creation. But they weren't alone. They had followers. If the others showed up thinking they could smash through Oberon's magical defenses and rescue me, they'd be overrun by sheer power of numbers.

It should have been a death knell to my fragile hopes, but those hopes had already been crushed. Dull resignation ruled my mind and body, bowing my shoulders like an invisible weight.

Two guards stepped forward and ripped Vale's embroidered jacket from my shoulders, leaving me once more naked. They took my arms, propelling me onto a stone platform I knew all too well. Time and nature hadn't yet toppled the dark-stained wooden post set in the center, illuminated by yet more torches. Those stains, I knew, were blood. Some of it was probably mine.

Unresisting, I allowed the guards to lift my arms, shackling them with rusty iron manacles so that I was basically hugging the hateful post, my cheek pressed against splintery wood. The iron tang of old blood tickled my nose, making my wolf stir restlessly.

"This is where your *friends* will find you, worm," Oberon said, dragging a taloned finger down the vulnerable skin of my back. "Broken and dying. Do you think they will weep for you? Or will they be too concerned for their own welfare, and immediately forget about you?"

I didn't know if they'd weep for me or not. And with the spell in place, I couldn't dedicate any emotional energy toward wondering about it. Inside me, my wolf whined a warning.

The talon reversed direction and slid up my spine. Harsh fingers tangled in my hair, yanking my head back until Oberon's decomposing face loomed in my vision, wavering in the firelight as the sun slipped below the distant trees.

"Bring me the cat-o-nine-tails," Oberon barked, spittle flying against my cheek.

It smelled like decay.

When I didn't respond, the king sneered at me in disdain. "Release the spell, witch. I wish to enjoy her screams and struggles as she dies."

The grip on my hair slammed my cheek against the rough wood and let go. In my peripheral vision, I saw someone hand Oberon a whip, the individual tails tipped with metal barbs like fishhooks.

"Yes, my king," Pavia said, and a clammy wave of magic shivered through me.

The unnatural apathy slid away like thick oil, and my awareness slammed back into focus just as a whistling noise announced the first lash of the metal-tipped cat-o-nine-tails.

Tearing pain exploded across my back in the same instant that my wolf wailed an eerie scream of rage. The shift overcame me, my body twisting as the change rippled outward.

THIRTY-THREE

AS MY BODY transformed into that of a wolf, my arms and legs grew thinner. My wrists, previously held tightly within the iron shackles, slipped free of the metal constraints. My shoulders and spine contracted, my body doubling over to land on all fours.

"Sire!" Pavia's shrill cry of warning drew my predator's attention.

She was only feet away, and already raising her hands to perform some kind of magic spell on me. I lunged despite my weakness after having been starved of food and water... despite the crippling pain of my torn back after the strike of the metal-tipped lashes on the cat-o-nine-tails.

Intense, animal satisfaction flowed through me as my razor-sharp teeth snapped around the witch's throat and ripped through tender flesh. Blood spurted, coating my muzzle and flowing down my throat. Pavia's scream choked off into liquid gurgling, her limbs flailing and jerking without coordination.

I tore at flesh and cartilage, my wolf's not inconsiderable weight bearing my victim's body to the ground. Oberon's roar of rage wasn't enough to distract me from shaking the flopping hunk of meat viciously—but the blast of powerful magic that bowled me over was.

It *burned,* the force behind it tumbling me across the rough ground. I tried desperately to get my legs under me so I could charge Oberon. Maybe I could rip out his throat as well, even though the thought of biting into that rotting flesh was repulsive beyond the bearing of it.

I was too slow. A second blast of magic flattened me against the dirt and cobbles, pinning me in place. It wasn't like the spell that had made me meek and compliant, or the one that had paralyzed me in the dungeon cell. This felt like a boulder had fallen on me. I kicked and clawed for purchase, whipping my head around wildly, but my body was trapped on its side by the crushing, invisible weight.

"You stinking pile of excrement!" Oberon ranted, his voice growing louder as he approached. "You useless, idiotic cur! I will flay your skin from your flesh an inch at a time! I will torture you to the brink of madness, and make you watch while I do the same to my ungrateful bitch of a daughter!"

The lash that tore into my side this time was magic, not braided leather tipped with sharp hooks. Again and again, Oberon laid into me, the pain of every fresh slash jabbing at my awareness like fire. My jaws opened to howl my agony to the world, but no sound emerged — the invisible weight crushing me didn't allow me enough air to cry out.

Oberon continued to scream all the things he would do to me… to Ember, until the sense of the words began to disappear beneath the growing buzzing sound in my sensitive ears. My vision dimmed, going red at the edges, then gray.

I was going to die here. This was it… this was my Oberon-shaped nightmare come alive. The gray and red swirling mist swallowed my vision completely, growing darker and darker until everything was black. Only the repeated lashings of magic against my vulnerable body registered along overstretched nerves. My fur grew wet and matted with hot blood.

As my consciousness fled inward, seeking blessed oblivion, a new presence wrapped around me. The sheltering warmth was both familiar and not, but it was so difficult to focus on anything through the sharp spikes of pain.

Without warning, the mental link flared to brilliant life, overtaking the torment of Oberon's unrelenting torture. My wolf whimpered, recognizing its source an instant before my human thought processes could catch up.

Vale.

It was my mate, reaching out to me through our bond. Comfort, reassurance, apology, and the promise of vengeance poured across the vibrant connection, blanketing me until the distant abuse of my body felt muffled and unimportant. I could feel his wolf reaching for my wolf, sense the overwhelming message through the bond—*hold on*.

But I had nothing to hold on to. Or… nothing except him, anyway.

Was this how the bond was supposed to feel? I clung to my sense of him, which now felt truer and more immediate than the cruel reality in which my body was trapped. Vale held me within the bond, a continuous litany of *I'm sorry, I'm so sorry, we're coming, you have to hold on*, playing through my awareness.

The feeling of being wanted, of being *loved*, was so shocking that I did as the voice asked, holding onto consciousness and life by my splintering claws.

When Oberon's attack ceased, the weight on my ribcage easing, it was such a shock that I gasped back into awareness. My vision wavered, and I blinked rapidly until I could make out the blurry outline of the corpse king. His back was to me. Beyond lay a flaming travel portal, and out of it stepped a familiar female figure with bi-colored black and platinum hair.

Ember.

Two more figures stepped out, flanking her. Cai and Tamlain. *No*, I wanted to whimper — terrified that they'd come here to accede to Oberon's demands. I couldn't be the reason for Ember's capture, *I couldn't*.

Inside my head, Vale continued to murmur reassurance. *Hold on, Darby. Hold on.*

"Daughter," Oberon sneered. "You are just in time to witness your friend's death."

"I strive to be punctual," Ember said, sounding like she was holding onto her temper by a thread. "Wow, no offense, but you look like total shit, *Dad*."

Run, Ember, run! I wanted to shout, but all that emerged was a weak, wolfish whine. *Get away! Get away while you still can!*

Brilliant light flared around the overgrown and ruined palace square. More portals opened. *Dozens* of them. I panted weakly past cracked ribs as fae warriors poured out of the dancing ovals of flame, weapons raised and magic flying.

Told you we were coming, Vale's voice whispered across the bond.

I couldn't see him among the sea of arriving forces engaging Oberon's guards in a fierce battle, but I knew he was here. Edric would be here, too, I thought with certainty. Dianthe as well.

Titania had sent a full battalion of warriors to defeat her resurrected husband, led by my mate and my closest friends. Bolts of flame and electricity flew around the clearing, missing me mostly by virtue of the fact that I was still splayed out flat on the ground in wolf form. Within moments, it felt like everything around me was on fire.

The torture post groaned and toppled from the platform, flames engulfing the ancient wood. The end landed less than a foot from my head, the heat from it singeing my fur and making the skin beneath feel tight and tender.

Electrified by the instinctive fear of being burned, I rolled onto my belly with a groan, cracked bones grinding together and blood still pouring from my wounds. A single thought filled my awareness, ringing like a bell.

Where was Oberon?

I whipped my head around, searching for him through the smoke and the flying bolts of magic. There. He was standing maybe ten feet away, hands raised to hold a shimmering magic shield in front of his body.

His back was still to me.

Fiery hatred unlike anything I'd ever known burned along my nerves, lending strength to battered muscle and sinew. My body wasn't working right. Something inside me was badly broken—maybe fatally so. It didn't matter, though. There was one more thing I had to do, and a little issue like being mortally wounded wasn't going to stop me.

I gathered wobbling legs beneath me and staggered forward, my entire focus on the abomination standing a few paces away. My head was buzzing again, even Vale's frantic cries of *Darby, Darby!* through the mate-bond growing distant and tinny now.

Oberon started to turn around, something having alerted him to my presence. With a low snarl, I stumbled forward and leapt for him, my jaws open wide.

THIRTY-FOUR

MY BODY CRASHED into Oberon's, the stink of death choking me even as my teeth closed on bloodstained ermine. I knew I only had one chance at this.

I locked my jaws, holding on with all my strength as Oberon cursed sharply. A fresh blast of magic blew me backward, shattering more bone and tearing sinew. My neck whipped around, my bodyweight jerking at the fabric of Oberon's cloak. The pain of my injuries was all-encompassing, but I *utterly refused* to relinquish my grip.

A tearing noise reached me through the buzzing sound in my ears. Everything felt like it was happening in slow motion. But the moment the clasp on Oberon's cloak gave way, time sped up again. I crashed to the ground in a tangle of heavy fabric, my legs feeling distant and numb.

A few feet away lay the burning torture post. The flames were even now spreading to the surrounding grass. Oberon screamed in rage, trying to climb to his feet. I steeled myself and shoved off with my hind legs, sickeningly aware of all the broken parts of my body fighting each other.

With the cloak still clamped in my jaws, I stumbled and dragged myself forward on my belly, pulling it with me until I could fling it over the burning post. The smell of scorched velvet and fur clogged my nostrils, joining the smell of my own blood as I collapsed. Behind me, Oberon's shrieks of fury grew high-pitched and desperate.

Using the last of my strength, I shuffled my front end around until I could see him through the growing haze of smoke and my own weakness. I wasn't entirely sure if what I was seeing was real or a side effect of my blurring vision, but his decayed features seemed to be melting like wax. He clawed at his face with skeletal hands, skin and muscle sloughing away as smoke rose in acrid curls from his body.

Greasy bones crumpled, toppling to the ground.

The darkness roiling around the edges of my vision rushed in, drowning me in sweet nothingness as the unbearable pain finally slipped away.

***

For a long time, I drifted. Occasionally, I thought I could hear voices calling out in the distance, full of fear and desperation. Trying to understand the words was too difficult, though—so each time I turned back toward the peaceful blackness.

One of those voices was more insistent than the rest, echoing through the aching caverns of my skull rather than teasing my ears. My wolf stirred weakly, whining in distress, but she was too feeble to turn toward the familiar presence.

More time passed.

The smell of smoke, charred flesh, and death that had seemed to cling to me like a second skin faded. My fragile, intermittent connection to the outside world seemed to flare brighter, and with more regularity. I started to wonder if I should reach for it the way my wolf had wanted to reach for the internal presence calling inside my mind.

Something about my body during those brief snatches of awareness felt... *different.*

I wasn't sure if I could trust my own impressions, but I didn't feel as broken as before. Did I dare believe that? Or would reaching outward bring me back to the painful agony of shattered bones and torn muscles?

And... really, shouldn't I be dead by now?

It hadn't occurred to me before this moment— but dying seemed to be taking an awfully long time, given how badly injured I'd been. Couldn't I just shuffle off this mortal coil like a normal person and be done with it?

A massive wave of denial slammed into me, like being slapped across the face by someone who was standing inside my brain. I gasped, catapulted unceremoniously back to full awareness for the first time since I'd seen Oberon fall on the battlefield.

"*Wha—?*" I croaked, my voice emerging like sandpaper scraping its way up my throat.

I was in human form, I realized as the rasping word passed my lips. How was I in human form? I'd been a wolf...

"Darby!" Three voices chorused in unison.

I blinked my eyes open, fighting eyelids stuck together with what felt like yet more sandpaper.

"Here, hold still." That was Ember. She sounded like she'd been weeping.

A cool, damp cloth wiped gently across my face, cleaning away some of the crusty mess around my eyes. I tried again to open them once it disappeared, and thankfully had more luck this time.

Everything was a blur, but it was immediately obvious that I wasn't where I had been before. The atmosphere smelled sweet. My surroundings were in a soothing palette of blues and greens. The air was cool, not hot and choked with smoke.

I licked my lips, but my tongue was dry, too, so it didn't help. Immediately, strong hands supported me from either side, easing me up by the shoulders to lean against a pile of... pillows? Was I on a bed?

Cool metal pressed against my lips, blessed water slipping into my mouth. I gulped and gulped, until the goblet disappeared.

"Easy," It was the voice from inside my head, only it sounded hoarse and frightened now. "Not too fast. You'll choke."

I leaned back against the luxurious pillows, having suddenly realized that my body felt... *okay*. Well, to be fair, it felt bruised and strained and exhausted. But it didn't feel horrifically shattered.

A blur of black and white and pale peach loomed over me. Slender hands clasped one of mine, lifting it. Ember again.

"Can you say something, Darby?" She, too, sounded frightened. Were we still in danger? This cool, comfortable room didn't *feel* dangerous.

I blinked rapidly until her worried face swam into better focus. When I licked my lips this time, it worked to wet them. "Ember? 'S everyone safe?" The words slurred drunkenly.

She sagged in relief, her head bowing over our joined hands.

"Oh, thank the Creator," said the male voice that had urged me not to drink too fast. It still sounded utterly wretched.

"Darby," Ember said, choking on the name. "It's okay. You're going to be okay."

"Th' others?" I insisted.

"Safe," she said, freeing a hand to brush hair away from my forehead tenderly. "Oberon and Pavia are dead. Their forces were captured or killed by Titania's troops." She hesitated, looking at me intently. "Pavia's throat was ripped out. Was that you?"

I nodded dumbly.

Safe. They were all safe.

I looked to my left and found Vale kneeling by the bed, looking as though he'd been felled by an axe. I looked to my right and found Edric hovering—trying and failing to school his features into impassivity.

Someone was missing. Ember had promised that everyone was all right, but…

"What about Aiwin?" I whispered.

Edric cleared his throat. "I won't lie to you. He was close to death when we found him. But Tamlain healed him while Dianthe was busy healing you. He's still very weak and bed-bound, or he would have been here."

I relaxed, knowing how skilled both Tamlain and Dianthe were when it came to healing injuries.

Edric wasn't finished, though. He dipped his head, loose blond hair hiding his face in shadow. "I owe you an apology, Darby, for how I treated you when I learned of your bond with Vale. And also for my own incompetence. I'm not good enough with healing magic to have helped you or Aiwin myself."

I reached out with the hand Ember wasn't holding and squeezed his arm to stop him.

"Doesn't matter," I told him. "You came." My gaze moved to include Vale. "You both came for me."

Vale's startling blue eyes flew to mine. He looked utterly wretched. "Of course we came."

Ember leaned forward and pressed her lips to the top of my head. "I think maybe I should leave you three to talk. Tamlain and Dianthe will be in a bit later to check on you. I'm *so* glad you're feeling better, my dearest friend."

I managed a tremulous smile for her. She returned it and let my hand go after giving it a final squeeze. A few moments later, I heard the door open and close softly.

Once she was gone, I turned to Edric, unable to face Vale quite yet.

His golden eyebrows drew together. "There was never any doubt that we would come after you, Darby. I'm only sorry that you were ever made to question that fact." A heavy sigh escaped him. "This hasn't really been the finest hour for any of us, has it?"

"That's a colossal understatement." Vale's voice was barely audible.

Part of me still didn't want to look at him; it was too painful. I made myself do it anyway. A deep, cautious inhalation proved that my broken ribs were healed except for some lingering soreness. That was good. I needed that fortifying breath.

Lifting my chin, I met his eyes. "You should know that Aiwin told me your secret, that you can't shift form. You mustn't blame him, though. We both believed we were going to die at the time. I think he was trying to make me feel better about you rejecting me."

At my words, Vale froze as though he'd been turned into a statue.

"Oh, dear," Edric murmured. "Well, I suppose this is a conversation we needed to have anyway."

THIRTY-FIVE

"I DON'T DESERVE you." Vale's head dipped — the proud alpha's shoulders slumping as he knelt by my bedside, unable to hold my gaze. "You should have a mate who puts you above his own vanity. I couldn't bear the thought of you knowing about my humiliation. I'm not a true shifter. I can't mate you."

I stared at the top of his head, aware that I should be relishing this after everything he'd put me through. *This was it.* Vale, who'd treated me like dirt, was groveling before me. Yet I felt… *nothing.*

Shouldn't I feel something about this? Maybe all my emotions had been burned out of me in that dungeon cell, at the same time my fear had been.

But that wasn't right, either. I'd been so relieved when Ember told me everyone was safe that I'd nearly passed out again. Relief was an emotion, wasn't it? Clearly, I could still feel *that* much, at least.

"You could have just told me," I said. "You must have told your friends at some point, since Aiwin knew about it. Didn't I deserve the same courtesy?"

"Of course you did." Vale lifted a shaking hand to cover his eyes, further hiding himself from me. "*Gods.* I don't deserve them any more than I deserve you."

"Maybe let us decide who deserves to be our friend and who doesn't," Edric said evenly. He didn't sound thrilled, but he didn't sound openly angry, either.

I glanced over at the aristocratic blond fae, only to find his mask of indifference firmly in place, smoothing his expression to unreadability. He met my eyes and quirked a slanted eyebrow, somehow managing to convey, *'Yeah, he's an idiot... but he's our idiot, so please try to cut him some slack.'*

I didn't really feel like cutting Vale any slack right now, even though I appreciated the fact that he'd brought help and come back to save Aiwin and me.

Vale lowered his hand and dragged his gaze up to mine. His beautiful blue eyes were bloodshot and red-rimmed.

"Oberon *hurt* you," he spat. "I felt your pain as though it was my own. I wanted to kill him for what he did to you. I wanted to rip out his intestines and watch him die over the course of days. But when I reached your side, he wasn't there. Titania said the bones lying nearby were his. I'd already missed my chance."

"Yes," I said. "It's true. Oberon hurt me. But so did you."

He flinched as though I'd physically struck him, but he didn't break eye contact. Oddly, neither did I—though I should have. I *always* had to look away when things got too intense. It was part of being an omega wolf.

This time, I didn't.

"You hurt me, as well," Vale said quietly. It wasn't an accusation, exactly. More like he was reminding me.

For a split second, I was confused. Did he mean when Oberon had been torturing me, and my pain had reached him through the bond? Then it hit me.

"Oh." I swallowed hard. I'd hurt him when I'd had sex with Edric… when his wolf had sensed its soulmate's infidelity. "Yes, you're right. I did. And I knew it, too. I told myself you deserved it for rejecting me." I lifted my chin. "I'm not sure I've changed my mind about that, actually."

"I do rather wish you'd mentioned that part at the time," Edric said mildly.

I cringed, because if there was a victim in all of this, it was him. Maybe Aiwin, too. "I *am* sorry for that, Edric," I told him. "That wasn't fair to you, and it wasn't fair to Aiwin, either."

To my surprise, Vale leapt to my defense. "Don't blame her. If I hadn't behaved like an ass, it would never have been an issue in the first place."

"That's true enough," Edric said dryly.

Vale met my eyes again. "You don't owe me anything, Darby Adalwolf. Like I said, I'm not a real shifter. That means our mate-bond is basically meaningless in the eyes of your society. You should choose someone better. Like Edric. Like Aiwin."

It would have been a pretty speech, if his wolf hadn't been howling its disagreement through the bond, thrashing and wailing and gnashing its teeth in denial.

"You're wrong about one thing, you know," I told him. "You are a shifter. Your wolf is still inside you."

Vale frowned, jerking back from the bed. "What do you mean? I have no wolf. I can't shift."

How could he think that? *Holy ancestors*, but the man was dense.

"That thing in the depths of your soul that's screaming right now?" I began gently. "*That's* your wolf."

Vale gaped at me, his lips parted, as though my words didn't make sense.

Edric sighed. "Vale, you're an idiot. Have I mentioned that yet? Anyway, this sounds like a conversation that should maybe wait for later. Right now, I think the three of us should go see how Aiwin is faring. That is, if you're feeling strong enough, Darby."

My heart skipped with excitement at the prospect of seeing my plain-spoken, flame-haired fae. Yes, the others had told me that he would recover, but I wouldn't truly believe it until I saw him for myself. "I want to see him."

"Then we'll see him together." Edric helped me swing my legs over the edge of the bed and supported me onto my feet. "Vale," he said sharply when I swayed, my knees threatening to give out.

Vale froze for a moment. I would have frozen as well, except I was wavering too much on my feet. Then he rose and hurried around the end of the bed to join us, taking my other arm. The contact warmed me from within like a hearth fire on a cold night. Our wolves strained toward each other, whining with desire.

I firmed my jaw and refused to acknowledge the instinctual, unwanted response.

The pair helped me shuffle out of the luxurious bedroom, into an equally elegant hallway. I recognized Titania's Summer Palace, with its flowers and branches woven inextricably into the architecture. It hadn't even occurred to me to ask where we were when I'd woken up. I'd been more concerned about all my friends being here and safe than with our physical location.

"Pardon me," Vale said, when we came upon a plainly clothed fae who had the look of a palace servant. "Could you see that General Tamlain and the Huntress Dianthe are informed that we have taken their female patient to visit with Aiwin in his room? I don't want them to find her gone and worry."

The servant curtsied. "I will see to it, Master Vale."

"Thank you." Vale dipped his chin in response.

I was forcibly reminded that Vale, along with his mother, had been among Titania's closest advisors for some time. *Of course* he'd be known and respected by the servants. He'd lived here in Titania's palace since she took control of Elfhame after Oberon's first death.

I wasn't sure why the realization jolted me so. Maybe because his interaction with the servant had been so civil, when I'd mostly known him as cruel and brusque. It didn't change any of the things he'd done to hurt me, but it was worth remembering that not only did Edric and Aiwin count him as worthy of friendship, but a powerful fae ruler thought his counsel worth listening to.

It was difficult to reconcile the two aspects of Vale in my mind, much less in my heart.

We continued down the flower-lined corridor at a snail's pace, Edric and Vale supporting me on each side. When we eventually reached an open door leading to another richly appointed bedroom, I let out a sigh of relief to see a familiar broad-shouldered figure propped up against a pile of pillows on the massive bed.

"Aiwin," I said, nearly sagging in the others' hold as my legs decided they'd had enough of holding me up.

"*Darby*," Aiwin said, sounding as relieved as I was.

Edric and Vale helped me the final few feet to the bed and sat me down on it. Dignity forgotten, I half-flopped and half-rolled into Aiwin's arms, burying my face in the crook of his shoulder and shaking.

His arms around me trembled as well. I could tell he was still painfully weak. We both were.

"Oh, lass," he said, stroking the back of my head. "I was so worried for you."

I took a deep, shuddering breath, not sure if words would emerge, or sobs.

"I t-tore off Oberon's cloak and threw it over a burning post," I managed, my voice wavering. "Just like you said. It worked. Aiwin, *it worked*. He's gone. Forever, this time."

Aiwin's hand stilled. Around us, the silence in the room suddenly felt very… *complete*.

"*You* killed Oberon?" Vale asked, and I managed to summon a hint of offense at how surprised he sounded.

I raised my head. "Well… yes?" I said, my flash of irritation going some way toward steadying my shattered nerves. "It was Aiwin's idea, though. I wouldn't have known what to do otherwise."

More silence.

This time, Edric was the one to break it. "You, uh… do realize that you're a hero of Elfhame now, right?" He sounded shell-shocked, but not as disbelieving as Vale had.

It took a moment for the sense of his words to penetrate. When they did, my thoughts stalled, crashing to the ground like breaking glassware.

I was *what*?

THIRTY-SIX

"I DON'T WANT to be a hero of Elfhame," I said blankly. My life was complicated and overwhelming enough as it was. By killing Oberon when I'd had the chance, I'd only been doing what any one of us would have done under the same circumstances.

"What *do* you want, Darby?" Aiwin asked, still cradling me close to his chest.

I chewed my lip, trying to get my brain working again. *What did I want?* It wasn't a question I'd devoted much time or energy to thinking about before now.

"I want..." I said slowly. "I don't know. I want there to be peace. I want to help Ember make the world a better place for people who don't fit in." I steeled myself to meet each of their gazes in turn. "I want to surround myself with people who care for me, and for each other."

Edric shared a glance with the others. "You know what? I think that sounds like a really good start."

A light knock on the doorframe cut through the moment. Dianthe poked her head in. "Ah. There you are. Time for a check-up. You two scared the stuffing out of us, you know."

"Sorry," I said meekly, knowing my cheeks were flaming at being caught in Aiwin's arms like this, with my disaster of a would-be mate looking on. The embarrassment grew exponentially worse when Tamlain followed Dianthe into the room, raising one sharp eyebrow at me.

Dianthe made shooing motions at me until I rolled out of Aiwin's embrace and sat up shakily on the bed next to him.

"That's better," she said. "I need to run a diagnostic spell on both of you so I can see how our repairs are holding up. Time for canoodling later."

"*Canoodling*?" Aiwin echoed in confusion.

"That's what the Earthers call it, isn't it?" Dianthe asked, sounding supremely unconcerned.

"*No*," I said firmly. "It's *not*. Also, you're making us sound like broken-down human automobiles. Like you're planning on checking beneath our hoods or something."

"Only magically," Dianthe shot back. "Do they have magical automobile mechanics in the human realm?"

"Not that I know of," I told her. "Maybe that could be your niche if you ever decide to move to Earth."

"Perhaps, for now, we should focus on the state of your healing," Tamlain said.

He'd never been one for banter, and frankly he still intimidated the hell out of me. I immediately snapped my mouth shut and nodded agreement.

"I'm feeling much better, General," Aiwin said. "You should check Darby first."

Dianthe pushed me down to lie flat on the bed next to him, while Tamlain moved to the other side, looking down at Aiwin.

"As there are two of us and two of you, that will not be necessary," he said. "However, your expression of chivalry is noted."

We lay back and submitted to being magically poked and prodded by the two powerful practitioners. I tried not to squirm, the places where I remembered being badly injured itching and tickling as Dianthe's magic washed through them.

"You'll do," she said when she was finished. "You need a *lot* more rest, though. And in case it wasn't clear from the context, 'rest' doesn't mean 'traipsing through the palace when you're barely strong enough to stand up.'"

"I would like to perform an additional healing spell on this dagger wound, once the flesh has had a bit longer to knit," Tamlain said, straightening from his examination of Aiwin. "Perhaps tomorrow. Aside from that, the prescription of more rest would seem to be applicable to both of you."

"Then Darby should stay here," Aiwin said quickly. "There's plenty of space, and otherwise she'd have to walk all the way back to her room."

"What an excellent idea," Tamlain said, utterly deadpan. "No doubt that would be the most efficient arrangement for everyone involved."

It was easy to forget sometimes that Tamlain had more experience than most people when it came to navigating complicated and unconventional romantic entanglements. I wondered what he saw when he looked at the four of us.

I cleared my throat. "Yes, that's what we'll do. Because… efficiency. And rest. Very important stuff."

Vale was looking between us as though he couldn't quite decide if we were screwing with him somehow.

Edric raised an eyebrow that mirrored Tamlain's almost eerily. "Vale and I will make ourselves available to watch over the invalids. We'll call you if there's any change."

Tamlain inclined his head in an abbreviated bow of acknowledgement, courtly as ever.

Dianthe snorted. "Right. You do that." She turned to me, her bright green eyes softening. "Rest well, Darby. You'll both be better before you know it."

<hr>

In reality, it was nearly two weeks before I could resume anything like my normal routine without feeling as though I was going to pass out after ten minutes of mild exertion.

I was appreciating the feeling of being able to walk from one end of the palace to the other, when a harried palace servant rushed up to me.

"Lady Darby," he said, bowing low. "Queen Titania requests your attendance in the throne room. May I escort you there now?"

Surprised, I glanced down at my simple tunic and soft trousers. It was hardly court attire, and Dianthe wasn't around to magic me up an appropriate dress to wear. After roughly half a second of thought, I decided Titania could go hang if she didn't like it. If it hadn't been for her crazy ex-husband coming back from the dead, I wouldn't be wandering around her palace in what was basically a pair of glorified pajamas.

"Yes, thank you," I told the servant, and followed him through the grand halls.

I could tell the poor man was torn between keeping a slow pace for my benefit and hurrying to keep his queen happy. But the truth was, I couldn't have hurried even if the place had been on fire. So, I shuffled along as best I could, and resolved to give Titania a piece of my mind if she got on the servant's back about it.

The doors to the throne room were closed when we finally got there, but the guards flanking the entrance opened them with a flourish at our approach. The servant bowed me in, neatly sidestepping the question of being berated for his slowness by turning and leaving as soon as I walked past him. After I entered, the doors silently swung shut behind me.

My attention fell on the dais, where the fae queen sat regally upon her throne—flanked by Zara standing on one side and Vale on the other. When I saw that no one else was in the echoing room, not even a single servant, I slowed, overcome by sudden wariness.

What was this about?

"Approach us, Darby Adalwolf," the queen commanded.

I did, my feet dragging with reluctance.

"Your Majesty," I greeted, bowing and trying not to wince as my muscles protested. "You wished to see me?"

I couldn't help glancing toward Vale as I straightened. He wouldn't meet my eyes. We'd had surprisingly little interaction over the past couple of weeks. Vale had fetched and carried attentively during my recuperation, but he'd avoided conversation with me for the most part—focusing instead on Aiwin when he spoke at all.

Now, he looked stony-faced but determined, though I wasn't sure about what.

He cleared his throat. "Darby," he said, "I feel it is important that the queen learn of the circumstances surrounding Oberon's second death, even if that knowledge does not go beyond this room. As you were the only known witness to what happened, I thought you should be the one to tell her."

After a brief moment of panic, I realized he was trying to give me an out if I needed it. I could tell Titania any story I wanted to. I could tell her that Oberon and Pavia had a fight about something, and that Pavia rescinded her animating magic before she died. I could tell her a stray bolt of power from the battle took him out.

The desire to lie was strong. But why? Titania hated Oberon almost as much as he'd hated her. It wasn't like she was going to be angry with me for killing him.

Decision made, I straightened my spine and raised my chin.

"We have Aiwin to thank for Oberon's demise, Your Majesty," I began. "He understood enough about the magic Pavia had used to theorize that if someone destroyed Oberon's bloodstained cloak, it would break the spell animating him."

Titania's regal brow furrowed. "And yet, Aiwin was discovered locked in one of the cells after the battle, near death. Are you saying it was he who destroyed my former husband?"

"No," I admitted. "I mean, not exactly. Aiwin was the one who came up with the idea. He was the one who knew what to do." I hesitated, then plunged onward. "*I* was the one to tear the cloak from Oberon's shoulders and burn it."

Understanding dawned in the queen's gaze. She exchanged a speaking glance with Zara, though I wasn't sure what was conveyed between the two.

"However," I continued quickly, "I would take it as a personal favor if that knowledge didn't become public."

Titania tilted her head. "You do not wish the accolades that would come with such a heroic deed?"

"*No*," I said with feeling. "No, Your Majesty—I really, *really* wouldn't."

She digested that for a moment. "Very well, child. If it is your wish, I will make a public statement that Oberon was killed during the battle by a person or persons unknown."

"Thank you," I said in relief.

But Titania wasn't finished. "Even so, you must accept my private gift for your valor."

I opened my mouth to protest. "Your Majesty, that's not—"

"Don't interrupt, child," she said severely. "I offer you the services of a valued advisor, Darby. Vale is now yours."

She might as well have smacked me across the face. I gaped at her. "I... you... *what?*"

Her gaze twinkled with secret amusement at my expression of shock. "I trust you will not make me repeat myself. Though I do intend to retain his mother, thereby ensuring that Vale will return often to visit us. Also, all the resources you and Ember require for your haven will be granted if they are within my power. You have both proven yourselves fast friends to Elfhame, and to me personally."

My mouth was still open. I regained enough of my wits to look at Vale, trying to gauge his reaction to all this. His expression was still hidden behind a stoic mask, but a nervous buzz of energy thrummed through the bond.

"Perhaps Darby does not wish—" he began, only for Zara to cut him off.

"*My son,*" she said sternly. "You should go with your mate. It is clear the two of you have much to discuss."

Now we both turned to gape at her, rather than each other.

"Mother! You *knew?*" Vale demanded, his voice rising with surprise.

THIRTY-SEVEN

"OF COURSE I KNEW she's your fated mate," Zara said patiently. "A mother can tell about these things, my dear one."

I snapped my jaw shut. Why was it such a shock to me that Vale and his mother were close? I knew how much Zara had risked to keep Vale safe from Oberon while he was growing up. I knew how much she'd sacrificed.

Among other things, she'd sacrificed Vale's ability to shift—or, technically, Titania had sacrificed it—to protect him.

Vale swallowed, visibly regaining his composure. "Mother—Darby doesn't want to be mated to someone like me. I'm not a true shifter, and…" He steeled himself, straightening his spine. "… and I've treated her abominably. My Queen, your gift is not a gift she is likely to want. With good reason."

My inner wolf whined softly in distress, despite my attempts to quash her reaction. I licked my lips, not wanting to do this in a public venue—but suspecting that might be the most effective way to get my point through Vale's thick skull.

"Or maybe," I began, "you could try letting me decide things for myself instead of constantly taking my choices away. You decided that you weren't good enough to be mated without even discussing it with me. Now you've decided how I feel about Titania's gift… *without even discussing it with me.* Do you sense a pattern developing here?"

Both Titania and Zara were staring at Vale with raised eyebrows. I couldn't even bring myself to regret airing this basket of dirty laundry in front of them.

"*Vale*," Zara said, in a tone of mingled surprise and disappointment. "Is this true?"

Vale stared straight ahead, his hands clasped behind his back and his expression pale. "Yes, mother. It's all true. As I said, I've behaved inexcusably toward her."

Again, my wolf wriggled and whined restlessly. I tried not to resent that animal part of myself, evidently so eager to let bygones be bygones and forgive Vale in response to the first kind words he'd spoken.

I squared up to him and lifted my chin. "You certainly have. And I just want to make sure you understand that you didn't reject me and humiliate me because you were trying to protect *me* from the mate-bond. You were trying to protect *yourself* from the mate-bond. You were the one who didn't want the humiliation, because you think your lack of shifting ability is somehow important to me."

Vale's face had been pallid before. Now, it was positively gray. Even so, his startling blue eyes met mine, unflinching.

"Yes," he said. "You are completely and utterly right about that. I know that apologies are often composed of trite and meaningless words. But you have my apology nonetheless." He took an unsteady breath. "I would make amends in some more concrete way, but I fear the best way I can do so is not to burden you with my presence any further."

I narrowed my eyes, not letting him break my gaze. Was this what being dominant felt like? This feeling that I was somehow in charge of the exchange? I wasn't sure if I liked it. It felt like a lot of responsibility.

"Ask me what I want," I told him. "Stop telling me what I *should* want, or what you think I want."

Beads of sweat dotted Vale's forehead. Both Titania and Zara were watching us with focused interest, but they didn't interrupt the conversation.

"Lady Darby," Vale said formally. "Would you prefer that I remove myself from your presence?"

Through the bond, our wolves yearned toward each other. For the first time I could remember, I wished—in part, at least—that my inner animal wasn't there. It was too much of a reminder of what I truly wanted and couldn't have.

I wanted to go back in time to our first meeting, and to have it go differently.

Unfortunately, that sort of second chance was beyond even fae magic.

"I don't know yet," I told him. "But I know I want you to truly understand why you were so cruel. Without that understanding, any conversation we have will be pointless."

His gaze dropped to the floor. "Again, you are correct. With your permission, I will speak to Aiwin and Edric on this subject. I owe them amends as well."

For the first time, a hint of guilt crept into my mind. "I think we both do." Clearing my throat, I mirrored his pose with my hands clasped behind my back. "One more thing, Vale. I already told you this, but you're wrong about your wolf. He's still inside you. Don't give up on him."

Zara straightened abruptly. "No. Vale's wolf was lost. It was the price of his safety."

"That's not true," I told her. "I can feel Vale's wolf through our bond even as we speak."

Zara turned sharply to Titania. "My Queen — is this possible? I attempted the wolfbirth ceremony. But there was nothing."

Vale still looked like a wraith, his eyes darting from me, to his mother, to Titania. His expression belonged to someone who didn't think he could afford hope, because it had been ripped away from him too many times in the past.

The fae ruler tilted her head, considering. "It should not be possible. I removed Vale's shifting abilities so Oberon would not be able to find him."

"With all due respect, Your Majesty," I said, "Vale's wolf was fated to mine. Our wolves are two halves of the same soul. You couldn't have destroyed that part of him without destroying that part of me at the same time — and my wolf is just fine."

Titania's attention fell on me, assessing. "How fascinating. You seem very certain of this, child."

I shrugged, suddenly uncaring that the gesture wasn't appropriate for a royal audience with a powerful monarch. "Like I said, his wolf is right there inside him. It's not the kind of thing you can mistake. Not through a fate-bond."

Vale made a low, choked noise, but when I glanced at him, he still stood unmoving.

"Look," I told him. "If you want to try and do something about this, come talk to me. In the meantime, talk to your friends and figure out the stuff you need to get figured out. I'll be around."

And then, with a formal bow and a polite request for dismissal from Titania, I turned on my heel and left the throne room. It would have been more dramatic if I'd been able to sweep through the doors with my back straight and my head held high. In reality, I shuffled out at the same invalid snail's pace as I'd entered.

Oh, well.

<hr>

Instead of going back to either my room or Aiwin's, I went looking for Ember. She and Cai had been going back and forth to Earth to make sure everything was all right with the Greystalker pack, while Tamlain stayed to help Dianthe look after Aiwin and me as we recovered.

When I arrived at the large suite of rooms the three of them shared, I was relieved to find Ember present. After a sheepish knock on the doorframe of the open door, I wandered in and flopped down on the empty chair across from where she was sitting.

"Hi," I said. "I think I might be an idiot. Am I an idiot, Ember?"

Ember sat back and regarded me for a moment. I couldn't hear either of her mates nearby; apparently, we had the suite to ourselves.

"I'm a little scared to hear what brought this on," she said eventually. "Maybe you better tell me what kind of idiotic thing you did before I answer that."

I sighed. "Well, for starters, I haven't told Vale to go jump off a cliff yet."

Understanding lit her gaze. "Oh. Well… I mean, I'm probably not the best judge of when to cut your mate loose…?"

"It was different for you, though," I said. "Cai was being magically manipulated when he rejected you. Vale just seems to be a self-absorbed asshole. Or, at least, he started out that way."

"And now he's changing?" Ember prompted.

I threw my hands up, although I was tired enough that it looked more like a listless wave than the emphatic gesture I'd intended. "Is he? I'm not sure. He seems to be. People change. But they also don't change, you know?"

My best friend chewed that over, nodding slowly. "Yeah, I do know exactly what you mean." Another pause. "Here's what I think. Every damn one of us, with the possible exception of Tamlain, has been a trauma victim for a good chunk of our lives, right?"

"Yes," I said cautiously, thinking of all the terrible things we'd been through.

"So," she continued, "on the one hand it's probably unfair to expect this guy—who was hunted by a mad king from practically the moment of his birth—to be some super well-adjusted paragon of mental health."

"Fair," I admitted.

"But, on the other hand, being that badly messed up can mean that someone isn't necessarily the safest choice for a relationship," she added.

"Also true," I said, and slumped back in the overstuffed chair. "*Argh.* I'm not sure you're helping."

She gave me a sheepish smile. "Well, here's the bottom line. Or, if not the bottom line, then at least something else to think about. Messed-up people have the biggest hurdles to overcome when it comes to change, but they also have the most to gain by changing."

I stared at her. "Wow. Deep."

She snorted and threw a cushion at me. It bounced off my chest and landed in my lap, because I was way too out of it to intercept it.

"What about your two pretty fae?" she asked, changing the subject. "Where do they come into all of this?"

I hugged the assault cushion to my stomach. "I don't know," I said plaintively. "I can't ask them to betray Vale. They're his friends."

"Well, I mean, you *could* ask," Ember shot back.

"Fine," I admitted. "I could ask. But what kind of person would that make me?"

"Someone who communicates and has conversations about important things?" Ember suggested.

I groaned and threw the pillow back at her. She caught the weak toss easily.

"Seriously," I told her. "You are the least helpful best friend *ever*. But… I'm glad you're here."

She gave me a wan smile and got up to hug me, tossing the cushion aside. "Not as glad as I am that *you're* here. Anyway—bottom line, you're going to have to talk to the three of them. And if you decide to give Vale another chance, all that says is that you're a sweet and forgiving person."

I snorted into her neck.

"You *are*," Ember insisted. "You've been there for me since we were old enough to walk, even when no one else was. You're not alone now. If Vale hurts you again, I'll have Cai rip his balls off, and then have Tamlain—I dunno—turn them into newts or something."

I blinked up at her. "*Newts*? Is… that actually a thing?"

She shrugged. "I don't see why not. Tamlain's very powerful, you know."

I couldn't help it. I dissolved into stupid giggles. Ember followed a moment later, until we were both clutching each other tight, laughing like idiots.

THIRTY-EIGHT

ANOTHER WEEK PASSED. Edric and Aiwin were friendly enough to me, but I no longer curled up in Aiwin's bed at night. Not as I had when we'd both been so terribly weak from our injuries. I caught them looking at me sometimes, though. I caught Vale looking at me, too.

On three separate occasions, I heard shouted arguments coming from Aiwin or Edric's rooms. The first two times, I acted like a civilized person and turned on my heel, marching away before I heard any details. The third time, I decided that if they wanted to keep their fights private, then they should be quieter, damn it.

Hovering in the hallway, I held my breath as Aiwin shouted, "You're an idiot! Can you not see what's in front of your stupid earthen eyes?"

Edric added something I couldn't make out, but Vale wasn't holding back. "I'm telling you to take her if she'll have you! You stubborn, pointy-eared fae—"

Something complicated and unpleasant twisted in my stomach. I hurried away, out of earshot, wishing I hadn't eavesdropped.

For the next two days, I stewed. Then, screwing up my courage, I cornered Aiwin alone in his room, late at night.

"Hello, lass," he greeted. "Didn't expect to see you here at this hour. What can I do for you?"

"Can I come in?" I asked, slipping past him when he obligingly stood aside, holding the door for me.

This room had become familiar and comforting during my long convalescence. It had also become a place of buried frustration as I grew stronger—feeling Aiwin's muscular body curled against mine; knowing it wouldn't go further than a comforting embrace.

He offered me an overstuffed chair by the fireplace and took the one opposite it. I examined his face in the glow of the banked fire... friendly and open, and so, so dear to me after what the two of us had survived.

"I feel stuck," I made myself say, still struggling with the concept of simply blurting out what I wanted. "And I don't know how any of us are supposed to move forward like this."

He took in my words, his green eyes holding mine, and gave me a slow nod. "I don't suppose we're helping much with that, are we?" he offered. "I'm sorry for that, Darby. It's just—"

I waited for him to continue, but he shook his head in a sharp, frustrated movement.

"It's just that you don't want to get too friendly with me when Vale is also important to you," I finished for him.

Aiwin blew out a breath. "Well... yes and no. It's partly that, but it's partly because neither of us are in a hurry to get our hearts broken."

My own heart flip-flopped unpleasantly. "What do you mean?"

Aiwin watched me closely as he replied. "Exactly what I say. I could try to dress it up as being selfless on our parts—as worrying about accidentally hurting you when you're already in a vulnerable position because of this blasted fate-bond thing." He scratched at the back of his neck sheepishly. "But you've already got one idiot refusing to let you see what he really feels. You don't need another two."

"No," I agreed emphatically. "I definitely do *not*."

Aiwin shrugged, as though I was making his point for him. "Exactly. So, that's the long and the short of it. Edric and I aren't in a hurry to fall for you any deeper, only to get shunted aside if you decide you want your real mate after all."

I thought about that for a minute.

"Do you know," I said, "I think you're one of the first people to ever talk to me like I wasn't made of glass." I paused. "Well, who wasn't also bullying me, I mean."

Aiwin snorted. "Seems a little daft to pussyfoot around things at this late date," he replied. "I need to ask you, though. In all seriousness, would you take Vale back after the way he acted toward you?"

I chewed the inside of my cheek nervously. That was the real question, wasn't it? The one I didn't want to ask myself, because I wasn't sure I liked the answer.

"Not..." I began cautiously. "Not unless he can actually look me in the eye and tell me what he feels for me. I don't mean telling me what he thinks I should do, or what he thinks is best for me. I've heard plenty of that already."

"Mab's tits, you and me both," Aiwin muttered. "It's embarrassing to have to say this, but I never realized just how far up his own arse Vale's head was until you came into the picture, lass."

It should have been funny, but it just made me want to cry. "If it's any consolation, my life was a lot simpler before he came into it, too."

Aiwin leaned forward, resting his elbows on his knees with his hands loosely clasped.

"Of that I have no doubt," he agreed. "That isn't quite an answer, though. And I'm sorry to push, but it's important. You're still open to having Vale as your mate, under the right set of circumstances?"

I rubbed my palms over my face, knowing that I had to be honest with Aiwin in this moment. "I don't think you understand what a damaged mate-bond feels like. It's as though something inside your body has been partially severed, but it will always be there. Hanging on by a scrap of flesh even as it festers and rots."

Aiwin made a low noise of distress.

I took in a steadying breath. "So, I suppose… the answer is yes? If I really thought Vale understood why he acted like he did, and if I knew for a fact that he cares for me and wants to be with me. But if I don't feel those things, I'm not willing to sign up for the heartbreak any more than you are."

"Thank you for being honest with me," Aiwin said. His usually open face was carefully controlled.

I shook my head. "Here's the thing, though. If Vale truly cared for me and was willing to respect my decisions—my right to make choices for myself—then he'd have to accept my feelings for you and Edric, too."

A flicker of something escaped from behind Aiwin's stoic expression. His wasn't a face meant for hiding things.

"You do realize he's been practically throwing us at you for the last week?" he asked.

I shifted uncomfortably. "I've, uh, heard the three of you fighting, sometimes."

"Damn *right* we've been fighting," Aiwin growled. "Because, as previously discussed, Vale's head is so far up his own arse that he has to eat every meal twice."

A choked noise escaped my control.

Aiwin waved it off. "So, he wants to pretend like he's fine with seeing you in our arms. Meanwhile, *you* want *him* to pull his head out of his arse and admit how he actually feels. Which, by the way, is like shit."

"Yes," I decided. "And I know he does. You forget, my wolf and his wolf are linked. He feels my pain, but I also feel his."

Now Aiwin's green gaze narrowed, a calculating glow kindling in his eyes. "Yes. About that. Maybe there's a way to nudge the pea-brained arsehole along, now that I think about it." The calculating expression collapsed into uncertainty. "If you trust me, that is."

And *there* was something I didn't even have to think about. "I trust you, Aiwin. You've never let me down or led me astray."

A look of pain flashed across his broad features. "I think I have, love," he said. "Not least when I stayed away instead of having this conversation with you sooner."

"I wasn't ready for it until now," I said simply. "Now, tell me about this cunning plan of yours. I'm intrigued."

His bushy red eyebrows drew together. "Easier to show you than tell you," he said, rising from his chair.

He extended his broad, callused hands to me, pulling me up with him when I clasped them. Then he was leaning down, slowly enough that I could have pulled back if I wanted to, but with clear intent. My heart leapt into a gallop as his chapped lips closed over mine, brushing chastely.

I gasped as the contact flared along my nerves in a cascade of heat, spreading outward like a warm wave. Pressing forward, I licked eagerly against the seam of Aiwin's lips, which parted beneath mine.

Through the bond, a familiar wolf bolted awake in alarm. In my mind, Vale howled as though his soul was being ripped in two.

THIRTY-NINE

WHERE EDRIC HAD been all gentle teasing peeking out from behind a courtly façade, Aiwin was more like a shifter when it came to coupling. My interlude with Edric had involved almost as much talking and banter as touching. By contrast, Aiwin didn't appear to have much interest in conversation.

Broad hands clasped the meat of my ass cheeks and pulled my hips flush with his—the hard line of his cock pressing against the crease of my thigh as I rose on tiptoe to get a better angle in the kiss. He grunted into the press of lips, taking effortless control and ravishing my mouth until my lungs burned.

Edric had let me up for air when I needed it. Aiwin seemed content to keep going until I fainted dead away from hypoxia, and apparently my libido was here for it. In some ways, I felt like Aiwin and I had always understood each other. And in this, too, he seemed to understand my wolf in ways that most other fae probably wouldn't.

I hadn't even realized we were moving until the back of my knees hit the edge of a soft surface. Aiwin tumbled me down onto his comfortable feather mattress. I lay there, gasping air, staring up at him with wide, wanting eyes.

I remembered something Edric had said to me in the heat of the moment. *'You have a wicked mouth indeed, but I am not such an oaf as to spill my seed down your throat with no warning. That sort of thing is more Aiwin's department.'*

A roar of desire rushed through me at the memory, nearly drowning out Vale's anguished howling through the bond. My need coalesced into a hot ball in my belly, heavy and liquid.

"I want to suck you," I said breathlessly. Then I hesitated. "No. That's not right. I want you to… to take my mouth."

Aiwin groaned. "*Goddess*, woman. You can't just say things like that."

I pushed myself up on my elbows and lifted my chin defiantly. "Yes, I can. I just did."

Who was this confident she-wolf, anyway? Where had she come from?

Aiwin let out a bark of laughter. "So you did, hellion. Get those clothes off, then. We're doing this properly."

He went to lock the door while I shimmied out of my clothing, making up in speed what I lacked in grace. When he returned, his expression was as predatory as any alpha shifter's. I took the hand he offered, and he used the connection to tug me around until I was lying on my back with my head hanging off the side of the bed, grinning at him from my upside-down perspective.

"Think this is funny, do you?" he asked. His own amusement tugged at his lips despite his best attempts to look severe.

I mock-pouted and batted my eyelashes. "Are you going to make me stop laughing?"

He unbuttoned the fall of his breeches one handed, pushing his underwear aside and freeing an erection that was as different from Edric's slender, elegant cock as it was possible to be.

Aiwin's stand was thicker by far; veiny and flushed with trapped blood, its head broad and mushroom shaped.

My mouth fell open. That was a mistake, because Aiwin stepped forward and rested one knee on the edge of the mattress, so his dick and balls were looming over my face. I moaned as he took advantage of my gaping surprise, feeding that fat cock past my lips and filling my mouth to bursting.

"Good girl," he said, the words sending a new wave of shivery heat through me. He nudged a little deeper as I squirmed, then pulled back and pushed in deeper still.

My wolf, caught between our mate's distant distress and the feast in front of us, whined low and then flopped over, baring herself to Aiwin's casual dominance. I rubbed my thighs together. They were slippery with excitement, and I groaned around Aiwin's cock again.

"Ah, look at you," Aiwin said, his burr more pronounced than usual. "Now, touch yourself. Shove two fingers into that tight little passage and use your thumb to rub your clit. Do it now, lass. Frig yourself hard and fast—but don't you dare come until I tell you to."

My chest hitched, my heart thundering as another pulse of dampness between my legs threatened to start a puddle on the mattress beneath me. Tentatively, I wriggled my fingers into my folds. Sparks flew from even that hesitant contact.

Aiwin pulled back and thrust into my mouth, his tip pressing against my hard palate so I had to swallow convulsively around him to keep from gagging.

"Stop pussyfooting around, little wolf," he teased. "Do as you're told."

I held my breath and pressed my middle finger and ring finger into my untried passage, letting out a choked yelp at the wonderful stretch and burn of it.

"Now rub your clit," Aiwin reminded me, his cock still half-choking me. "Nice and fast, mind."

The angle was weird. I had to twist my wrist to get my thumb where it needed to be, and then the first brush nearly made me come undone.

"*Ah*," Aiwin scolded, bringing me back from the brink by pulling back and thrusting deep again. "None of that, now."

I had no leverage, and no room to squirm away. My wolf wriggled ecstatically on her back, thrilled at the feeling of being properly taken in hand. My awareness squirreled back and forth between the unbearable pleasure of my own fingers working frantically against my pussy and clit, and the frightening yet somehow liberating sensation of helplessness at having my face fucked.

I was going to come. How could Aiwin possibly expect me not to come? What would he do to me if I lost control before he gave me permission?

I wasn't allowed to stop touching myself, or even slow down. The feeling of Aiwin's thick cock nudging deeper into my throat with every stroke was physically frightening in some ways, but it wasn't doing a damned thing to calm my excitement.

At the edge of my awareness, Vale's wolf snarled and slavered its rage. I grabbed onto that delicate connection with all the focus I could muster, letting my mate's pain and despair spill into me. And that was better. *That* was what I needed to control myself.

You could have had this, I sent along the bond. *And if you didn't want it, you could have shown me enough respect to tell me the fucking truth rather than treating me like garbage. You think you have the right to be upset that I'm in Aiwin's bed?*

The snarls turned into anguished howls of pain, and the guilt I should have felt over my moment of cruelty was buried somewhere beneath incandescent physical pleasure, coiled in my womb like a volcano ready to erupt.

Rough fingers stroked my chin. "Such a good girl," Aiwin said. "Make yourself come for me. Don't hold back."

The cock in my mouth shoved deep, removing every single thought of Vale from my mind. I couldn't breathe… didn't really want to as I rolled my thumb over my aching clit and felt ecstasy crash over me like a wave. My body jerked, muscles no longer under my command.

Aiwin fucked into me without restraint, thrusting in to the hilt and pulsing thick, hot come down my throat. Gradually, my body went limp, completely spent. But Aiwin was still coming, pulling back so the last few spurts filled my mouth.

He was breathing hard when he pulled out, leaving me with a mouthful of bitter-salty spend and not sure what I should do with it. I made a tiny noise of distress. Immediately, a broad hand cupped the back of my head, lifting and supporting it. Aiwin's other hand settled over my throat.

"Swallow, lass," he said hoarsely. "Let me feel you swallow it down."

I gulped, a convulsive movement. Then I worked up some saliva and swallowed again, my throat bobbing under the heavy palm covering it. It was a bit like swallowing raw oysters, and with that strange thought, my uncertainty fled.

"*Mab's green garden*," Aiwin said, giving my throat a final stroke and sending my wolf into paroxysms of happy pleasure beneath the possessive touch. "You are utterly perfect, and Vale is a fucking idiot."

I hummed, my awareness going soft and fuzzy as all of my muscles turned to goo. Even Vale's howls felt distant and unimportant. Aiwin arranged my body properly on the bed, my head resting on a pillow and a crisp sheet pulled over my lower body. He kissed my forehead.

"I'll be right back, love."

When he returned, I had a vague sort of impression of a damp cloth cleaning up the mess I'd made of my thighs. Then a solid form slid in next to me, tugging the blankets up and cuddling me close. I buried my nose in the familiar scent and breathed in. When I breathed out, sleep overtook me without a struggle.

The following morning, I woke with a feeling of deep rest and renewal, except for a slight ache in my neck and a rasp in my throat that would almost certainly disappear once I ate breakfast.

Aiwin was fast asleep next to me, snoring softly. A strange reticence discouraged me from waking him. It wasn't that I believed we'd done anything wrong, but the idea of speaking to him right now seemed hopelessly awkward. Had he done what he'd done last night solely for the effect it would have on Vale? Or had it been for himself as well?

The idea of asking either of those questions felt overwhelming when I hadn't even had a cup of tea yet. So, I did the omega thing and snuck out of his room wearing yesterday's clothes, ready for my private walk of shame back to my own room in the palace guest wing.

I opened Aiwin's door silently, crept out, closed it behind me with care, turned around… and nearly stumbled over the crumpled form of Vale, who was huddled against the corridor wall, looking up at me with red-rimmed eyes.

FORTY

THE SALTY CRUST of dried tear tracks marred Vale's perfect cheekbones, and dark circles underlined his startling blue eyes. I stopped dead, frozen in place in the grand hallway of Titania's palace.

Be strong, I thought. *Darby, if there was ever a time you needed to grasp your courage, it's now.*

Vale's lips moved, his mouth opening and closing before words finally came out.

"I can't…" he swallowed hard. "I… can't do this. I'm sorry. I tried. I thought I… I could do the right thing and let you go."

"I wasn't yours to begin with," I managed. "I'm not an object for you to keep or give away. I'm a person. I'm your *mate*, Vale."

"I know," he whispered, drawing his limbs beneath him as though to rise.

I took a step back, unable to stop myself—but Vale didn't climb to his feet. Instead, he moved to kneel in front of me, his hands clasped together in supplication as he looked up at me with tear-swollen eyes.

"Please, Darby," he began, "I beg of you. Please find it in your heart to give me a second chance. I know I don't deserve it. I know you'd do better to choose Aiwin. Or… or Edric. They're both better people than I am. But if you can find an ounce of forgiveness for one who treated you so badly, I want to do better. I want to become the kind of person who owns up to his mistakes and atones for them."

I stared down at him… the proud royal advisor groveling on his knees with his beautiful face stained by weeping and tinged by exhaustion.

I had brought Vale to this. Me, the lowest of the low in my pack. Somehow, I had not one, but *three* gorgeous males ready and willing to do my bidding. My wolf let out a small yip, pawing at me with a front paw as though to say, '*And what are you going to do about it?*'

I paused, holding myself as still as if I'd been turned to stone. What *was* I going to do about it? The realization that I had all the power in this situation — *that I could make whatever choice I wanted* — slammed into me like a boulder. There was no one to tell me that what I chose was right, or wrong, or brave, or stupid.

It was completely up to me.

I lifted my chin, looking down at Vale imperiously. "You have my permission to court me," I told him. "You are a shifter, whether you choose to believe it or not. So, act like one. Show me why I should take you back."

Vale let out a huge gasp of breath as though he'd been holding it in anticipation of my reply. His shoulders slumped in clear relief. Honestly, for a moment there, he looked like he was in real danger of passing out.

"Thank you," he breathed. "Darby, thank you. I'll win you back. No matter what it takes."

"We'll see," I told him, and hurried away before I could start second-guessing myself. My heart was pounding as though I'd run a race, and as I fled

Vale's presence, it occurred to me that he wasn't the only one in danger of fainting on the spot.

———◆———

I spent the day immersing myself in work. Now that Titania had agreed to throw her entire support behind Ember's vision of a commune where anyone who needed help and support could get it, there was an amazing amount of work to be done.

Dianthe still insisted that I take it easy and get plenty of rest, but today, I needed work as a distraction. I caught Ember shooting me curious glances as the afternoon progressed, but she restrained herself from asking until we were walking back to my quarters that evening.

"Well?" she demanded as we approached the door to my room. "You've been a thousand miles away. Are you going to tell me what's going on? Is it Vale?"

I flushed, not having been aware that I was so easy to read. I'd thought I was doing an excellent job of focusing on the work and pushing Vale out of my thoughts. Ember knew me too well, though.

"Erm... kind of," I said, opening my door and gesturing at Ember to precede me. "Sorry if I was—"

Ember stopped cold in the doorway, so abruptly that I almost ran into her back.

"What... in the *world*?" she asked.

I peered around her, taking in the profusion of huge, floral bouquets decorating every flat surface in the room. My jaw dropped. Ember stepped aside, and we both entered the room, looking around.

Titania's summer palace was a marvel of architecture, magic, and nature combined. The very walls and ceilings hung with flowering vines, perfuming the air with sweet nectar. The amount of effort needed to find flowers that could upstage the ones already present in the palace must have been staggering.

Some of the blooms were as long as my forearm, and the colors were like nothing that I'd ever seem on Earth. Individual petals might shade from blue to violet to pink, while others were a crimson so deep it was nearly black. The fragrance was almost overwhelming.

"I, uh, might've given Vale permission to court me," I blurted, realizing Ember was still waiting on an answer. "It… looks like he's started?"

"Good goddess, Darby," Ember said, sounding blank. "Does he think he can drug you into submission with magic pollen?"

Now that she mentioned it, the heavy floral scent *was* a bit on the hallucinogenic side. I could taste it clinging to the roof of my mouth, and I felt a sort of goofy sense of wellbeing plucking at my awareness. A slow grin tugged at my mouth.

"Maybe?" I said. "It's not going to be that easy for him, though."

Ember shook her head fondly, pulled me in, and pressed a smacking kiss to my forehead. "You go, girl. Make him sit up and beg."

I huffed. "Go on. I'll meet you and the others for dinner in a bit."

After splashing water on my face and changing into a more formal gown, I made my way to the dining room where I often shared meals with Aiwin, Edric, Tamlain, Cai, and Ember. Tonight, the servants bowed as I entered, and I discovered the most succulent wild boar I'd ever eaten waiting for me.

"The kitchens received instructions that you and your friends should have the most exquisite cuts of the day's catch, courtesy of Master Vale, Lady Adalwolf," said the head servant.

Ember whistled low, catching my eye with a wink.

Over the following days, almost every time I left my quarters, some new gift was waiting when I returned. Flowers, bottles of fine mead and wine, exotic fruit, beautiful clothing, expensive jewelry — some of it magical.

Of Vale himself, there was very little sign. To be fair, I had no idea how much time and effort it must be taking him to acquire the gifts and sneak them into my room on top of his usual daily duties. Or maybe these gifts *were* his daily duties now. After all, Titania had basically gifted Vale to me. It sounded like he was no longer required to attend her along with his mother.

Being courted with extravagant gifts fit for a princess was utterly alien to my life experience. So much so that it took me a couple of days to stop waiting for someone to jump out and deliver the punchline to the practical joke.

"Why would you not consider such gifts your due?" Dianthe said around a mouthful of juicy, perfectly ripe bengala fruit on the fourth day.

She'd been making herself free of my quarters since hearing about my sudden bounty of fine things, and I was happy enough for the company. If nothing else, having a second person there prevented me from giving in to the occasional urge to down an entire bottle of the expensive wine in hopes that drunkenness would help the world start making sense again.

I frowned. "I'm nobody. These gifts are for an important person. A noblewoman or…"

"A king-killer?" Dianthe suggested wryly.

My heart stuttered over its next beat. "How do you know about that?" I demanded.

A slow smile graced her lips. "I didn't until just now. Thank you for confirming it."

I cursed myself internally. "So, you guessed?"

She shrugged and took another bite of the fruit. "Yes. Who else could it have been? You were alone with Oberon in the middle of the battlefield. But my point is, whether you choose to acknowledge it or not, you are an incredibly important person in Elfhame's history now. A hero, in the truest sense of the word."

My cheeks flamed. "I wish people would stop saying that."

Dianthe looked supremely unconcerned. "Does not a hero of Elfhame deserve a few fruit baskets and bottles of wine?"

"And diamonds?" I muttered.

"And diamonds," Dianthe said firmly. She tossed the remains of the fruit onto a convenient tray. "Come. We're going hunting. You clearly need to get out of your own head for a bit."

I agreed with a sense of relief. At least in the forest, I could hand the reins over to my wolf and stop thinking for a while.

It was a lovely day. The woods were filled with the intriguing scents of game, and before long I was happily stalking a stag with Dianthe moving silently beside me. We'd just maneuvered it upwind of us and were splitting up to flank it when the sound of someone crashing through the brush sent the animal fleeing into the trees.

Dianthe popped her head up from where she'd been hiding and shouted, "You have *got* to be kidding me!"

I sniffed the air, three familiar scents reaching my sensitive nose. Straightening into human form, I felt the magically imbued necklace that had been one of the gifts weave clothing around my naked body.

"Edric! Aiwin! Vale! What are you doing out here?" I asked, stepping forward to meet them.

"Hunting," Edric said dryly, holding up a brace of fat birds resembling pheasants. "A certain someone insists that he needs to find the finest meat and fowl on a daily basis. I can't imagine why."

Vale looked vaguely uncomfortable at having met me out here. I wondered if it was because he was hunting as a human, whereas I always hunted as a wolf.

"The three of you are damned inconvenient," Dianthe said. "I hope you realize that. This is the second time you've spoiled our hunt."

Edric bowed to her. "Once again, we can only beg your pardon, huntress. And hope that our bounty makes its way to your table in lieu of your lost stag."

Dianthe made a *hmph* sound, but I didn't think she was truly upset.

A sudden idea came to me as I looked at Vale, and I couldn't seem to shake it. A little voice in my head whispered *why not?*

"Vale, I want to draw out your wolf. Can we try it here?"

Vale went very still. "What, *now*?" He sounded almost frightened.

"Why not?" I asked. "It will either work or it won't. Now or later, it hardly matters to the outcome. In your place, I'd want to know as soon as possible."

Dianthe looked between us and took a step away. "Um, no offense, but this sounds like a *'you'* conversation rather than a *'me'* conversation. Have fun; be safe. Don't be a stranger, Darby." With that, she darted forward and plucked the game birds from Edric's grasp. "I'll just take these off your hands, shall I?"

After giving me a quick, one-armed hug, she cast a portal and disappeared through it.

Edric frowned at the place where she had been. "Did she just steal our game?"

I rolled my eyes at him. "She's taking it back to the palace kitchens, that's all. Now, come on. We're doing this."

Silence settled over the clearing.

"Should Edric and I make ourselves scarce as well?" Aiwin asked.

I sighed. It had taken me long enough, but I was finally learning that the best way to get what I wanted is to ask for it.

"No, this is for all of us. I won't choose between you." I pinned my gaze on Vale, who still stood frozen in place. "And if that's going to be a problem, now's the time to speak up."

FORTY-ONE

VALE LICKED HIS full lips. "My instincts cry out in pain at the thought of you with another male."

I winced internally, even though I'd already known this to be true. I'd heard Vale's wolf howling its agony inside my mind when I'd been with Edric and Aiwin. That didn't mean it was the answer I wanted to hear.

Vale wasn't finished, though. "Nevertheless, I know that I am unworthy of you. That isn't just words. It's the truth. And these two fae are my closest friends. My only real confidantes since childhood."

I let that penetrate for a moment.

"Okay. That was almost an answer," I said. "But not quite."

Vale squared his shoulders. "Their presence—in this clearing, and in your heart—will not be a problem. Edric, Aiwin... please stay."

The two friends relaxed, their tense postures easing.

"Thank you, Vale." Edric inclined his head, clasping his hands behind his back. "We truly have been doing our best to navigate this complicated situation while causing the least possible collateral damage."

Vale shot Aiwin a quick glance that seemed to say, *'Have you, though?'* Aiwin gave him a flat stare in return, no apology in his expression.

"This situation only became complicated in the first place because Vale decided to make it complicated," I reminded them... and possibly, myself.

The barb hit home, and Vale cast his eyes downward. "Yes. That's the truth, and I have no defense against it."

"Just so we all agree," I said. "Now, take your clothes off."

Vale's head shot up, color flooding his cheeks.

I shrugged, unmoved. "You're about to turn into a wolf," I reminded him. "You can do that with clothing on, I suppose—but I honestly wouldn't recommend it."

"For the last time," Vale said. "*I can't shift.* Titania took the ability from me when I was a babe."

"And yet, here we are," I said sweetly. "So. *Clothes. Off.*"

To demonstrate—and not at all because I was enjoying torturing him—I pulled my necklace over my head and handed it to Aiwin even as my magically conjured clothing dissolved. Vale's eyes looked like they might bug completely out of his skull.

The fae, meanwhile, were staring straight ahead, standing very still, like soldiers at parade rest.

"Lesson one," I began. "Shifter society doesn't make a big deal out of nudity. Fancy magic pendants are all well and good, but most shifters wear simple clothing and take it off when they're going to shift. When they shift back, they're naked until they return to wherever they stashed it, and *no one cares.*"

Vale hesitated for a long moment; his gaze fastened on my fate mark. Then he cautiously moved his hands to the fastenings of his tunic. His fingers were shaking.

I crossed my arms, watching the show and not letting him off the hook. *Ancestors*, he was beautiful. He lacked the bulk of many shifter males who'd spent their lives wrestling for dominance and running down wild game. But every muscle was painstakingly defined, from his broad shoulders to his trim waist, and down to his shapely calves. I couldn't see a scar or imperfection anywhere on him, except for the matching fate-mark to mine inscribed over his heart.

He straightened and tossed his buckskin trousers aside, his gaze drawn to my body like iron filings to a magnet. Color still tinged his high cheekbones. Was he embarrassed because he was hard for me? His flushed cock jutted out from a thatch of black hair, and his hands twitched by his hips as though he was fighting the urge to cover himself.

I raised an eyebrow.

"Kneel," I told him, channeling every alpha I'd ever watched performing a wolfbirth ceremony.

His Adam's apple bobbed. I knew this would be hard for him. He was proud, and he was also damaged. Plus, it wasn't just *me* watching him submit. His friends were here, too. But he clenched his jaw and dropped gracefully to his knees in front of me.

I joined him, kneeling to face him and holding my hands out for his. Honestly, I had no idea what magic pack alphas used to draw out a young shifter's wolf for the first time. It didn't matter, because I had my own magic… my own connection to Vale's wolf.

Vale lifted his hands to mine, tangling our fingers together. He was still trembling.

"Don't be afraid," I told him, and unleashed my wolf into the bond.

She sprang forward joyfully, finally free to unite with her fated mate. I felt as much as heard the answering whine of excitement from Vale's wolf.

How ironic that it was only the human parts of us that had made this whole thing such a nightmare. Left to their own devices, our wolves would have joined joyfully the moment we'd first laid eyes on each other. They cared nothing for ego or status or shame.

I felt the two animals meet in the space between us, wagging and wriggling with unadulterated joy. Vale let out a quiet gasp, flinching as though he'd been struck. I squeezed his hands tighter.

"It's going to be okay," I whispered, and closed my eyes, drawing my wolf back to me.

As I'd known he would, Vale's wolf followed, manifesting in the real world. The air in front of me twisted. The hands in mine contracted into furry paws. I let them go.

In front of me crouched the most impressive huge black wolf I'd ever seen. Vale yipped, and an instant later, I had a lapful of giant canine licking excitedly at my jaw and cheeks.

"Will you look at that?" Aiwin murmured.

My wolf was leaping and cavorting in impatience. Before I could regain control of her, I was shifting as well, my senses transforming until all I could see and smell and taste was *mate*. Every complication fell away… every memory of hurt gone in an instant.

Vale leapt up, scenting the forest around us. *Run with me*, he sent through the bond.

And so, I did.

"Well, *shite*," said a rapidly diminishing voice from behind us. "Should we follow them?"

And then, barely audible, "I think we'd better."

The trees and brush blurred around us as we ran, free and together, our tongues lolling and our lungs panting. Vale's furry body brushed and bumped against mine, teasing. Warmth spread outward from my heart, becoming heat, becoming an inferno of need.

I nipped at Vale's jaw, teasing him in return— my excitement only increasing when I noticed two more familiar wolves chasing us.

Want, I thought, my need becoming overwhelming. *Want, want, want, want…*

Vale tackled me playfully to the ground, sniffing all along my sides and flanks. I whimpered, desperate for touch—and a sudden realization sent me shifting abruptly back to human form. My mate followed, breathing raggedly as we lay tangled together on the ground, naked.

The inferno growing inside me didn't ease, and abruptly—painfully—I knew exactly what this was.

Two gray wolves charged up to us, transforming into Aiwin and Edric as they crashed to a halt a few feet away. Vale stared up at them, a growl rumbling in his chest.

"Are you two all right?" Edric asked, taking a cautious step back.

I licked my lips, trying to drum up some moisture in my mouth.

"I'm…" I rasped. "I think… I'm going into heat. The bond must have triggered it." I swallowed hard, my throat clicking, and looked up at them helplessly. "It's… I don't know how to… it's my first time."

FORTY-TWO

VALE PUSHED AWAY from me as though it tore muscle and sinew to do so. He scrabbled backward, his nostrils flaring, scenting the air.

"Edric, Aiwin," he said in a voice like gravel. "You have to get her away from me. I won't be able to help myself. You're stronger than me. Bind me magically, so I can't follow."

His words didn't make any sense. "Wh-what?" I asked.

Vale's blue eyes met mine, burning with an inner light. "You don't want me, Darby. Not for this." His fingers dug into the forest loam, as though he was trying to anchor himself against my rejection.

I blinked, tears spilling over. "Of course I want you!" I cried. "*You're my mate*! You're all my mates and I *need* you now!"

My emotions were going haywire right along with my body. A terrible fear that all three of them would turn their backs and walk away gripped me.

Edric raised a hand toward me, like someone quieting a wild animal. "Darby. We're here. We'll always be here when you need us. But please — what do you mean by *heat*?"

I wrapped my arms around myself and started rocking, because none of my mates were wrapping *their* arms around me.

Vale answered, his tone shaky. "It's a mating drive. Like a rut. I've only heard about it, never seen it — but now I can smell her, and I can't *think* —"

He looked like he was about to lunge for me... or possibly *away* from me. Aiwin's heavy hand landed on his shoulder, grounding him. Vale flinched, his eyes wild — but he didn't move to shake off the grip.

"Darby, quickly," Aiwin said. "You want to... mate with all of us? I mean, as some sort of permanent ceremony? Where we all have sex together?"

"Yes!" I sobbed, cradling my aching belly. "Please don't abandon me, *please*! I'm so empty — it hurts!"

Vale growled again, jerking his shoulder fitfully against Aiwin's grip. The two fae exchanged a wide-eyed look. Then Edric seemed to shake himself free of his paralysis.

"My family's hunting lodge," he said. "I'll portal us there. Aiwin, spell her to prevent conception. I don't know that she can make a rational decision about that kind of thing right now."

"Especially since the last fae-shifter hybrid nearly destroyed both realms," Aiwin muttered. "Vale, come on. We're going."

I hunched miserably, not able to follow the sense of what they were talking about. Edric cast a portal, and Vale sprang to his feet the instant Aiwin let him go, rushing forward to scoop me up in his arms. Aiwin pressed a hand to my aching abdomen, murmuring an incantation. A tingle radiated from his fingers straight to my womb, and I moaned, writhing in Vale's grip.

Vale leapt through the portal, carrying me as though I weighed nothing, with Aiwin and Edric hot on our heels. We landed in a rustic building, spacious but with the faintly musty air of disuse.

"Servants?" Aiwin said tightly.

"None," Edric replied. "Mab's *tits*, Aiwin. My family might technically be nobility, but we aren't *that* rich. Come on, there's a bedroom through here."

I clung to Vale's shoulders, aware that my fingernails were probably leaving marks.

"You're all right, lass," Aiwin said, stroking my sweaty hair away from my face.

But I *wasn't* all right. I was terrified. What if they changed their mind and decided I wasn't worth their time? What if I was too needy, too raw... what if my animal nature disgusted them?

Vale clutched me closer to him. "No, no, no," he murmured. "No, Darby—*stop*. No one's abandoning you."

I could feel his distress through the bond, and it only made my own distress worse.

"Here," Edric said, "put her on the bed. Darby, do you need—"

As soon as my back hit the soft mattress, I lunged an arm out and grabbed Edric by the wrist, dragging him down with me. Since I hadn't let go of Vale either, the three of us ended up in a tangle.

"I think what she needs is sex," Aiwin said dryly. "Not sure how much clearer she has to make it. Vale, are you going to be able to handle having us here? Seeing as how you growled at us earlier like you wanted to rip our throats out..."

Vale was nosing along the swell of my breast. His answer hummed along my skin, making me arch. "I don't know, I've never done this either. Fuck! I need her so badly..."

"You and she should go first," Edric said. "Maybe take the edge off."

"And if you try to harm anyone in this room," Aiwin said, "I'll put you under a paralysis spell so fast you won't know what hit you."

"Yes," Vale said, as he worked his way down my stomach. "Yes, do that. *Goddess*, Darby—you smell so good."

I cried out as Vale dove between my legs and started devouring me. Edric managed to get himself righted on the bed and pulled my upper body half into his lap, supporting me. Vale's need swirled together with my own through the bond, driving my wolf crazy.

I wanted to drag Vale inside me and make him live inside my ribcage forever, next to my heart. I wanted to kill and fuck and feast and never, ever stop. I wanted—

Vale's tongue dragged over my clit, and I came with a howl, arching off the bed. Before I knew what was happening, Vale flipped me over, tumbling me off Edric's lap and onto my front. He crouched over me, dragging my hips up so I was kneeling. His big cock pressed at my entrance, and I rocked back with a snarl.

He felt huge compared to my own fingers, when Aiwin had told me to touch myself. The stretch was almost painful—a deep burn that felt like it was splitting me in two. I didn't care. Let me bleed… let me rip my own body open to accommodate him.

"Easy," Edric said, and the word drew another growl from me.

I didn't *want* easy. Also, why was he still wearing clothes? Vale thrust into me, his hands gripping my hips with bruising force. It was perfect—the feeling of being full to bursting finally cutting through the sea of need I'd been drowning in.

Edric's breeches tied closed with a complicated pattern of laces. I stretched toward him, scrabbling at the knots, whining in frustration. Before I could start ripping at them with teeth, the fabric disintegrated beneath my touch in a tingle of magic, leaving only bare, pale skin.

"You're welcome," Aiwin said, with the same hint of dry humor from earlier.

"Thanks," Edric gasped, at the same time I craned forward and swallowed his cock. He was painfully hard, seed leaking from his tip.

I hadn't anticipated how Vale's wild thrusts would drive me onto Edric's length, practically ramming him down my throat. But my wolf had swallowed bigger game than this, and I wasn't about to pull back when I finally had almost everything I wanted.

I wasn't the only one on a hair trigger, it seemed. After only a couple of minutes, Edric's hand tightened in my hair as though trying to tug me away. "Darby, I… I'm…"

I grabbed his thighs and let Vale push me onto him so deep that my nose met crinkly golden curls.

Edric made a choking noise and went rigid, his cock throbbing and pulsing as he spent down my throat. A rumble of a satisfied purr escaped me, at least until the hand in my hair grew more insistent, Edric pulling me off as his body shuddered, oversensitive.

Vale took that as motivation to plow into me with his full strength, even as I slammed back against him in brutal counterpoint.

He dragged me up by the shoulders, both of us balancing on our knees. I didn't expect the sharp pain of his teeth closing on my shoulder, but my wolf wailed her ecstasy as the mating bite threw both of us into a full-body orgasm.

The bond exploded like a glittering sandstorm. Before, it had been a distant thing; something I had to reach for. Now it was all around me, as clear and immediate as the bed beneath my knees and the air in my lungs.

And... it wasn't just Vale. Two other familiar presences circled in the background—one sleek and mercurial, the other bluff and earthy.

"What the—?" Aiwin said. "Edric, can you feel that?"

Edric moaned, his spent body arching weakly. "I... what's happening?"

Vale and I slowly toppled forward onto the bed, our muscles going limp as the climax faded. I burrowed my face against Edric's trembling thigh, relishing Vale's weight on top of me.

"I just spent in my bloody trousers," Aiwin grumbled. "That's what's happening."

The mattress dipped, its frame creaking as Aiwin settled on it heavily.

"Should've dissolved your clothes at the same time you did mine," Edric mumbled. "But, seriously, why can I feel three other people in my head?"

"Mate bond," I slurred, already feeling fresh stirrings of arousal.

"Yes, but we're not shifters," Edric said—since apparently, he'd mistaken me for someone interested in holding a conversation.

I growled at him to get the point across. Vale, still half-hard and sheathed inside me, rolled his hips, and the growl tailed into a happy whine.

"Could it be the blood vow?" Aiwin asked, sounding way too coherent for someone who'd just come in his pants.

Vale was hardening inside me, his lazy thrusts gaining more purpose… and suddenly trying to follow the back-and-forth between them felt like far too much effort.

━━━◆━━━

By the time Vale finally needed a rest, Edric and Aiwin were recovered. I was beginning to trust that the connection between my mates and me wouldn't suddenly be ripped away.

Gradually, my desperation mellowed into a haze of waxing and waning pleasure. Edric and Aiwin had this thing where they put me on my back and took turns mating me, pulling out whenever they got close and switching places. They drove me to climax after climax that way, keeping it going for what felt like forever.

Aiwin also had a trick with magic that he pulled once while Vale was fucking me—a slender, invisible shape easing past the tight ring of my ass and slowly gaining length and girth as my interior muscles loosened. I was pretty sure that was what had been happening when I left the livid bite mark on Edric's inner thigh—though really, they had only themselves to blame.

Time was meaningless, but the sun was pouring merrily through the window when my body finally threw in the towel, and I fell abruptly asleep with Aiwin rocking into me from behind.

When I woke up, the light was gray and uncertain. I had no idea if it was dawn or dusk, much less what day it was. I sat up in a rush, then immediately regretted it when every muscle in my body protested at once.

"Ow," I whimpered.

Two larger bodies had been flanking mine on the bed. They both sat up as well—Aiwin on my left and Vale on my right.

"All right, lass?" Aiwin asked.

I prodded at the mate-bond. It was still there, in all it's three-fold glory. "What...?" I began, then stopped and tried again. "How...?"

Edric came into the room. He was dressed, his hair as neat as ever in its complicated, fussy plaits, and he was carrying a plate of food. My stomach rumbled.

"We think it was the blood vow," he said calmly, putting the plate down on a table. He stuffed a few pillows behind my back and handed me the food.

I tore into it. "What blood vow?" I managed around a mouthful of venison.

Vale shifted uncomfortably. "When we were young, after Edric recovered from the unicorn attack, Aiwin suggested we make a vow that we would never be parted. We sealed it with blood."

"Blood and magic," Aiwin clarified.

I frowned, stopping with my hand halfway to my mouth. "So, it was a bond? A magical one?"

"That's right," Edric agreed. "Apparently, it was enough that when Vale's mate-bond with you solidified, we were dragged in as well."

"Which is not a complaint," Aiwin said quickly.

My mind was whirling—a fact not improved by having three other people in it. "Tamlain has a bond with Ember," I said slowly. "But it's not through Cai. It's Tamlain's own magic, Ember says."

"That's a slightly different situation," said Edric, "since Ember is half-fae. But I do intend to have a word with the general at some point, assuming you don't mind."

Talking about our friends made me realize something that nearly had me choking on my venison. "Ember! Oh, no! She must think we're all missing! Goddess, what day is it?"

Nightmare scenarios of Ember assuming we'd been kidnapped, of Titania sending forces across the kingdom to look for us, swept through my head. My mates inhaled sharply in reaction to my panic, but their calm reassurance immediately flooded the bond.

"No, no—I sent a message to Ember and her mates outlining what happened shortly after we came here," Edric said quickly. "In, er, the most delicate terms I could manage."

A flush of pink darkened his cheekbones. I suspected there were only so many ways to say 'Darby is in heat, and we all need to have constant sex with her until she gets better' in *delicate terms.*

I slumped back against the pillows, lightheaded with relief. "Oh. Well. That's all right then. It's not like she doesn't turn into a raging sex-slut four times a year as well."

Aiwin raised an eyebrow. "Four times a year, you say?"

I shrugged. "Give or take. Goddess, that's exhausting. I feel like I've been tenderized."

Vale shifted position and winced. "Same. But worth it."

I silently agreed, aware that the others could 'hear' me through the bond.

Aiwin's expression grew serious. "So, you're all right with this, then? With the bond? We didn't exactly have a chance to discuss it first, and I don't get the impression it's the kind of thing you can undo after the fact."

Old patterns of thought immediately reared their ugly heads. Did Aiwin mean that he regretted it? Did Edric? They'd been dragged into my mate bond with no warning and now they were stuck with me until I died—

"Stop," Edric said kindly. "Look inward, Darby Adalwolf."

I let out the breath I'd been holding and consciously turned my focus toward the bond. It was full of uncertainty, yes—but no doubt. My three mates didn't know exactly what the future might bring. However, none of them harbored regret.

Aiwin cleared his throat. "Growing up, we always knew that a romantic relationship might tear the three of us apart... or at least weaken our bond. Then all three of us ended up falling for the same she-wolf. Life's funny that way."

A tremulous smile curved my lips. "So, I ended up with a package deal?"

Aiwin chuckled. "Looks like it."

"I still can't quite believe I'm here, after... well... *everything*," Vale said quietly.

"Same," I said, echoing him from earlier. "But worth it."

"We'll need to go back soon," Edric said. He huffed. "I doubt Aiwin's parents will care, and I'm sure mine will come around to the idea, since I'm a second son. Zara only wants Vale to be happy—but what about your parents, Darby?"

I went very still.

My parents.

My extremely conventional traditionalist parents, who'd already suspected—quite correctly—that I was being inappropriate with Edric.

This was going to be interesting.

EPILOGUE

"YOU *WHAT*?" my mother said, her voice rising to a volume that turned a few heads around us.

I'd taken a day to recover and steel myself before returning to Earth with my three mates in tow—reassured that Ember had delivered a message to my parents that I was safe and would visit as soon as possible to let them know about everything that had happened.

We'd found them working in the newly established school building near the edge of the settlement. The learning center wasn't running at full capacity yet, but there were a few youngsters and several other staff members present while we finished working out the kinks.

Suffice to say, this wasn't exactly the venue I would have chosen for this conversation. Fortunately, the handful of random teachers and administrators in the room decided quickly that this wasn't an exchange they were interested in sticking around for.

"I went into heat," I repeated, once the others retreated and gave us the room. "And now I have three mates. You've already met Edric. This is Aiwin, and this is Vale, whose fate-mark matches mine."

My three gorgeous males stood behind me silently, a solid wall of muscle and magic. I couldn't deny how reassuring that felt.

Less reassuring was the way my mother's jaw hung open, and the way her complexion went pale for a moment before two high spots of color rose in her cheeks. Her shocked gaze bounced between the four of us as though she wasn't sure where to look.

"Three?" she managed at last. "You… you can't have *three mates*! That isn't how it works! What will people think?"

"I guess they'll think that my heats are really interesting?" The words slipped out before I could stop them. I blushed and glanced around guiltily, confirming that we were still alone in the room.

Mother made a choked noise, the red spots on her cheeks turning blotchy.

Before I could either double down or lose my nerve and stammer an apology, my father spoke up.

"Now Freida," he began. "Be careful what you say next. Do you really want to insult our pack alpha's choices?"

My mother blinked—probably as surprised that he'd spoken up as I was. "What are you talking about, Grigori? This has nothing to do with Cai Greystalker!"

I raised my eyebrows, waiting for her to figure it out. My father wasn't so patient.

"Ember has two mates," he pointed out. "One of whom is fae, I might add."

Mother's mouth opened and closed a couple of times. "That's different," she said weakly, but I could see the fight going out of her. "It's… this is our little Darby… the *scandal*…"

Aiwin cleared his throat and stepped forward. "I know this whole thing is unexpected, Madame. But we're all deeply honored to become part of your clan. We hope you'll also consider yourself part of ours. I'm a nobody—"

I made a noise of protest, and Aiwin put a quelling hand on my shoulder.

"—but Vale's mother is a close advisor to Queen Titania, and Edric—"

"My family holds some small status in Elfhame," Edric said humbly.

"He's nobility," I corrected.

"*Minor* nobility," Edric clarified. "And I'm only a second son."

"Plus, all three of them have saved my life," I concluded.

Vale had been awfully quiet during all of this. My mother's eyes landed on him. She looked bewildered, but no longer distraught.

"And you don't mind sharing your mate?" she demanded.

Vale dipped his head in a shallow bow before meeting her eyes. "These men share a blood bond with me. They are closer than brothers… they are my better nature. Had I not behaved like a cad at our first meeting, perhaps Darby and I would be bound in the normal manner. It is better for all of us that we are not. This is how things were meant to be."

My mother wasn't a high-status wolf. Not in the way Vale was. Yet she managed to hold his gaze as she drew breath to reply.

Before she could, the sound of childish shouting and a series of ominous thuds reached us from another room across the hallway, breaking the tense moment. Without needing to exchange a word, Vale,

Edric, and Aiwin hurried toward the commotion, with my parents and me hot on their heels.

Three youngsters aged perhaps ten to twelve years were tussling in an activity room that should have been empty at this time of day. My mates each grabbed one of them by the scruff and pulled the combatants apart, still shouting and swinging their fists wildly.

All three were male—two shifters and a pale, slender fae. The fae child, struggling mightily in Vale's grip, let loose a weak bolt of magic aimed at the other two. Edric flicked a careless hand up and blocked it with an invisible barrier that coruscated with pale sparkles as the feeble attack hit it.

"*Enough*," Aiwin growled, in a tone that made the shifter boys immediately stop fighting and show throat. I wondered if he'd learned that trick from Vale.

The fae youngster stood with his fists clenched at his hips, his chest rising and falling like a bellows. He raised a hand to point at the other two with a trembling finger.

"They called my magic weak!" he accused.

"Well, it does appear to be a *bit* weak," Vale pointed out mildly.

"He called us a pair of stupid animals!" one of the shifter boys snarled.

Aiwin sighed. "And trying to pound him into the floor with your fists argues against this *how*, exactly?"

Edric turned the youngster he was holding to face him and crouched down, putting them on an equal footing. "You know, the first time I saw my friend over there, I thought he was a grimy little shifter savage."

"*Oy*," Vale said.

"Don't feel bad," Aiwin said. "He also thought I was a grimy little fae peasant."

"You *were* a grimy little fae peasant," Edric retorted.

I hid a smile, watching the children forget their quarrel in the face of this good-natured back and forth. Beside me, my parents were standing very still, following the exchange closely.

"The point is," Edric went on, "the three of us ended up being fast friends despite our differences."

"And that one over there?" Vale pointed at Edric, his attention settling firmly on the fae boy he was restraining. "His magic couldn't so much as light a candle when he was your age. He got better, though."

Edric snorted. "Thanks to a lot of help from my friends."

"Really?" asked the fae child. "Your magic got stronger?"

Edric wiggled his fingers and sent licks of blue flame into the air, where they formed into the shape of a dancing unicorn before extinguishing. "I do all right for myself. And so will you. But that will be a lot easier if you let other people get past your walls so they can help you learn and grow."

The children exchanged wary looks, but all the hostility had drained away to sheepishness.

"Now," Aiwin said, "run along to wherever you're supposed to be right now, because it's a fair bet that you're not supposed to be in here."

"We're not in trouble?" asked one of the shifters cautiously.

"Not from us," Vale said. "But if it happens again, that might change."

With a final suspicious look at each other, the three hurried out of the room, giving my parents and me a wide berth. My mother leaned toward me, speaking too quietly to be overheard. "All right. Maybe I was a *bit* hasty."

I couldn't help the smug smile that tipped up the corners of my lips.

That night, we stayed in the same vacant student den where I'd spent my first night with Aiwin and Edric. After the scene at the school, my mother had softened considerably toward my unconventional mating—a process that had probably been helped by her gradual realization of what it would mean for our low-status family to have mate-ties to Elfhame nobility of both the shifter and fae varieties.

We were sprawled in a pile on the thick fur rug in front of the hearth, my cheek resting on Edric's lithe chest as Vale curled against me from behind.

"I trust we didn't disgrace you too badly," Edric teased.

I snorted. "Mother will come around soon enough. Father likes you already. He's just keeping quiet about it because he has to share a den with her."

I was relieved there hadn't been more drama. We'd visited the others' families before coming to

Earth, since they were closer. Zara had been surprised but thrilled for us. Aiwin's huge, extensive family had welcomed me with literal open arms. Edric's noble parents had been taken aback, but flawlessly polite. It was clear that they loved Edric and wanted him to be happy, even if the shape his happiness took was unconventional.

All in all, I'd gained an extensive new family support system that spanned two realms, and I was in mild shock. With Titania still espousing complete support for our little sanctuary in the Greystalker packlands, I was feeling positively giddy with thoughts of the future.

Then Aiwin spoke, and my mind crashed to an abrupt halt.

"Do you want children, Darby?"

"We couldn't really ask you before the heat," Vale added softly. "Everything happened so fast."

I made myself stop and really think about it for a minute before answering.

"I do," I said carefully. "The thing is, I don't care if they're mine biologically or not." I met Aiwin's eyes, and then Edric's. "I know you're both worried about hybrid children after what happened with Ember. And I think you're right to be. But there are other children here who need a family. I think we should consider being that family."

Aiwin's beautiful smile spread across his face. "Ah, lass. You're heart's as big and deep as the ocean. I think that's a wonderful idea."

"So do I," Edric said gently, the words rumbling beneath my cheek.

I craned around to see Vale, the only one of my mates with whom I might safely have my own biological children.

"Families of choice are the most important families of all," he said, including the others in his gaze. "But if you ever decide you want to carry a pup of your own, I'll happily give it to you."

I twisted my neck enough to accept a kiss from him. "Thank you. All of you."

Aiwin stretched and settled back among the furs. "We were thinking of building our own place here in the settlement," he said. "After all, we're going to spend a lot of time here, and we can't keep using a den meant for your students."

I rested my chin on Edric's chest to look at him, suddenly worried. "I've uprooted you," I realized. "I didn't even ask if you wanted to spend so much time on Earth, just because this is where my life is."

Edric had been idly stroking my hair as we spoke, but now he flicked the back of my head lightly. "Stop. You spend time on Elfhame, too—not just Earth. Our families are only a portal away whenever we want to see them."

"You're our home, Darby," Vale said quietly. "A place is just a place."

"What he said," Aiwin agreed. "Mab's hairy legs, Vale. When did you become a poet?"

Vale freed an arm for long enough to throw a pillow at him, and Edric snickered like a schoolboy. I felt their lightness through the bond, and it buoyed my own heart.

"You know, we might have an opening for a poetry teacher at the school," I suggested.

Vale groaned.

Aiwin laughed aloud. "Hire Edric. He's the one with the classical education."

"It's not a terrible idea," Edric mused after a brief pause.

"It's not," I agreed. "And we can talk more about that… *tomorrow*. Right now, I want to curl up with my mates and forget about the rest of the world for a bit."

Three warm bodies closed around me. Three warm minds cradled mine in love and support, and for a few blissful hours, we did exactly that.

finis

For more books by this author, visit
www.otherlovepublishing.com